HOUDINI PIE

PAUL MICHEL

B&H Bennett &
Hastings Publishing

Bennett & Hastings titles may be ordered through booksellers or by contacting: sales@bennetthastings.com or writing to 2400 NW 80th Street #254, Seattle WA 98117. Promotions material for your bookstore may be obtained by e-mailing Mary Myers (mary@bennetthastings.com) or inquiries@bennetthastings.com

Edited by Adam Finley

Cover Design by Larry Cyr
www.larryccyr.com

ISBN: 978-1-934733-55-4

Library of Congress Control Number: 2010921327

For Cathy and Joe

HOUDINI PIE

PROLOGUE

OXNARD, California in 1910 had a population of nearly four thousand souls. Charlie Gates figured that if only ten percent were suckers, he would be out of debt before summer. One buck per sucker would net him four hundred dollars. Subtract the costs of production, packaging and advertising and he'd soon be sitting on something in the vicinity of three hundred and thirty dollars, split three ways.

Charlie was twenty years old. He had no job, no prospects. His wife Vera was pregnant again, still two months to go and already as big as a zeppelin. A hundred dollars would come in mighty handy. It was worth a shot.

"Stardust Pills," he called them, "A Patented Mixture of Rare Herbs and Essential Substances, to Counter the Deleterious Effects of the Terrible Halley's Comet." The Comet's tail, as everyone knew, contained the mysterious poison cyanogen, which the papers had been saying for months was nasty stuff. People were buying asbestos masks, building underground rooms and taking mail-order potions to keep them safe from Halley's astral spew. Charlie figured the Pills were a sure thing.

He had two partners. Abe Beasly was as tall as a transom and as skinny as a sapling. He wore a punched-in top hat and clunky boots with wooden soles. His father was an apothecary. His mother had run away when Abe was three. He was in charge of making the Pills in the back room of his old man's shop on C Street. The ingredients were random: a pinch of this, a cup of that. Whatever was handy and cheap. He rolled the boiled-down goop into little brown balls the size of lemon drops. Charlie called them squirrel turds.

Charlie's pal Warren was short and bespectacled, and so smart it was scary. He was nuts about this Comet business, and had read all about it in the newspapers at the Carnegie Library downtown. It would be at its closest point to earth, he said, near the end of May.

The Pills went on sale the first of April. Sales were brisk from the start. People bought pills for themselves, sent them to relatives and mixed them into their kids' oatmeal. Abe's share of the money went mostly to the local pool hall. Warren bought books. Vera browsed a Sears and Roebuck catalog. Charlie worried. Things were going a bit too smoothly.

The City of Oxnard planned a celebration for the night of May 21, a Saturday, to commemorate the ground-breaking for a new Chinese pagoda at Plaza Park. There would be speeches, a parade, a baseball game, a tug-of-war. Charlie and the boys produced a batch of slightly larger pills, flat and round like overcoat buttons, that he dubbed his "Last-Minute Emergency" line. They came three to a package, at a dollar-fifty each.

The big day dawned bright and clear. Charlie set up under a palm tree at the corner of the park.

"Last chance!" he hollered at the milling crowd. "We are now fully within the tail of the Comet. It may be lovely to look at, but …"

"Charlie," said Warren. "Look."

A dozen men were walking purposefully toward them in the twilight. Charlie's huckstering faltered on his lips. A crowd gathered slowly around them.

"What do you suppose they want?" Charlie whispered.

"I don't know, but they're not looking at the Comet."

Forty degrees above the eastern horizon Halley streaked uncannily across the firmament. Not a head was craned to watch it. All eyes were on Charlie.

Leading the group was big John Stokes, manager of the Oxnard Livery. His expression was a combination of boiling fury and crippling discomfort. He was bent forward oddly at the waist. Many of the others were similarly hunched over.

"So you're Mr. Stardust," Stokes said.

Charlie extended his hand and spoke with exaggerated civility.

"Charles Gates," he said. "I don't believe we've had the pleasure …"

"Can the cute stuff. My wife made me take one of your goddamned Pills last night. I been shittin' my guts out since."

An ugly murmur of assent rose from the men behind him.

"I don't understand. There have been no reports of …"

"All we want to know is what did you put in these goddamned pills?"

Charlie swallowed hard. He didn't know. He hadn't even been in the room when Abe cooked them up.

"Well?" said Stokes.

A hoarse shout came from the back of the crowd. It was Thomas Rice, one of the Oxnard City Councilmen, and a well-known shark with a pool stick. He was dragging a sorry figure wearing a punched-in top hat.

"Here's the man," he roared.

Rice deposited Abe at Charlie's feet. The crowd moved closer. Abe's face was green, his eyes bloodshot, his collar torn and his nose recently bloodied.

"They made me tell them," he said.

"Not exactly," countered Mr. Rice. "Seems that Mr. Beasly has been bragging all day about the killing he and his friends have been making. What did you say was the magic ingredient this last round, Mr. Beasly?"

"Castor oil," Abe muttered.

"Speak up," said Rice. "I'm not sure that everyone heard you."

Abe cleared his throat, but didn't lift his head.

"Castor oil," he said, a little more loudly. "Mixed with some sawdust."

"*Sawdust?*" said Charlie.

"Helped hold them together," Abe sniffed. "You wanted them so damned big."

Warren was making small squeaking sounds in his throat.

"What was your part in this, young fellow?" Rice asked Warren.

"I ... I ... mostly kept the books, sir. The money, I mean."

"I suggest that you go get it."

Warren was off in a flash. Charlie took a step as if to follow.

"Not so fast," came John Stokes' growl. "We ain't done with you."

The big man held out his fist and opened it. On his palm lay three big Pills.

"Taste of your own medicine," said Stokes. "Eat 'em up, now."

"But I ..." Charlie began.

"One at a time," Stokes said. "There's gonna be some poisonous vapors in your house tonight, but they ain't gonna have anything to do with the Comet."

The men howled. Charlie smiled weakly and reached for a Pill. The feel of it in his hand—slimy, slightly sticky—was repulsive. People had *eaten* these?

"Down the hatch," said Stokes.

Charlie got home shortly after midnight. When he staggered up Downing Street he was alarmed to find Doctor Broughton's brand new Model T in front of his little cottage. As he came up the steps he heard the jagged cry of a newborn.

Broughton was sitting at the kitchen table; his tie undone, his sleeves rolled up and a tumbler of whiskey at his elbow.

"Put up a fight, he did," he said, "but we got the little giant out safe and sound."

There were two nurses in the front room. One cradled a bundle of towels. Charlie peeked inside it at what could not possibly be a newborn. It had a head the size of a melon and arms as thick as his wrists. Its eyes were an impossible, unearthly blue. Charlie whistled softly, then headed for the stairs.

"She's fine," said one of the women. "The doctor is a wizard with the stitching."

Vera lay propped against the pillows, her face as pale as the sheets.

"We got us a boy," she said with a weak smile.

"One at least," said Charlie. "What are we going to name it?"

Through a gap in the curtains they could just make out the smudge of the Comet against the sky.

"Why," she said, "I think we should call him Halley."

Charlie didn't answer. He raced down the stairs, through the back door, and to the outhouse, where he sat with the door flung open. He cursed the Comet silently while all his schemes and fortitude gushed out of him like a stinking waterfall.

So close, he thought. So goddamned close. Damn Abe. Damn that John Stokes. Damn Warren. Damn it all. What are we going to do now?

CHAPTER ONE

THE LITTLE GIANT

HAL GATES came home on a Thursday afternoon in October 1918, swinging his books from a handle of braided twine. Though he was in only the fourth grade, Mrs. Perluski's class, he was the biggest boy in the school. To his mother's relief he was a good pupil: studious and polite, qualities she attributed to her side of the family. They certainly weren't evident in her husband.

Hal found his father as he'd found him every day since early summer: sitting in a straight-backed chair in the kitchen, hunched over a drugstore cane. He wore a black eye-patch and he had one leg in a filthy plaster cast. He had a scraggly beard, he needed a bath, and his face and shoulder muscles twitched spasmodically. A squadron of horseflies buzzed around him.

"Oh, it's you," he said. He straightened up, put down cane and lifted the patch.

"How was school?" he asked.

"All right," Hal answered. He rummaged in the icebox, empty but for a half-brick of lard and a plate of stale biscuits. He took a biscuit, nibbled tentatively at its edge, and set it back on the plate.

"Nobody come today?" Hal asked.

"Nah," said Charlie. "Quiet all day."

Charlie had been in a minor accident in the spring. A drinking buddy had gotten him on a roof repair crew at the Carnegie Library and he'd fallen asleep in the sun and slipped off and onto the ground fifteen feet below. To Doctor Broughton's amazement he wasn't seriously injured, just a mild break of his fibula. The leg healed by the Fourth of July, but events of an international scope persuaded Charlie that it was not the best time to be strutting around Oxnard as an able-bodied man.

There was a war on, and the U.S. finally had entered it. Conscription had started up the year before and there was a push on to round up evaders, and those who claimed to be conscientious objectors. Charlie's objections weren't especially conscientious; he just didn't want to get shot at. He decided to lay low a while, reckoning that nobody would yank a cripple out of bed and put him in a uniform.

In July there came disturbing rumors that the round-up was proceeding in earnest. Charlie decided to become utterly undraftable. Hence the twitch, the cast, the eye patch and the avoidance of the bath. "They may find me," he said, "but they sure as hell won't want me."

As Charlie wouldn't leave the kitchen and Vera was out doing whatever work she could find (laundry, house-cleaning, sewing, cooking, even a few stints in the beet fields outside town), Hal effectively became the man of the house before he had mastered his multiplication tables. He got himself and his little sister Sarah ready for school and out the door each day, helped her with her homework at night (she was a year older, but struggled mightily with her lessons), and had sole responsibility for the scraggly vegetable garden in the back yard. "A little hard work never killed anyone," Charlie would say, stretched out on the sofa in the front room. "When I was your age ..."

"Oh, hush," Vera would say. Usually he would.

Sarah was late today, staying after school to wrap bandages for the War drive. She was a dreamy, quiet girl, prettier than anyone gave her credit for, content in her private world of pressed flowers, secret sketchbooks and walks on the beach. Her marks were poor but passing, her demeanor sad and distant. Hal loved her fiercely. Just last week he'd overheard a fifth grader refer to her as a "spook" and he'd blackened the boy's eye. He received a double detention at school, but Charlie had approved wholeheartedly.

Vera was due home soon. Hal went out to the garden and returned with a limp head of broccoli, a pencil-thin cucumber and three knobby potatoes.

"I guess I can do something with these," he said.

"Sure could use some meat," Charlie answered. "When's the last time we had a bit of meat? I don't see how a boy your size is supposed to stay alive on rabbit food."

Hal sighed. When his father got on one of his meat kicks there was no stopping him. Either Hal snuck into the emergency money Vera kept in an empty cold cream jar and went into town for a couple of anemic chops or a skinny chicken, or Charlie was likely to drag out his old bicycle from behind the outhouse and pedal up and down Harbor Road after midnight, looking for fresh road kill. When he found something, God forbid, he would skin it on the spot and bring the carcass back for stew. Raccoon, squirrel, skunk, rabbit, porcupine—he wasn't choosy about, or even always certain, what he'd found. "A man needs flesh," he'd say when he had eaten, a line of brown gravy running down his chin. Hal preferred to raid the cold cream jar.

He met Sarah on his way out the door to the butcher.

"He wants meat again," Hal whispered. "I'll run over to Steiner's." That was the Bavarian butcher on Magnolia Avenue, a suspect figure since the War started, but the cheapest in town.

"I'm not hungry," she said. "I might just lie down."

"I'll bring something up to you."

She squeezed his arm as she passed. Her hand was hot as a skillet.

"Are you okay?" said Hal.

"Just tired."

She smiled her thin little smile and went upstairs.

Vera was in the kitchen when Hal returned. A cup of tea steamed at her elbow and her head nestled in her arms. She jerked it up when Hal came in carrying a small brown package.

"Him and his meat again?"

Their eyes met. Hal shrugged. She knew where he got the money.

"I'll make a soup," he said. "I dug some spuds from the back."

"No you will not," she said. "I'll make the dinner. You go and play."

Men were scarce in Hal's life—men, that is, who seemed to him anything like what it was worthwhile trying to become. Many of the young fellows in town had shipped off in the last year, to training camps or to Europe itself. (The first few of them had started to come home, in boxes as often as in sleeper cars.) Uncle Abe, as Hal had always known him, had signed up in June and was off serving in France. Uncle Warren, too nearsighted to be a soldier, had left town a few years back.

It was mostly through his mother's eyes that Hal saw the world. He could do little wrong in their light. Not that he was a problem child, but he did get into fights a lot. Because of his size-- it was clear that even if he stopped growing by the time he reached puberty, he'd still be one of the biggest men in Oxnard--, there was a certain kind of boy that couldn't resist trying to best him. Hal took on all comers. He fought them reluctantly but efficiently, with an uncanny sense for matching the intensity of his victory to the strength of the vanquished. He hurt no one more than he had to.

Under the back stairs he kept a baseball and a glove. He took them most evenings to the brick wall of an old building a few blocks away. It was part of an abandoned shoe factory that now sat crumbling in the shadow of three enormous date palms. Hal would pace off fifteen steps, kick a line in the dirt and start firing away. A chalked rectangle on the wall represented a stingy strike zone. Inside it the bricks were chipped and darkened by the impact of his bruised and battered ball, many stitches of which were already broken. He'd throw, he'd field the bounce-back, and he'd throw again. And again. And again.

Tonight he threw until sunset. He whistled a tune as he walked home—*It's a Long Way to Tipperary, it's a long way to go* …. Everyone was singing it these days. Overhead a hovering hawk waited lazily for the first of the night-critters to make their tentative, fatal forays into the open space along the road. Hal watched the bird with his head tilted back. It would be alright to be a hawk. As long as he was eating rodents, it would be better to have them fresh.

His father was sitting on the front porch steps. He'd gotten a cigar someplace, and was curled up in a posture of unusual bliss for a man in his circumstances. Hal was tossing the baseball up and down, still whistling, letting the odor of just-made stew pull him up the stairs.

"There he is," said Charlie, exhaling an enormous blue cloud, like his own private weather. "My own spittin' image. How old are you, now, anyway?"

Hal's eyes opened wide. Wasn't that a father's job to know?

"Eight," he said.

Charlie whistled softly through his teeth.

"Hell, you're one tall drink of water. But I guess you've heard that before."

"I guess."

Charlie smoked. Hal stood by him, waiting to be dismissed. It was fully dark now, and very quiet. The stars sparkled the sky from horizon to horizon. Charlie knocked his cigar against his cast.

"You hear anything about the War today?" he asked. Hal kept his ears open for news and rumors, and his eyes open for used papers for Charlie to read. He'd picked up neither today, but it always helped to tell his father something.

"They say the Hun is pulling back," he answered.

This was the same news Hal had delivered on Monday. Charlie didn't seem to notice. He sucked his stogie and popped three ragged smoke rings into the darkness.

"You bet your ass he's pulling back," he said. "That dog has had his day."

"How come you didn't go?"

Hal's own words surprised him. Looking at the globe at school he would imagine how far it was to that distant fistful of countries where the fighting was, and what it was like to be there. He'd heard the men outside Josie's barbershop say that it was "Hell in the trenches." Trenches were holes in the ground, he knew, and Hell was the biggest hole in the ground of all, so he pictured them as some sort of openings to where the Devil himself lived, like stairways strewn across a field with bombs dropping all around and men fighting, real fighting with guns and bayonets and no crying 'uncle'. He tried to see his father fighting, with his fake cast and eye patch, sucking his cigar and smelling like last week's dishwater. He couldn't bring the picture into focus.

It was too dark to read Charlie's expression in the long silence that followed, except once, when the cigar glowed bright and Hal could see his eyes, not angry as he expected but half closed and studying him through the smoke.

"I've got a family," said Charlie, soft enough that he might have been talking to himself. "If I go off to fight the Hun, who stays here to take care of you and the girls?"

From inside came the pounding of feet, first on the stairs, then crossing the living room. The front door banged open. Vera held the limp form of her daughter in her arms.

"Run for the doctor," she said. "Quick."

Hal looked at his father.

"You know I can't run …" Charlie began.

"I wasn't talking to you," Vera snapped.

She turned to Hal. Sarah's head fell backward, her hair reaching the ground.

"Run I said."

Doc Broughton's house was on Fifth Street, on the other side of Plaza Park. Hal's legs were long, and the streets flew by beneath him.

Overhead the stars seemed close enough to touch. When it was dark in Oxnard, Mrs. Perluski said, the sun in France was shining on the trenches. Hal wished he was old enough to go fight the Hun. He would send them down those stairways into Hell. You bet your ass he would. But he was only eight, and his sister needed the Doctor. So he ran faster.

..

Sarah died three days later. That was quick for the influenza, though not as quick as some. She'd been young for a victim. Not as many small children died as adults. Thousands and thousands and thousands of them. Over a hundred in Oxnard alone. There was no bright side to her death, of course, but Hal had to admit that it brought some changes to the Gates' house. On the morning of the service Hal didn't even recognize his father when he came downstairs, and he was about to ask the stranger what he wanted when he spotted the familiar twinkle in Charlie's eyes. The cast, eye patch and twitch were gone. He'd shaved his beard and found a suit somewhere, and a white shirt and a pair of shiny shoes. Vera straightened his tie and kissed his cheek, something Hal wasn't sure he'd ever seen.

"Aren't you worried the press gangs will take you?" Hal blurted.

Charlie drew back his shoulders.

"Let 'em try," he said.

..

Life after the funeral was hard to get used to. Not only was Sarah gone, which left a hole in Hal's heart as well as an empty bed in the room they had shared, but his parents were different people; people he found himself having to get to know all over again. Especially Charlie. He didn't revert to his draft-evading self. One of his buddies found him a job doing clerk work in the mailroom at the Courthouse, sending out jury notices and keeping track of all the requests for exemptions, mostly from grievers for victims of the influenza and the war. He left for work each morning at eight o'clock and came home sober in time for dinner every night. It was as if Hal's father had moved out of the house and a new man had moved in.

The most alarming transformation came on a day in late December, when Charlie announced at breakfast that he would be going into the office late, as he was stopping off to register at the temporary Selective Service Registration office on Hill Street.

"Man's got a duty," he said.

Vera set her coffee cup down carefully. Hal saw that her hand was trembling.

"What are you thinking?" she said sharply. "You want to go over there and get yourself gassed? Haven't you been hearing the stories?"

The Armistice was already a month old, signed about the time Charlie last changed his undershirt. Hal had heard the chances of new recruits seeing combat were slim-to-none, but he bit his lip so as to afford his father his moment of bravery.

"What I'm hearing is that Kaiser Billy is pulling back," Charlie said. "Now that we've got us over there in force just need a few more doughboys to finish the job."

"Simple as that, is it? Leave me and the youngster to fend for ourselves?"

"The 'youngster' here is practically my size."

"He's eight years old."

"Almost nine," Hal piped up.

Charlie smiled.

"'Atta boy."

Vera had no need to worry. Charlie came home for lunch that day as usual, banging open the new Kelvinator (bought on credit) and whistling "How I Hate to Get Up in the Morning." Hal sat at the kitchen table, eating a peanut butter sandwich.

"So," she said. "No uniform?"

"Exempt on two counts," he answered. "Seems they don't have a pressing need for married men, for one. And because of my job I am officially an Officer of the Judiciary. So it's stateside for me. Somebody's got to keep the home fires burning."

"God help the home fires," Vera muttered.

She would go out at night alone sometimes after dinner. These visits did not sit well with Charlie, who would wait up for her. The hissing discussions they would have when she came home kept Hal awake. From Charlie came "ridiculous," "charlatan," and "gullible." His mother spoke less, but he heard her say "contact," and "manifestation," and "scientifically proven." He asked her about these outings one day when his father wasn't around.

Vera explained that she had met a woman in town named "Madeleine," who had house parties to which some of the local ladies came, especially those who had lost their children to the fighting or the flu.

"Sad parties?" Hal asked

"Not really," his mother said. "Sometimes Madeleine helps us—well, talk to the ones we've lost. From the other side, you know."

"From heaven?"

Vera smiled.

"Sort of like that." she said

"Do you talk to Sarah?"

"We're … looking," said Vera. "There are so many."

"Why doesn't Daddy go to the parties?"

She put her hand on his head, then let it drop to his shoulder. It felt heavy there.

"Your father doesn't want to hear the voices."

"Will you take me instead?" he asked.

Vera took both his hands in hers, and looked him straight in the face. "Maybe someday," she said.

··

That summer, Hal played on his first real baseball team. None of the other kids guessed that he was three years younger than them, as he towered over the tallest by a head. He pitched mostly, and he was more or less un-hittable. Sometimes he'd float one in slow and let a poor kid have a poke at it, just to put the ball into play. When he came to the plate himself the other teams just played him deep and prayed.

Hal was happy. The War was finally over, and the horrors of the influenza. Sarah's death was still sad, but its immediate sting was fading. Vera kept up her visits to Madeleine, but Charlie didn't wait up anymore. Hal would let himself fall asleep as soon as he heard her footsteps coming home. This was a summer he wanted to last forever.

Its end was sudden, and it arrived by train. On August 15, with his ball team unbeaten, the backyard tomatoes in fat, full fruit and the first day of school still three eternal weeks away, Uncle Abe came home. Charlie brought him home to Downing Street. To Hal's delight Abe grabbed Vera around the waist and twirled her like a square dancer. She laughed and seemed not to mind. Then he looked at Hal.

"I'll be good goddamned," he said, "if you are the same kid I knew a year ago."

Hal blushed. Abe turned to Vera.

"I am truly sorry," he said, "about—you know."

The light faded in Vera's eyes.

"It all happened so fast," she said.

"There's been a lot of changes," he said. "Bad and good."

"This calls for a drink," Charlie announced. And out came the whiskey.

Charlie didn't make it into work the next day, nor the day after, and then came the weekend and there was no reason not to celebrate a little longer. Vera didn't complain. She cooked and laughed and drank and let Abe waltz her around the room while John McCormack sang *Roses of Picardy* on the brand new gramophone. It was good to have Abe home. If only Warren was there, it would be just like the old days.

Monday morning dawned. Charlie had taken Abe out to one of the fruit pickers' tent camps after dinner the night before, and they hadn't returned by breakfast. Hal went to school. When he came home at noon his mother was sitting at the kitchen counter looking like she'd swallowed a rock. It seemed she'd walked into town to the Courthouse mail room, to see if Charlie had come straight to work. But they didn't know where he was at the mail room. He hadn't worked there for several weeks. One of the women took her aside and explained that there had been an "altercation," as she called it, between Charlie and a man from the Temperance League named Hopkins, who was circulating a petition for a ban on alcohol sales in Ventura County. Charlie had taken a swing at him. When the poor guy came to, Charlie had cleaned out his desk and gone. Mr. Hopkins still worked in Records, she said, if Vera would like to see him. But Vera had seen enough.

By the time the anniversary of Sarah's death came around in October, things were pretty much back to the old ways at the Gates'. On many mornings Hal found his father still awake from the night before, sitting at the kitchen table, sometimes talking to Abe and sometimes just talking. The Kelvinator had been repossessed, as had Doc Broughton's Model T. The salary Vera thought they'd been living on turned out to be mostly credit. Charlie was nonplussed. *Income*, he said, was a word for working stiffs. What Vera and Hal needed to get used to was the notion of *fortune*, for things were about to change in the Gates household, and once they turned the corner there would be no looking back. He had a plan, he said. Abe was part of it too. There were changes in the wind, he said. Soon they'd know. Soon enough.

Soon was a rainy Friday after school in January. Hal came home with a pit in his stomach, for he'd been in a fight again. Edgar Hopkins, sure enough the son of the man from the Courthouse, finally had worked up the nerve to ambush Hal on the way home from school. The scuffle was short. There were four of them. Once Hal recovered from the initial assault it had taken him only six punches to end the fight, and six only because Edgar, who believed he was fighting for his family's honor, took three blows to the head before he fell. Hopkins was a teacher's pet; he'd have a tale to tell. Hal figured he'd best tell his side first.

The moment he stepped inside the house he knew that this was not the time for confessions. Abe was there along with Charlie and three men Hal didn't recognize. They were sitting at the kitchen table with glasses in their hands. The strangers wore dark suits, felt fedoras and thin moustaches like his father had grown after Sarah's death. The table was covered with maps, and some other papers that looked to be ledgers. Stacked in the empty space where the Kelvinator had been were a dozen crates of brown bottles. From the front room Hal could hear his mother sobbing.

"This your kid?" said the oldest-looking of the three strangers

Charlie nodded.

"Halley," he said, for some reason using his son's full name.

"He sixteen yet?" said the man. "He know how to drive a car?"

"Nine," said Charlie.

"Nine what?" said the man.

"He's tall for his age," said Charlie.

"Holy Toledo," said the man. "Does he drink?"

"Plenty of time for that," Charlie said.

"Besides, nobody drinks anymore," said Abe. "It's the law."

The men all laughed. Hal stepped sideways past them and into the living room. Vera was huddled in a corner of the sofa. She reached for him, drawing him to her. He could not imagine why.

CHAPTER TWO

HOUDINI PIE

"FLASH the light once when the coast is clear."

Hal nodded. He *always* flashed the light and, so far, despite a couple of close-calls, the coast had always been clear. Clear enough for Abe or one of the boys to make it onto the street or into the woods, or even a couple of times into the air in a rickety biplane, with the cargo that had been the Gates' life blood for almost ten years now. Charlie was a bootlegger, and a damned good one. Hal was his right-hand-man. And tonight, once again, the coast was as clear as an Oxnard summer sky.

Anyone paying attention had seen Prohibition coming, of course, what with the Temperance and Anti-Saloon Leagues and Kraut-bashers all having their say. The only thing a hard-working honest drinking man could do was to learn to like home-brewed beer and weather out the righteous storm. Unless he was a man of imagination and ambition, that is. During the year between ratification of the 18th Amendment and the dark day that it became law, they'd developed one of the most sophisticated distributorships south of San Francisco. Charlie was the mastermind. Abe's job was to know the market, the competition, the networks and—most of the time—the whereabouts and disposition of the Law. Vera reluctantly took on the role of bookkeeper. Hal was the workhorse.

He started out digging holes, the summer after his thirteenth birthday. Charlie and Abe somehow had appropriated title to the old shoe factory on King Street. Construction had been abandoned long before Hal was born, after a foundation had been poured and the rudiments of a steam tunnel excavated below grade. It was in this semi-basement space that Charlie set his son to work. At first it was weekends only, "nothing that will interfere with his precious schoolwork," Charlie said. And at first he'd worked for free. Eventually Charlie paid him, ten cents an hour. Vera bit her lip and entered his salary in the book. Despite her misgivings, she recognized the prudence of keeping their enterprise a family business.

Thirteen had felt different. Life pressed in, shimmering with colors, alive with sounds, rich with smells he had never noticed before. It was as if someone had sprinkled salt and pepper on a world he had been eating plain. Hal threw himself into the digging, feeling the muscles in his arms and back tighten like ropes in the sun. He dug until he was hungry and thirsty and his muscles burned. And he dug some more.

Seven years later, waiting for the umpteenth time for the coast to be clear, Hal had not dug anything in ages. They had plenty of store-houses by now. Besides, playing 'lookout' was far more important. Rival distributors sprang up every day. Worst were the outright "robbin' hoods;" thieves who preyed on established bootleggers, raiding caches and sabotaging deliveries. Monitoring their whereabouts became even more demanding than keeping track of the Law. Tonight the drop was a school house outside of town. The buyer was a swell named Baxter, a lawyer who was throwing a party to celebrate his daughter's engagement. Baxter insisted on inspecting the goods before transfer, a ritual that usually consisted of drinking an entire bottle of the evening's booze of choice (Scotch, tonight) with Charlie and Abe, while Hal kept watch.

Hal lit matches at ten minute intervals and studied in their light from a book propped against the steering wheel. He didn't know what he would do after high school. His grades were good enough for college, but college cost money and although it seemed to Hal like there was a fair bit of it around, Charlie would hear no talk of more schooling.

"Twelve years of sitting in a desk getting spoken at is more than anybody should put up with," he said. "A high school education was good enough for me and Abe."

"And Warren?" Vera asked.

Hal barely remembered his other "uncle." Warren had gone to college years ago, someplace in Colorado. He sent letters at Christmas and on Vera's birthday. They focused on his travels all over the U.S.; Europe, a couple of times South America, even Australia. Charlie was confused, always looking for the angle in Warren's itineraries, seeking the profit motive that would inspire a man to spend a month in Italy, or endure a steamer trip to Indonesia, or spend the weird months Warren described wandering the deserts of Arizona and New Mexico.

"What the devil is out there but scorpions?" Charlie would wonder. "Maybe he's looking for oil. I bet there's untold crude under them mountains."

"Seems like he spends most of his time with the Indians," Hal would answer, squinting to read Warren's tiny, precise handwriting.

"They know where the damned oil is," Charlie insisted. "You mark my words. He'll be rich as Croesus in five years. Let's hope he remembers old friends."

The letters were a little weird. Warren would go on and on and on about this or that cemetery or tomb, or about the odd customs and stories that he picked up on his travels. Vera read them over and over. Hal wasn't sure exactly what the connection was between Warren's letters and his mother's obsession, but clearly her enthusiasm was wrapped up in her long-standing quest to reach Sarah. Madeleine had passed away after a few years of fruitless séances, but Vera never had let go of her mission. Left to her own devices she was game for any strategy she could find. She read tea leaves, she bought a Ouija board, she tried self-hypnosis, and she attended meetings of every spiritualist group she could locate.

She even built a crystal radio. Everyone was building them. Hal had made a couple himself in high school science class. But his had not been intended, like Vera's, to pick up signals from the "world of the physically departed." The idea made such perfect sense to Vera that she was taken aback by Charlie's stock dismissal of "hocus pocus quackery," or, as he inexplicably referred to her spiritual endeavors, "damned Houdini pie."

The set was made partly out the sole of one of Sarah's old slippers. Vera intertwined strands of her daughter's yellow hair with copper wire wrapped meticulously around the shoe. She set the crystal in the cradle of a mood ring that Sarah had bought at the Ventura Country Fair. Snippets of ribbons, pressed flowers, dresses and even bits of under things were pasted here and there on the apparatus, which was contained in a cut-out jewelry box. Vera managed to incorporate a pair of her daughter's earmuffs into the headphones she used to listen to broadcasts, or to monitor incoming projections.

For hours she sat on the sofa in the living room, the earmuffs on her head, sliding the steel tuning needle slowly up and down the copper wire coil. Sometimes she would stop and lean forward, a look of rapturous concentration on her face. If Hal was in the room he would freeze, his pulse quickening. Then Vera would relax, Hal would return to his schoolwork and Charlie, if he was present, would cackle and pour another jot of whatever he was drinking.

Baxter was taking his sweet time sampling the goods this evening. Two hours was too long. Hal opened the door quietly and lowered himself to the ground. He needed to pee, and he needed to know what the hell was going on.

The drop-off was a good twenty miles inland, but the air was so still Hal could swear he heard the surf beyond the hills. The splash of his stream on the orchard dirt was so loud it embarrassed him, even though he was alone. He buttoned up and realized as he started for the road that the night was less quiet than it had been when he'd left the truck. He froze and tried to pinpoint the difference.

The sound was distant but growing. An engine. Hal slipped back inside the truck cab, then immediately decided that might not have been the best thing to do. If the whine meant trouble, a hundred-proof laundry truck might be the last place he would want to be associated with Hal Gates.

The whine stopped. Hal exhaled a deeply-held breath.

The light on the schoolhouse porch went out. Then on. Then out again.

Hal started the truck and lurched out of the orange grove, directly into the path of a shiny black Marmon with its lights out. He acted purely on bootlegger's instinct—to run. He spun the truck around and shoved the gas pedal to the floor, working through the gears until he was flat-out hauling it in the direction not of the barn but of the schoolhouse itself. The big Marmon, its lights on now, was in hot pursuit. Hal knew the car could outrun, pass and block him, knew that his flight would be short and futile. Then what? Make a dash for it on foot? They wouldn't hesitate to shoot him, he knew. There were ugly stories of how agents treated bootleggers out in the country with no witnesses around. The Marmon's lights were right on his tail; he could hear it roaring behind him, and then, sure enough, the *pop* of a revolver, then another. The schoolhouse was to his right. They would hear the gunfire, of course. Would they come to his aid? He leaned on the horn, yanked the steering wheel to the right and bounced across the field. They sure as hell better.

He didn't see the ditch. The left front truck wheels were suddenly suspended in air. His shoulder hit hard against the driver's door. From behind him came the sound of breaking glass, then the sound of shouting. Hal shook his head to clear it, made a quick bodily inventory—nothing broken, nothing gashed—and roused himself to a kneeling position. The truck was completely on its side. He straightened himself slowly, pushed open the passenger door above him and hoisted his torso free of the cab.

Another shot rang out, then another. In the interval between them Hal was thrown back against the door frame. He thought he might have been hit, though he felt no pain. More shouting, and dark shapes approaching, lanterns swinging in the air. The roar of the Marmon in reverse, a squeal of brakes, a couple more shots—different this time, the ringing of a rifle, not the pop of a handgun—then another roar as the big car sped away.

Men surrounded the truck. Hal saw Charlie, Abe, and a few strangers—one holding a deer rifle—and a fat, florid man with a drooping moustache he took to be Baxter; the only face in the lantern-light that was looking not at him, but at the tail lights of the retreating car. From the back of the truck came the smell of alcohol.

"You okay?" said Charlie.

Hal was too stunned to speak. Baxter turned to several shadows hovering at the edge of the group.

"Might as well unload anything salvageable," he said.

Hal was led to a classroom that had been turned into a temporary speakeasy. The teacher's desk was covered with bottles and set-ups; ginger ale and tonic water and a galvanized bucket of ice. Next to them stood a wind-up Victrola, its needle riding the dead band at the end of a black disk, filling the air with a rhythmic hiss and pop. Hal excused himself and found the boys' bathroom across the hallway. Beneath the glare of a bare bulb he examined himself. His left shoulder bore a green and purple bruise as big as one of his own handprints. There was a painful knot on his head where he must have struck the door. Most frightening was something he didn't see until he was taking his shirt off for a careful wash-up: a bullet hole, near the breast pocket, blackened around its edges. Another half inch and he'd have taken it in the chest.

Back in the classroom everyone talked at once. Charlie approached him, Abe in tow. His father's eyes were red, his tie askew, his smile lopsided.

"What's the damage?"

The hole in the shirt was visible, but neither man noticed it.

"Bunch of bruises. I'll live."

Abe staggered to the makeshift bar and returned with three glasses. He gave one to Charlie, one to Hal, and kept one for himself, which he raised in the air with a grin.

"Here's to close calls," he said.

Hal looked into his glass, half-full of amber liquid the color of unhealthy pee. Booze. He'd never even tasted it—never really wanted to. It paid the bills, it kept the family together, but it didn't appeal to him the way it did other men. Tonight it had almost killed him. He supposed he ought to make its acquaintance. He lifted the glass to his lips and drained it. It was just as he'd expected—neither bad nor good, really; just an earthy burning in his throat and a sharpness in his nose. Abe offered a refill. Hal took it down in one more quick gulp and set his glass on the desk.

"Can we go home now?" he said.

CHAPTER THREE

WAITING OUT THE STORM

O N Hal's twenty-first birthday, Vera broke her leg. She always over-did his birthday. One year—third grade, was it?—she came to school in a clown suit to surprise him on the playground. In sixth grade she brought little cakes for the whole class at lunchtime. In high school she'd insisted on parties. This year she outdid herself. Maybe she was trying extra hard to counter the aura of gloom that had settled over the town—over the whole country—in the year and a half since the Crash. After the first shock there had been optimism. Surely things wouldn't get as bad as the papers were saying. But they had, and fast. Businesses failed so quickly that men left for work in the morning and were queuing up for bread lines by sundown. Farmers looked to the banks for loans, for seed, for fertilizer, and to pay their desperate help, and the banks did not look back. There were riots in L.A., lootings in San Francisco, a rash of burglaries in Ventura. After a while the violence subsided and the populace fell into a gray funk of despair.

Vera's accident happened while she was putting up Christmas lights, part of her birthday surprise for Hal, who would be arriving late with Charlie after a routine run. All across the roof line she had built a chicken wire frame on which she wired the shape of a comet in white bulbs, streaking through the sky. Below, in red, she was writing her son's name. She slipped while making the "H." She was still on the ground when the boys got back from their run. They were surprised, all right.

Home from the hospital two days later, a new white cast encasing her leg from pelvis to toes, she tried to joke about it all. *What I have to do around here to get a little attention?* Hal got up on the roof to untangle the mess of wires. He looked out over the familiar Oxnard rooftops, the twin smokestacks of the beet factory on Wooley Road, the palms at Plaza Park, the unfathomable Pacific in the distance. It was pretty, it was home, and it was driving him crazy. He'd had his fill of Oxnard. Down in the city, even with the Crash—well, there must be opportunities for a young man.

Hal was by far the biggest man in town. He'd stopped growing at six-foot-nine-inches in his socks, then spent a couple of years filling out. His hair was thick, curly and the color of corn silk. If he didn't keep it cropped close it stuck up like a cockscomb, which made him seem even taller. His torso was as big as a pot-bellied stove, but there wasn't an inch of flab on him. Despite his height and girth, his face remained pre-teen: round cheeks and hairless chin; his blue eyes wide and clear. But even if those eyes could find a place for him to go, how could he leave his mother behind?

Vera's leg healed slowly. The cast turned a dingy yellow. Doc Broughton had long since passed away, but his successor, young Doctor Stevens, came by the house to smile and counsel patience. Hal saw worry in his eyes. His mother, never a robust woman, was wilting worse than ever. She lost weight. Her skin was the color of the cast. Her hair was dry and thin. Getting to her bedroom required both Hal and Charlie to carry her, moaning, up the stairs. By mid-July she no longer left the couch at all except to use the outhouse. The downstairs took on an unpleasant, sweetish smell. Charlie never set foot there except on his way to bed. Many nights he didn't even come home to sleep.

As '31 dragged into '32, the Great Depression—that's what they were calling it now—got worse. The bootlegging stayed steady, but it got harder for Hal to feel good about it, surrounded by so many signs of desperation. Only Charlie seemed content.

"We're just waiting out the storm," he would say.

On a hot morning in the middle of June, the telephone rang. Vera picked it up in the living room. Hal was reading the paper in the kitchen. The radio played softly in the background; a thin guitar and a high, sad yodel. Charlie was pouring coffee, his hand shaking as he splashed over his cup onto the table.

"Rough night?" said Hal.

"I feel worse than I look."

That was hard for Hal to imagine. As he turned back to his paper a shout came from the sofa.

"That's wonderful!"

"What the hell?" Charlie said.

Hal set the paper down. What, indeed, could possibly be wonderful?

··

Uncle Warren was coming to visit. Hal went into town for groceries and came home to find Vera transformed. She'd put on a long blue skirt he had never seen; an old-fashioned thing that fell nearly to the floor and covered her injured leg. Her blouse looked new, but it had been so long since he had seen her properly dressed that he didn't remember what clothes she owned. Her hair was washed and brushed. She wore lipstick and moved with the aid of only a cane.

There were fresh flowers on the kitchen table and not a single dish in the sink or drainer. The Victrola was open, its speaker horn raised. There was a smell of baking.

"I tidied up a bit," Vera said.

Warren arrived at six o'clock, pulling up to the curb in a shiny white Studebaker.

"He's heard all about you," Vera whispered to Hal. "Don't be surprised if he acts like you're a long-lost friend."

She opened the door and for several seconds simply stood, rooted and speechless. Finally Hal heard her laugh, only it was not any sound he'd ever heard from his mother; a high, descending trill, like he imagined a tropical bird might make.

"My goodness," she said. "Do come in."

Hal did not recognize the man who stepped over the threshold. He was ordinary looking, in a tan suit rumpled from travel, with a plain oval face, black-framed glasses and a high forehead sloping to baldness. His only remarkable feature was his eyes, an unusual brownish green, which he blinked rapidly.

"Vera," he said.

He took her hand and gave a sort of bow. Then he looked at Hal.

"And this," he said, "must be the famous Halley Gates."

Warren's grip was strong. He looked Hal up and down.

"You're even bigger than I pictured you," he said. "Vera, you must have had some lumberjacks on your side of the family."

Vera laughed the bird-laugh.

"Or Charlie's," she said.

"Yes, of course," said Warren. "Though it doesn't seem likely."

At that moment Charlie arrived, carrying two brown shopping sacks up the steps to the back door. There was a moment of handshakes, grins and back-slapping. Charlie led everyone to the kitchen.

"Who wants a beer?" He dug into one the bags. "I got this from a guy at the auto shop. It's the real thing too, none of this homebrew crap. Cold to boot."

"Sure," Hal said. "A cold beer sounds just fine."

His father handed the bottle over.

"Tea for me," said Warren. "If there is any."

Vera got up to put the kettle on.

"So what's it been, pardner?" Charlie began. "Ten years?"

"Fifteen," said Vera.

Charlie whistled.

"Holy Toledo," he said. "A lot can happen in fifteen years. Hell, a lot *has* happened. I'm trying to remember even what the occasion was."

"Christmas," said Vera. "Warren was in town visiting his mother."

"You write this all down someplace?" Charlie said. Then he tilted his bottle back, drained it, and cocked his head toward his son.

"Guess this guy has grown up some," he said.

"There's an understatement," Warren said.

"You ever have any kids?" said Charlie.

Vera slapped her husband on the knee.

"Don't you think he'd have told us if he'd gotten married?"

"I didn't ask that," Charlie said. Warren forced a laugh.

"Well, it's no to both. Just never could see myself settling down."

"I know what you mean," said Charlie, nodding slowly as though the topic was suddenly a grave one. "The life of a family man. Who'd have thought it of any of us, back in the old days? Sometimes I can hardly remember a time I didn't have two more mouths to feed besides my own."

"Or three," Vera added softly. Charlie squinted at her.

"Yeah," he said. "Or three."

Charlie reminisced for a while. Warren laughed at a couple of anecdotes about old teachers and pals, and of course the Stardust Pills story, all of which Hal had heard before. When talk finally turned to Warren, he had other tales to tell.

His life had been a travel book. From Oxnard he'd gone to Colorado, where he managed a degree at the School of Mines, a program financed over five years of odd jobs—accounting, mostly, though he'd also been a camp cook, a grade-school teacher, an Indian interpreter, an insurance salesman and an intermittently successful poker player. During and after his school years he had traveled. Usually he was looking for stones. Rocks, gems, minerals, ore deposits and even once—in Brazil—the oil Charlie assumed had made his fortune. But there had been no fortune. There had been paychecks, and winnings, and a few foreign investments to which he made vague allusion, and somehow he'd come out all right. Warren freely acknowledged that he had been lucky. He wondered about the Gates'.

"Could be worse, eh?" he asked. "I didn't see the wolf at the door."

"We manage," Vera said.

They ate by candlelight—Vera's idea—in relative silence. Relative, because Charlie could not be awake and silent at the same time. He talked about the Depression, the cops, the coming elections, and the trials and tribulations of running a business.

"There are big changes coming," he said, spearing a pork chop.

Warren agreed.

"By the time this young fellow is our age," he said, nodding at Hal, "he'll hardly recognize the world we live in now."

"Gets so I hardly recognize it myself," Charlie said. "I mean, what kind a world is it where a man can't buy himself a damned drink after a hard day's work?"

"Legally, you mean," said Hal. "It's not so hard to do otherwise."

"Well, yeah," Charlie said. "Thanks to guys like us."

Warren fixed his attention on Hal.

"So what about you? You're full grown now, and then some. What have you got in mind?"

"For what?" said Hal.

"For your future. There's a wide world out there. Big strong fellow like you ought to be able to find a way to make a living in it."

Hal cleared his throat. He wasn't sure what to say. His father was.

"What the hell?" said Charlie. "He's got a job. And a roof over his head, and three squares a day. More than a lot of fellows can lay claim to."

Warren kept his eyes on Hal.

"As long as you're satisfied," he said.

"Satisfied?!" Charlie exploded, slamming his hand on the table. "Since when has 'satisfied' had anything to do with making a living?"

Hal took a breath.

"The work's not so bad."

"'Course it's not," said Charlie. "And somebody's got to do it."

Vera got up to clear the table. Warren put his hand on Hal's arm.

"I've got a few things in my car," he said, "if you could give me a hand."

Hal followed his uncle to the Studebaker. The night was cool, with a west wind carrying the smell of the sea. Warren opened the trunk and dragged out two fat leather suitcases, plastered with travel stickers, and a cardboard box tied with twine. Hal hefted a suitcase in each hand and followed his uncle back up the walk.

Vera was making coffee in the kitchen. Charlie had relocated to an overstuffed chair in the living room.

"Gather 'round," Warren said. "It's Christmas a little early."

One suitcase was full of presents. Warren handed them around with obvious delight. Most were for Vera. They brought a glow to her eyes and a blush to her cheeks. There was a hand-knit shawl from Ecuador, a Japanese kimono, crystal salt and pepper shakers from Boston, a turquoise necklace from New Mexico. There were books, too: a volume of poetry, an Atlas with maps in rich, bright colors, a book about the Pueblo Indians. And there was a geode the size of a grapefruit, broken cleanly in two, each cavity lined with crystals of astonishing colors, indigo and purple and shimmering silver that caught the light of the table lamp and held it in infinite, flashing depths. Vera gasped. Even Charlie was impressed.

"This cost you a bunch?"

"I found it," Warren said. "On a hilltop in Utah. There were thousands of them."

"Just laying around?" Charlie squinted. "For anybody?"

"Anybody who wants to climb around like a mountain goat in the burning sun," said Warren. "There's no money value to them. The Zuni Indians believe them to be very powerful. 'Thunder rocks,' they call them. In their mythology ..."

Charlie waved his hand.

"Enough mumbo jumbo," he said. "I thought you might have something here."

Warren handed Hal the final parcel from the suitcase, which looked to be nothing but a wad of brown butcher's paper. Hal pulled it open and found a scuffed baseball with an inked signature that he saw, looking closely, was that of Babe Ruth himself. He looked up with a grin.

"I've been carrying that around for you for years," said Warren.

Charlie made a snorting sound. So far there had been no gift with his name on it. Hal tossed him the ball. Charlie nodded at it, frowning, as if assessing its authenticity. Warren reached for the cardboard box and passed it to him.

"Hope they fit," he said.

When Charlie peeled back a corner of the box his face brightened. He lifted out a pair of boots, one in each hand. They were an unusual style, not quite riding boots, not quite dress-up, with sharp toes and thick heels, made of some kind of tooled leather in fantastically intricate designs that shimmered in the light. It was hard to pin down their color: partly brown, somehow violet, with winks of green and purple. Charlie whistled.

"Where in the world ... ?"

"Arizona," said Warren. "Lizard skin. Made by the Hopi. Very old."

"Lizards?" Charlie squinted. "Must've taken a few."

"Fewer than you'd think. I suspect they are iguana. Some of those beasts are more than two feet long. The old Indians raise them like pets."

Charlie kicked off his shoes to try the new boots on. Hal's hand shot up to his nose. Vera blushed and looked away.

"Hurry up," Warren laughed.

They fit perfectly. Charlie stood, holding a trouser leg high to admire one.

"Where the hell you get these?"

"Oh," said Warren, "I won them, in a manner of speaking."

"Poker game?"

"Something like that," Warren said.

"I'll be skunked," Charlie said. "They fit like a damned glove."

"Just don't take them off again while I'm in the county, okay?" said Warren.

He winked at Hal. The room grew quiet. Vera settled back into the sofa cushions, her new shawl pulled up to her neck. She yawned. Warren began to tidy up. Charlie clicked his heels, lit a cigarette and went to have a pee off the porch.

"I made up your sister's old bed in your room," Vera said to Hal. "You can show your uncle the way."

When Hal awoke early the next morning, the other bed was empty and Warren was gone. He found Vera in the kitchen, wearing her new kimono, her crutch leaning against the table by her side. Her eyes were puffy.

"He had business in Los Angeles," she explained, before Hal had said a word. "He put on the coffee before he left, bless him."

Hal poured a cup. The linoleum was cold on his feet. It was barely past dawn.

"He left this," Vera said. She held up a folded paper. Hal took it from her.

Halley,
My apologies for the graceless departure, but duty calls. We'll
meet again soon. In the meantime, take care of your mother.
                                        Warren

"He said it won't be so long again before he's back this way," Vera said.

Hal looked up. Vera reached for his big hand with her small one.

"You will take care of me, won't you?" she whispered. "No matter what?"

She squeezed. Hal squeezed back. Of course he would. No matter what.

CHAPTER FOUR

WORK FOR AN HONEST MAN

AFTER Warren left Vera slipped into a perpetual stalemate of con-valescence. Her leg got neither worse nor better. Doctor Stevens prescribed exercises, baths and compresses, and he tried to take her off the crutches and wean her full-time to the cane. Vera would have none of it. She would pull her Ecuador shawl tightly around her shoulders and bury her nose in one of Uncle Warren's travel books. Those were her good days. She nearly lost interest in her crystal set, though sometimes at night if Hal came in late he would find her wearing the old wired earmuffs, sliding the tuner up and down the coil, with the shoe box on an end table between the halves of Warren's thunder rock.

Abe had missed Warren's visit. He'd been away for a few weeks; "on business" is all he or Charlie would say, which was odd, as they typically didn't keep the details of the enterprise so secret. Hal told him about Warren on a drive one afternoon to Valencia. They were going to take inventory of a rented bourbon storage cellar Charlie had established in the barn of a hard-luck soybean farmer. Abe was twitchy about something. During the week he'd been back from his trip he'd spent his time hunkered in the kitchen, chain smoking Camels, drinking moonshine he'd bought from a Chinaman in Ventura and playing countless losing games of solitaire. When Charlie was home Abe would lure him away on walks to Plaza Park or down to Treacher's Diner, or even just to stand out front by his beat-up Ford, his hand on Charlie's shoulder and his lips close to his ear as though he had secrets he didn't want the air to hear. If the business telephone rang he would rush to answer it. His moves were even more herky-jerky than usual, causing Charlie on more than one occasion to tell him to light someplace goddamn it.

The closer they got to Valencia the odder Abe's behavior seemed. Normally a gleefully reckless driver, he was navigating the route with unusual care, driving under the speed limit, leaning over the steering wheel with his eyes scrunched up as though he was trying to read tiny print on the windshield.

"Tell you what," he said as he finally took a bone-jolting, dirt-road turn off the main highway. "Bootlegging is a rum job. You don't need to go telling your daddy this, but I've made up my mind. End of the year, I'm done."

Hal nodded, saying nothing.

"I mean it," Abe said. "You and him can run the business without me."

Hal had heard this rant before. He didn't want to debate it at the moment. He just hoped Abe knew where the hell they were going.

"Swear to God," Abe insisted.

"So what will you do?" Hal offered. "Pack oranges? Pick beets?"

"There's plenty of work for an honest man out there," Abe said. "Maybe not in Oxnard. Maybe a guy has got to hit the city. Make his own opportunity. There's gonna be changes soon; big changes, everything right like the old days. Who wants to spend life looking over his shoulder? Enough is enough."

As if on cue, somebody took a shot at them. Several shots, actually. They came from off to the right, where a field sloped up to a tangled row of trees and three low shacks that looked like chicken coops. Dirt puffs in their path showed where the shells hit. Abe shoved his foot to the fireboard and the Ford barreled ahead.

"Shit damn!" Abe yelled. "I told you!"

More shots, and the whine of shells as they sailed over the car. Hal dropped to the floor in front of the passenger seat, though the space was far less than his body required. Abe looked angry and scared, but not surprised.

A single slug nipped the left back wheel well with a ring like a big cow bell. Off-road now, Abe jerked the car back and forth, crushing soybeans all around, fighting his way back to level ground. Hal tensed for another shot. None came. Abe found the road, and all at once they were cruising again on the dirt track. Hal poked his head above the window. The ground leveled off. The outbuildings receded beneath the new horizon. He fell back into the seat, his heart pounding.

"Friends of yours?"

"Swear to God," Abe said, his eyes fixed on the road ahead. "I've had enough."

Soon the hills got steeper. The Santa Susana Mountains loomed ahead like a gray-green wall. Hal noticed the air growing hazy, and then a smell of smoke that quickly became overpowering. The haze settled into a cloud that hugged the ground like a dirty brown blanket. Abe took a wide turn around a low hill of fig trees and the source of the smoke came into view: A barn was ablaze, flames leaping forty feet into the sky. Black smoke billowed from its wide door and upper windows. The charred shell of a flat bed truck stood in a gravel turn-around. There was no one in sight.

Abe stopped the car. Hal could hear the crackling flames. Bits of ash as big as ball gloves swirled in the dirty air around them.

"Our destination?" he coughed.

Abe slammed the car into reverse and spun backward off the road. He drove back the way they had come.

"How much liquor you figure was there?" Hal said when he could breathe again.

Abe laughed.

"Not a drop. Not by the time they torched it. That hooch is well on its way to Los Angeles by now, I guarantee you."

"And the welcoming party?"

"Just keep low as we go by. I reckon they've had their fun."

Hal nodded. All in a day's work.

"I'm not looking forward to telling Charlie," he said.

"Oh, I don't know," Abe said softly, almost to himself. "I suspect he won't be so terribly shocked."

"What the hell is that supposed to mean?"

"It's not for me to say, son." Abe answered, biting his lip. "All I know is this game's gone on too long."

They drove the rest of the way in silence. Abe was lost in his thoughts, and Hal didn't know what to say. Abe was all but suggesting that Charlie had had something to do with the fire. Then why had he sent them all that way? Just to have proof of a job well-done? That didn't make any sense. Did he know about the gunfire too?

They got to Downing Street shortly after eight. Abe grunted good-bye and sped away from the house like a taxi in a hurry. Hal stood on the sidewalk and stretched his long arms up toward the stars, arching his back and neck, straining to loosen the kinks of the drive. He went around to the back door, as was his habit. One step inside the kitchen, he knew something was wrong. There was a smell of burning, and for the second time that day Hal wrinkled his nose and felt smoke sting in his eyes. He looked at the stove. Two withered chops sizzled in a cast iron pan, coal black in a grit of their own scorched fat, with the blue gas flame still under them. Hal shut off the valve, grabbed the pan with a dish towel and ran it out to the back steps, where he hurled it into the garden. Back inside he went to the living room, where Vera ought to have been but wasn't. Her shawl was on the floor, her radio sat on the table, and her crutches leaned against the sofa.

"Ma!"

He found Vera upstairs. He couldn't remember the last time she'd been upstairs. But there she was in bed, the sheets up to her chin. Her expression was oddly peaceful.

"He's gone," she said.

"Where?"

She looked toward the window.

"He wasn't sure. He just didn't want to be here, in case they came."

"Who?"

"He didn't say."

"How did you get up here?"

She looked out the window.

"He's still pretty strong for a man his age."

There was nothing to say to that.

She didn't tell him much more over the next few days, during which time she did not leave the upstairs bedroom, not even to use the outhouse, which meant that Hal had to take on the maintenance of the porcelain chamber pot, along with caring for her in new ways—cooking, bathing, reading her to sleep. Not that he had much else to do. There was no sign of Abe. The phone in the living room was silent, as though the news of Charlie's departure had reached his customers already, which for all Hal knew it had. All Vera would say is that he wouldn't be back soon. And Abe? Forget about him, she said. And the business? There is no business, she said. Not without Charlie.

Hal counted the money in the strongbox Vera kept behind a stack of pots in high kitchen cupboard. He didn't look at the ledger—he didn't want to know, just now, what promises or pay-ups might lurk in the future, he just wanted to know what cash they had at the ready. He counted the bills onto the kitchen table: Sixty-one dollars. How long could they live on sixty-one dollars?

He was going to have to find a job.

Finding steady work in Oxnard, California in 1933 was about as easy as finding an iceberg. Whatever one was or wasn't willing to do, there were ten men already waiting for a chance to do it. They lined up at dawn on Commercial Street by Plaza Park, waiting for drivers in flat-bed trucks to round up whatever labor was needed for the day, in the beet fields or the factory, or the walnut or orange groves or the strawberry fields. Sometimes a road or bridge crew would need bodies to haul gravel. The work was always hard, usually dirty, and often dangerous. Trucks rolled up with a driver pointing and shouting, and in a push and scramble of limbs the flatbed would be overfull of the lucky, with the un-lucky lobbing catcalls and occasionally rocks as the truck pulled away. Often the vehicles didn't even stop; they just rolled through, gathering men like bad meat gathers flies. By the time the sun was fully up and the last truck had gone, the men still standing far outnumbered those who, today at least, might not go home empty-handed—provided they actually were paid for their work. But the prospects of just a noon meal, which even the crooked bosses provided, made them luckier than the guys who got left.

There was a complex pecking order among the men. When Hal began showing up at the truck lines, the top spot was held without challenge by a man called "Rex." Like many of the men, he knew about Hal's previous livelihood. Rex made it clear from Hal's first day on the line that he had little regard for "the bootlegger."

"Thinks he's hot stuff," he would mutter. "Thinks he's the big dog now."

Rex was shorter than Hal by a foot, but if Rex didn't outweigh him it was close. And though Rex carried a second man's-worth of excess flesh around his middle, he had at least another man's-worth of muscles, too. It was said he'd been a sailor, a blacksmith, a boxer, a stevedore, a logger and a circus performer. Rex neither confirmed nor denied any rumors. He had a little retinue of thugs and ne'er-do-wells who sought safety, and a kind of notoriety, in his shadow. He was fiercely protective of his status, even as Hal's size and strength made him a favorite of the bosses.

"Hey bootlegger," Rex growled one Monday morning, as the en-gines of the day's first trucks growled faintly in the distance. The sun was a half-hour from rising. The buildings on Commercial Street were squat shadows in the misty dark. The darkness was punctuated only by the dancing red embers of cigarettes. Hal didn't answer. He wasn't looking for trouble, and Rex seldom was looking for anything else.

"Could be your luck day, bootlegger," Rex continued. "Maybe they need a truck full of rum runners to piss into some whiskey bottles. Then you can peddle them to the Chinamen on Eighth Street. Make your daddy proud."

A few of the men laughed. Hal clenched his fists but still said nothing. The engines got louder. A half-dozen fellows uncoiled themselves from under the park's palm trees, where they'd slept the night. They joined the hapless swarm now jostling itself into a semblance of order; the assertive in front, newcomers in the rear, the middle tier the most agitated as the men nudged and leaned into position.

A horn bleated. A couple of men hollered. They knew this truck; a beet factory flat bed, a decent shot for inside work. The beet bosses provided coffee, too, and breaks every three hours. There were worse ways to make a dollar.

Rex raised his arms. Headlights flared as the truck approached. A drooping cowboy hat was thrust out the passenger window, along with an arm, limp against the door panel, rising slowly as the vehicle approached. The horn bleated again.

"Twelve men! Two days work! No slackers! Let's go!"

Rex grabbed the truck's side panel and hauled himself up and over with one arm. As his second man helped the third man up, a red face poked out of the window.

"One of you men Gates?" he hollered.

"Ain't no Gates here," answered Rex. But Hal answered louder.

"That's me."

Having been singled out, Hal couldn't very well turn the job down. He held up his hand, and the vehicle came to an idling stop.

"Says here Gates picks own crew," yelled the driver.

Hal thought fast. Two new men on the truck stood with Rex like statues. One was an ex-con, the other a well-known card cheat. The red face poked out again.

"Christ almighty, girls, doesn't anybody want to work today?"

Hal leaped up onto the flat bed. He pointed to the crowd, at two tall boys he used to play ball against and two husky men he thought might be Rex's boys—a conciliatory gesture, he hoped. He banged three times on the side panel, the signal to shove off.

If the truck made it out of the park with Rex and Hal both in the back, that would mark Rex as part of Hal's crew. Everyone present knew what was at stake. The men on board pressed against the panels to give the two giants room.

"Look …" Hal began.

He wasn't sure what to say. Rex didn't wait for him to decide. Without word or warning he threw a beefy, round house punch that caught Hal below his right eye and sent him flying off the truck. He hit the curb hard. The truck began to move. A few of the men aboard grabbed Rex by the elbows and hurled him off the flatbed too. This surely would be a donnybrook for the ages.

Except that there was no fight. As the truck pulled away, Hal lay stunned. Rex stood over him, snorting and fuming. A murmur rippled through the men. The rising sun behind the hills sparked a glint on Rex's right hand—a row of brass knuckles. He slipped them into a side pocket when he saw where the men's eyes wandered. Hitting without warning was one thing. Hitting with brass knuckles? Even his own boys grumbled in disgust.

More headlights gleamed: Another approaching vehicle; a white Studebaker cruising down Commercial Street, veering toward the crowd. Rex muttered a curse.

Hal moaned and sat up. The car rolled to a stop. Two men emerged. Both wore new suits and crisp fedoras. One was stocky and blue-eyed, with a fresh face and shiny shoes. The other man, older and bespectacled, shook his head when he saw the situation.

"Gentlemen," he sighed. "This is not an auspicious beginning for future business partners. You need to become acquainted properly."

Hal squinted at the voice, familiar yet out of context. His head hurt, his back hurt, his face hurt. And his pride hurt. Fair or unfair, he was the guy on the ground looking up. This had never happened before.

The human images came into focus. Hal didn't recognize the stocky fellow. The man with the glasses was Warren.

Chapter Five

Forgiveness is Not Cheap

T HE Plan was either simple or stupid, depending on how you looked at it. Hal had heard it explained a half-dozen times now, and each sounded loonier than the last. But no matter how silly it seemed, Warren's way of describing it made you *want* to believe him.

"I have developed a machine," he would begin, "the construction of which is within the abilities of any industrious Boy Scout. Its theoretical basis is not so simple. It is designed to locate sympathetic vibrations of matter. In this case of gold."

This certainly was an attention-getter. Without it, Warren's follow-up, in Hal's opinion, was enough to have him locked away. But these were bitter times. A mention of gold caused even the most dubious audience to relax its guard.

"My device is in effect a radio X-ray machine," he explained. "It relies on the essential magnetism of sympathetic parts, which will reveal themselves in spite of intervening obstructions. In that way it acts much like a conventional X-ray, though it will allow the detection of organic and inorganic forms alike, based on their unique vibrational character. Let me explain: Each substance possesses a unique vibratory frequency; its own signature, if you will. Imagine the humming of a violin string. It will induce a similarly-tuned piano string in another room to sing out a note of the same pitch. That is an oversimplified example, but it gives you the general idea. Like locates like. Give me the part, and I am able to locate the whole."

How *exactly* did his instrument work? Warren smiled.

"Simply enough," he said, "that if I were to tell you the precise construction, you could go home and make one for yourself. Until my patent is secure, the details will remain secret. But I can assure you that it has been tried, tested and perfected. I am basing my professional reputation on its success."

The machine was not especially impressive: a tripod about waist high, within the legs of which was suspended a glass cylinder holding a brass pendulum. At the pendulum's bottom a silver needle was fixed above a finely etched grid. At the top of the tripod was a box, the size of two bricks side-by-side, mounted on a geared swivel. It had three dials, a switch and two knobs. There was a smoked glass window on its side, through which Warren could observe a contraption that looked to Hal like a bubble level mounted on a tiny apple corer. That was all there was to it.

"You can find gold with this?" Hal asked.

"I can find most anything," Warren said. "But gold is what we're after."

He sat Hal down at Vera's kitchen table one evening over tea, with a tablet of paper and a mechanical pencil. The X-ray gizmo, lovingly unpacked from its canvas bag, stood next to them. Warren spoke precisely, occasionally pausing to sketch something on his pad and slide it across to Hal, who would glance, nod noncommittally, and slide it back. Compared to what his uncle was telling him, Vera's crystal radio was no more Houdini Pie than a pencil sharpener.

"At first I was simply seeking minerals," Warren said, "running tests with different substances at various depths beneath the earth: iron, copper, mercury, tin. And of course the precious metals as well. I was looking for signatures identical to those I discovered—or created—above. I did my research in Los Angeles, where I lived for a time long before we met. I rented a room near the old Fort Moore, off Broadway. That's where I started seeing things that I couldn't explain."

"What does this have to do … " Hal began.

He heard a book slam out in the living room—his mother's way of telling him to shut up and pay attention. Warren continued.

"As well as identifying sympathetic substances, the X-ray makes it possible to determine—roughly, of course—the shapes and sizes of objects, as well as of voids. I began to find tunnels. More than you can imagine."

"Utility tunnels?" Hal knew about these, as he'd hidden booze in many and himself in more than one.

"Much deeper," said Warren. "And far older."

"Tunnels for what?"

"Gold. Vast quantities of it. In chambers the size of warehouses, far beneath the city."

"Ore deposits?"

"No. A treasury."

"How deep?"

"A thousand feet. Give or take."

"But that's …"

"I know. Impossible. But the machine doesn't lie. It's down there."

He had been sketching quickly as he spoke, and now he shoved the tablet Hal's way across the table. It depicted a crazy geometry of interconnecting lines, some straight, some jagged, some like the strands of a broken spider web. At several of their intersections were squares and rectangles.

"A rough approximation," said Warren as Hal frowned at the drawing. "The definitive map is still under construction."

"And how did this gold get down there?"

"That's the best part," said Warren. "The part that's going to change *everything*."

According to Warren, the tunnels were more than five thousand years old. They had been dug by ancient ancestors of modern day Hopi Indians, who once had lived in the vicinity, and who had been seeking escape from a cataclysm.

"An asteroid impact, maybe," said Warren. "Or a tremendous tidal wave. Or a volcano. They must have seen it coming. Tunnels that deep take time."

They were dug, he said, using a "corrosive acid" that could eat through rock. It must have been effective—he'd calculated over sixteen miles of caverns and passages, including narrow air chambers that extended all the way to the Santa Monica beach.

"They were a very advanced race," Warren said. "Capable of engineering feats beyond our own. And, like the Aztec, they had a particular fondness for gold."

"How in the world do you know this?" Hal asked.

"I have friends among the Hopi. I know many of their legends. I have spoken to their elders." Warren paused, ran his tongue quickly along his upper lip, and spoke in a whisper. "And yes, there is a map."

The story got stranger still. Hal motioned for his mother to join them, which she did with a smile a decade younger than her years. Warren's voice rose, earnest and almost pleading. Hal felt as though he was the grown-up in the room, listening to a couple of eager children trying to convince their parents of something they feared would be seen as ridiculous. Except that "ridiculous" hardly did it justice.

These ancient peoples, it seemed, were not precisely people. "Lizard men," Warren called them, with as straight a face as if were saying "Chinamen." According to his sources they had lived not only in California but all over the West for millennia, until some unidentified disaster had driven them below ground. Warren didn't explain exactly what was "lizardly" about them, and Hal wondered if he was supposed to imagine snouts or scales or tails or all of the above. He waited for a chance to interrupt.

"So are they still down there, these lizard guys?"

Warren's eyes glowed.

"Nobody knows," he said. "That's one of things I hope we learn when we dig."

"When we dig?"

"Of course. The whole idea is to dig."

"A thousand feet?"

"That's the depth at which I've located the chambers. If we reach more shallow tunnels sooner, we may use them as access. We won't know until we sink the shaft."

Hal began to glimpse his future in the enterprise. Digging. Warren needed a workhorse, and Vera had volunteered her son. Common sense told him that he ought to get up and walk out on this lunacy now. But there were at least two strong arguments against common sense, and they were oddly and inextricably intertwined: One was Vera, sitting to his left, smiling her loony smile. The other was the image of the breadlines he saw every day on "C" Street. Warren was offering a job. If he refused, what would his options be?

There was a knock at the back door. The screen rattled, the knob turned, and two men entered the kitchen.

One was the stocky fellow who'd arrived with Warren in the Studebaker at Plaza Park. He looked as dapper as he had that morning, though under the overhead lamp his skin didn't seem as young as it had in sunlight. The other visitor was Rex. He looked unusually civilized tonight, in a light gray suit that stretched to accommodate his massive frame. He grunted at Hal, shook hands with Warren and nodded at Vera.

"Welcome, gentlemen," said Warren, as though it was his own house they were entering. "This is my friend Mrs. Gates. I believe you've met Halley."

He beckoned to the men to step forward.

"Let me introduce my business partners. Mr. McCreery and Mr. Martin."

Rex was McCreery. Martin didn't say what his first name was—indeed he said almost nothing at all. They sat down on either side of Warren. Hal wondered if Vera would resent the intrusion, but she just blushed and busied herself making more tea. The men sat silently deferential in Warren's presence.

"We are putting together a plan for our investigation," Warren said. "Most of the pieces are in place. Mr. Martin has a strictly financial interest. Mr. McCreery is able to supply the required engineering expertise. He also has some important contacts in the community, of whom I will speak shortly. Mr. McCreery?"

Rex reached into his inside jacket pocket and pulled out a folded piece of paper: a map of downtown Los Angeles, the sort put out by the Chamber of Commerce, showing parks, major streets and key public buildings in oblique view. There was writing on it; arrows, circles, a few scribbled words. Warren nodded and continued.

"This is not the map to which I've alluded. That is not yet in our possession, though we expect it soon." (Here he shot a glance at Rex.) "This diagram is based on secondary research. I have identified three likely points of entry—all within a radius of less than a quarter-mile, in the vicinity of North Hill Street. Look."

He pointed to a spot near the old Fort Moore.

"Were we planning to dig a mere hole in the ground—something basement-sized, say—we could rely on darkness, or some temporary camouflage to shelter us from prying eyes. But we intend to operate openly. To be taken seriously. We will need the County of Los Angeles to provide the appropriate permissions. They will be reluctant. You, Halley, are the key to their cooperation."

Hal leaned forward. Surely he had heard Warren wrong.

"You're mixing me up with somebody," he said. "I'm an unemployed guy from Oxnard. I figured you wanted me to dig. I'm not key to anything."

"You are mistaken," Warren said. "You have influence you don't even realize."

He turned to Vera.

"How about some more tea, my dear? Hal here has so much to learn."

The next morning—or rather, later that morning, after Warren, Rex and the Martin guy finally had left, Vera and Hal sat for a while in the kitchen. They would talk later, Hal knew; for now it was enough just to sit and absorb the strangeness of the long night. Hal had agreed to nothing, refused nothing, acknowledged nothing, yet he knew that his life had been altered. "A lot to learn," Warren had said. The understatement of a lifetime.

Charlie's customers in L.A. had been the wealthiest of anyone they did business with. Charlie would boast about the parties he'd allegedly made possible, dropping the names of producers and movie stars as if they were old friends, claiming to have met Charlie Chaplin and Eddy Arnold and W.C. Fields. Hal had been to a few fancy houses up in the Hills and in Burbank, but for the most part he'd experienced the mansions only through their service doors. Their occupants were anonymous to him—though not, it appeared, to Warren.

"Think back," his uncle had said last night. "You and Charlie made a half-dozen trips to a hacienda-type place in Hancock Park. Just last year. Remember? Long crescent drive out front, steep hill in the rear, date palms along the alley, Venus de Milo fountain, climbing bougainvillea. All grade A, first-rate European product—Macellan's, Courvosier, Dom Pérignon. Twenty-one cases of German beer. Sixteen bottles of Jameson's. Seven cases of Russian vodka. Ring a bell?"

How the hell did Warren know these details? There had been a handful of jobs to that address. Hal remembered a party at the place, with a jazz band and a magician. One of the guests—a regular swell, by the looks of him, in a white linen suit—had invited Hal and Abe in for a drink. They'd stayed maybe twenty minutes. Hal got nervous about fraternizing with the clientele, which was strictly forbidden. Abe couldn't believe that Hal was dragging them away. It wasn't every day that two small town bootleggers got invited into a house in Hancock Park.

The party had been a birthday bash, Warren explained, for the mistress of none other than Frank Shaw, the newly-elected Mayor of Los Angeles. At the time, he was a member of the Los Angeles County Board of Supervisors. It seemed that Mr. Shaw had spent nearly twelve thousand dollars on the Gates' family booze in the past few years, and directed twice that much business Charlie's way. Every other time Hal and Abe had driven to the city, Warren said, it had been at Frank Shaw's request.

"Shaw is obviously a very influential man," Warren explained. "A few words from him to the Board and the acquisition of a permit would become a simple matter."

Vera had been through the books. It was all there—dates, quantities, dollars. Orders in Shaw's handwriting. Even a photograph—where had it come from?—of Shaw and Charlie at a party, clutching glasses of something that certainly was not lemonade. There was more than enough evidence without it to put the mayor's job in jeopardy, should the *Times* get hold of the evidence.

"What about us?" Hal asked. "We weren't exactly model citizens."

"Nobody will care about us," she said.

"It's blackmail."

She shrugged.

"All Warren needs is a permit. A scrap of paper. The rewards could be more than we can dream of. They could change everything."

There was that *change everything* again. Warren had only hinted at what was likely to change, apart from getting rich; a great idea, Hal thought, but hardly "everything." More likely they would simply waste a lot of time. But Hal knew that in the end he would go along with them—against his judgment, instincts and common sense. Because his mother wanted him to. Because he could not refuse her.

Though he hadn't slept all night, Hal took a walk to think. The rain had stopped hours before, but the morning air was still chilly as shreds of gray mist rolled in off the ocean. National Beet was putting together a baseball team, he'd heard. They were going to do some barnstorming up and down the coast. Maybe he couldn't support Vera by playing ball, but he could bring in a few more bucks. Maybe one of the minor league teams might give him a try, if a good word got out about him.

He shook his head, trying to make sense where there was nothing but nonsense. Even the lizard talk hadn't been the weirdest part about last night. When his uncle and the boys finally had bid farewell, Hal had followed them out to their cars on the street. Warren paused dramatically, as though he'd made a momentous decision that couldn't wait, even after all that had been said indoors.

"Halley," he said, annoying Hal with the use of his full first name. "You will recall when I returned to Oxnard and located you on the street. A compromised position, resulting from an altercation with Mr. McCreery."

Hal winced. He'd been hoping that no one would mention it.

"I have interviewed witnesses to the event, and Mr. McCreery himself, and I've learned that the encounter was not what would be considered a fair fight. Is that so?"

Hal shrugged. He could still feel the metal knuckles on his cheek. He had a score to settle someday, but this was hardly the time. Warren had a different idea.

"I am depending on you and Mr. McCreery in a venture that will require complete cooperation. We must not have any festering resentments. Are we agreed?"

Hal said nothing. Rex looked away.

"Forgiveness is not cheap on Downing Street. I might have expected no less from the son of Charlie Gates. There seems only one alternative. Mr. McCreery?"

Rex nodded, barely, in apparent acquiescence. Hal wondered what in the world.

"Good," Warren said. "Halley, you now have the opportunity to hit Mr. McCreery, in return for his attack upon you at the Plaza. Hit him as hard as you like, anywhere you like. He has promised not to defend himself. Once you have hit him, any bad business will be finished. Go ahead, young man. Give it all you've got."

Hal was speechless. He could not take an undefended swing at Rex. In a fair fight he'd be happy to knock him into the middle of next week.

"Forget it," he mumbled.

He turned his back, waved vaguely at Warren and the others and trudged back up the walk to his mother. When he got to the door he heard the sound of an engine starting behind him. As he reached for the knob he realized that his right hand was knotted into a fist so tight his nails drew blood. Vera had gone to bed. He was relieved that he didn't have to talk to her.

Chapter Six

Unfulfilled Desires

M ADAM EDITH was working too hard. You could ask anyone—or at least anyone who was paying attention (her daughter, maybe; her son, forget it). Everybody had the same questions: When would things get better? When would their jobs return, their investments recover, their property be worth something, their farms bounce back? As hard as Edith tried to help them, what she wanted to say was: *Ask me something easy.* Because who in the world knew?

Her mother Madeleine had been a medium up in Ventura, through the Great War and after, when what people wanted mostly was news of their dead—their husbands, brothers and sons killed in France, or their loved ones cut down by the Spanish flu. Edith had been just a girl then, setting the séance table, lighting the candles, cranking up the Victrola for a departed's favorite song. She never really believed her mother's incantations and contortions. Madeleine naturally was offended by any inference of chicanery.

"There's nothing phony about it," she would huff whenever Edith screwed up the rare courage to inquire. "It's the presentation that puts bread on the table. You keep your lip zipped and you might learn something."

Edith learned all right. She learned that it mattered the way you opened a door, or answered a phone, or shook hands with a stranger. She learned that the rich and powerful, even more than the poor and the humble, delighted in prostrating themselves before anyone richer or more powerful than themselves. If you presented yourself the right way, they would fawn in your presence. When her time came to follow in Madeleine's footsteps, Edith mastered the role.

Her reputation grew. Lawyers and judges, doctors and professors, farmers and shopkeepers, authors and actors: all would appear at her door with bared heads and ravaged hearts, asking for a glimpse at the road map of their lives. Edith led them from her entry hall to her "Reading Room." She wore a floor-length, purple robe covered with tiny blue stars and a tightly-wrapped turban of saffron silk. She spoke softly, but with great authority. She improvised.

"I see a great confusion in your affections," she might offer. Or: "I see a difficulty in letting someone go."

Eyes would grow wide in recognition.

"There is a fear in your household. The sight of an abyss."

Who *wasn't* afraid these days? The tears would flow.

She was raising two children on her own. Isabelle was her lovable but difficult daughter. Willful, irreverent and beautiful, twenty years old, she lived her private life in one of the three bedrooms of Edith's rented house in Pico Rivera. By day she worked at the public library. On weeknights she hauled home shopping bags brimmed with books— philosophy, history, natural science and novels by authors with unpronounceable names. On weekends she went into the city, staying out until daybreak with groups of men and women Edith did not know, dancing the nights away as if there were no Depression, no whispers from the neighbors, and certainly no Prohibition.

She had her father's color, eyes and lips, and the combination broke Edith's heart. Her husband was dead more than nine years now, drowned in a sailing accident, a pleasure trip to the Channel Islands on a summer day in 1925, he and two friends and their ridiculous assemblage of whiskey and fishing gear, intent on catching a tuna. He'd insisted that their first child, a boy, be called Reginald, after a character he admired from a book. Reginald was not quite sixteen when his father died. It was hard to say whether Fenton would have been proud of him.

A scholar young Reggie was not. He was held back twice in grammar school, and was always the oldest, biggest and worst behaved student in his grade. His father would hear no criticism of him. "He's just growing into himself," he insisted. "A fine lad." Within six months of Fenton's death the boy was arrested three times for fighting, and this in a district of south Ventura where fighting was an accepted way of life. Reggie's fights were especially violent and frequently unprovoked, as though the injustice of his father's death had unleashed a vendetta against any constraints of rules, rights or logic. If an accident can take my daddy, he seemed to say, then there's no reason I shouldn't take you.

Fenton's death had left Edith with no pension and no savings. It was financial desperation that first drove her to advertise as a psychic. Reggie's notoriety persuaded her to call herself Robinson—her deceased mother's name—as no one needing solace was likely to seek it at the house of a McCreery. Isabelle followed her example. Only Reggie still carried the family surname.

"You bring shame on us," Edith told him. "What would your father think?"

"He's dead. He don't think nothing."

Isabelle was four years younger, but she was the one person who could exercise any control over him. Her disapproval hounded him, nipping at his heels, squaring up to him across the dinner table. She didn't have to say a word. A frown, a shrug, a flip of her dark, straight hair or (worst of all) a single tear would sink Reggie into a swamp of black remorse. If she seemed especially upset with him, he might clean up his act for a week or even longer.

"Can't you talk sense into him?" Edith pleaded as her daughter got older.

"I can't turn him into something he's not," Isabelle would say.

"You bring out the good in him."

"Never for long."

When the Depression hit Edith moved to from Ventura to Pico Rivera, southeast of Los Angeles. She had only one marketable skill—her knack for the psychic vision, or rather her vision of the psychic knack, and there just weren't enough customers around Ventura and Oxnard to keep her crystal ball burning bright. (She didn't actually use a crystal, though she kept a glass ball on the mantelpiece for show.)

Isabelle was certain that her mother was not truly a Believer, at least not like Grandmother Madeleine had been. And to her mind, to say you were a psychic but not to believe it made you a fraud. Having a scamp for a brother and a fraud for a mother didn't sit well with her. Edith tried to explain.

"I'm a performer," she said. "I don't pretend to have special powers. I'm very careful about that. If people make certain assumptions …"

"You know they do. They think you can see things."

Edith regarded her daughter. Headstrong, sassy, and more fragile, perhaps, than she herself knew. What did the future hold for her?

"Well maybe I can," Edith said. "A little."

"Oh, mother. Honestly."

Reggie visited twice; briefly at Christmas and again in March. He was alone, hurried, mysterious. Out of Edith's earshot, he confided to Isabelle that he had, of all things, a girlfriend. He didn't see her often, he said—she'd moved back to Phoenix to take care of on her father. Her name was Rose. He lowered his voice, though there was no on else in the room.

"She's a half-breed," he whispered.

"You're going to introduce her?"

"Introduce her? I plan to marry her."

"What's stopping you?"

Reggie squirmed in his chair.

"She's got to get her old man's permission. He's not very keen on me."

Isabelle raised an eyebrow.

"You're going to change his mind?"

"You bet I am. I got stuff in the works. You'll see."

..

Tonight Edith's client was an attorney from Los Angeles, a return customer: short, perhaps fifty, bird-faced and balding, with bags under his eyes. He had come to Madam Edith as a skeptic, on the referral of a friend. She was surprised when he returned for a second session. She was certain she'd disappointed him with generalities, offering a menu of choices when what he wanted was a recipe for success. For Mr. Timothy Gavin was really a simple case. He wanted to be wealthy, a common enough ambition of the day. He'd lost his job with one of the big law firms downtown; and though had retained a few clients, he was barely scraping by. No matter what the papers said about the Depression, he saw wealth around him every day, and he was certain it escaped his grasp due not to any lack of talent or even anything as simple as hard times—it was some singular, reversible twist of Fate that mired him in less-than-modest means. He was determined to identify it. He was also lonely. He'd described to Edith his passionless marriage, his distant, grown children, his long office hours. It became clear to her that what he needed more than a psychic revelation was simply someone to talk to. He paid her in cash up front, so she was happy to oblige.

Gavin wrestled himself out of his raincoat in the narrow front hall, shook it out and hung it on an iron coat stand. He mumbled an apology about dripping onto the floor, and looked up with a nervous little smile that dissolved instantly in surprise. Edith followed his gaze over her shoulder and saw Reggie, with a scowl on his face, sidestepping out of the hallway through the kitchen door.

"My son," she said. "Visiting for a few days."

Gavin nodded.

"He seems familiar. May I ask his name?"

"Reginald," she said.

"Doesn't ring a bell," said Gavin. "But I can't imagine forgetting a man of his appearance."

"He takes after his father. Rest his soul."

The Reading Room was lit by candles. Edith sat in an overstuffed chair with her back to a bricked-in fireplace. Gavin sat facing her across a small round table made of dark, purplish wood. Right off the bat he was telling her about a dream he had, something about being a knight on a flying horse, then he was talking about one of his children, who years ago had fallen off a bicycle, and how his wife blamed him. He babbled disconnectedly, drumming his feet beneath the table.

She listened politely, looking as sage as possible, her hands in front of her face, the tips her long fingers touching in front of her nose. Then her attention must have wandered, for she realized that Gavin now was going on about some sort of opportunity that had come his way, a chance to make a bit of money on the side for one of his clients. He talked fast, his feet still thumping. He couldn't tell her the details—not yet—but it was something he was "hesitating on," as he put it, because—and he had trouble spitting it out—it "might not be completely on the up and up." He wouldn't be more specific except that whatever it was he was planning to do, it might make him rich overnight.

"I know you don't see everything that's going to happen," he said earnestly. "But do you get any kind of fix on this? Do you imagine me in prison? Disbarred? Or ..." (he forced a laugh) " ... as an eventual man of leisure?"

Edith didn't know what to say. She had told Gavin before to be wary of his "tyrannical passions" and his "lust for the ephemeral;" phrases she used with her more blatantly greedy clients. Now she was being asked, in a way, to be a psychic accomplice to some sort of shady business. What if this "caper," as he'd called it, was discovered, and somehow—she couldn't think how, but somehow—her knowledge of it was revealed? Her flimsy little business could survive neither the prosecution nor the publicity. She drew herself up tall in her chair and folded her hands on the table.

"Your conscience is troubling you," she said, in what she hoped was a sufficiently mysterious tone.

Gavin put his hands on the table. His tapping feet slowed but did not stop.

"That's the thing," he said. "I mean, it isn't. I figure a guy has got to make a buck somehow. This client of mine—he's a pretty important swell. He didn't get where he is today by listening to his conscience."

"Then why have you come to me?"

"It's not the thing I'm worried about," he said. "It's the consequences. I figured that's your department."

What a remarkable man, Edith thought. Like a Catholic seeking absolution from a priest *before* his sin. She'd seen plenty of remorse in her job, plenty of fear of retribution. She had never seen anyone try to settle it all out beforehand.

Edith lifted her hands to her temples. She was prone to headaches these days. Sometimes it helped to press the sides of her forehead. She was not unaware of the effect the gesture had on clients. After a moment she spoke:

"I see agitation in your life," she said. "Not punishment so much as unrest. I see deeds undone and desire unfulfilled. I see that no lasting good will come of your schemes. Beyond that, all is in shadow."

That was reaching a little maybe, but she hoped it would do the trick. Vague yet certain, like a psychic should be. She was condoning nothing, forbidding nothing; taking no sides, risking no complicity.

Gavin bit his lip and nodded slightly. Finally his feet were still. It was warm in the room. The candlelight glistened off the sweat beads on his forehead.

"Then it seems," he said softly, as if to himself, "that I've got a decent chance at this. No visions of shackles, at least. Agitation is something I'm used to. I could just use some money to go along with it."

His feet did a quick roll on the carpet, and then stopped abruptly. He winked.

"And as for unfulfilled desires, it's time I headed home."

He tipped her handsomely, a whole extra half-dollar, as they walked to the front door. She handed him his raincoat, noting that he craned his skinny neck to see down the hall as he put it on. She followed his gaze, and he cleared his throat.

"Is he in town long?" Mr. Gavin asked.

"My son?" Edith said. "A few days. Would you like to meet him?"

She made a move as if to call down the hall, but Mr. Gavin put a hand on her arm.

"No, no. I don't want to bother him. I'm sure it's a coincidence. I don't know anyone from Oxnard."

Edith smiled. What a funny little man.

"I hope I've been helpful to you in some small way."

It was her standard parting phrase, simple and humble.

"Oh you have," he said. "Quite."

Directly above her, at the window of his room, Reggie watched the stranger leave. He had heard every word in the Reading Room, standing in the hall with a tumbler against the plaster wall. He wasn't surprised that the lawyer had recognized him—it had been only a week since they'd met, briefly, in an office in the new City Hall downtown. They hadn't spoken directly, and of course he'd been introduced by his own name, Mr. McCreery, and not his mother's, and for that matter as "Rex," not "Reggie" (a name only Isabelle and his mother still used), so he could understand the man's uncertainty. He didn't much care. He was more interested in this "caper" Gavin spoke of.

That's what the meeting had been about, with those men from the County Board; what everything had been about since he'd met Rose's father, and Warren, and the world of opportunity had been laid before him like a red carpet.

He didn't understand exactly what the lawyer was referring to, about something not being "on the up and up." Everybody had an angle on the Plan, after all. The partners—among whom he proudly counted himself—stood to gain the most, of course. As for the fat cats on the Board, he assumed they'd worked out a deal among themselves whereby something less than their share would make it to the public coffers. Hell, maybe none at all. Maybe that was what had Edith's guest sweating. The best part of what he had overheard was simply that Gavin—and therefore the whole gang, including (and most importantly) the new Mayor himself—appeared inclined to go ahead with it all. That had not been clear in the meeting Rex attended.

He wondered where the bootlegger's son would fit in. What a weird coincidence *that* had been. Of all the guys Warren could have picked. It had been a near thing, out on the sidewalk, when Warren told the kid to hit him. What the hell was he *thinking*? A roundhouse from Gates would have sent him into the next county. Apparently Warren knew just what he was doing. Rex had walked away without a scratch. The suits were talking. The pieces were falling into place. Rex watched Gavin get into a Ford parked at the curb. It pulled away in the downpour. Yes, the pieces were falling into place; one, two three. Just like Warren said they would.

CHAPTER SEVEN

MAN OF THE HOUSE

T HE National Beet team was called the Sheiks. Hal didn't like it. He would have preferred the Indians, the Sharks or the Flyers, but those names all were taken by other teams in the local amateur leagues. The Sheiks were barnstorming upstarts, the newest outfit around. They were going to have to prove themselves.

The season was scheduled to start in April. Hal went to his first practice at the beginning of February. Everybody knew he had been a player, but then Ventura County was full of guys who *used* to play ball. Funny things would happen to them. They would quit for a year or two, get married maybe, or just be gone a couple of seasons hoboing around. They'd return with rubber arms, double vision and the reflexes of a potted plant. Baseball wasn't something you could turn off and on like a light switch. Hal was going to have to prove himself, too.

Of course he would pitch. Hal's fastball had made his name in high school, and the Sheiks' manager—a skinny wise guy named Lucky—remembered watching his own son flail at Hal's heat in a few mercifully bygone innings. Lucky liked the game rough, mean and fast, and encouraged his players to bring a boxing ring mentality to the field.

"We call it hardball for a reason," he told Hal the first day. "I want every player in Southern California to get a taste of your heater. The kind where they can count the stitch marks on their rib cage. Starting with our first game. It's against the Angels from L.A. The Coast League club."

"Christ," said Hal. "Why would they want to play a bunch of nobodies like us?"

"Exhibition," said Lucky. "They pick teams they figure they can wallop. We might just have a surprise for 'em. I want you on the mound every day until then."

So Hal pitched. A lot. He worked when he could. There had been no sign of Rex in the labor lines. He could count on two or three days a week hauling or picking or painting down at the docks in Hueneme. He spent less and less time at home. It wasn't so much Vera's company he was avoiding as his own. It didn't seem right, wasting away every night in the same room he'd grown up in, reading Zane Grey novels from the Carnegie Library. He was bored. Since the repeal last year of the Volstead Act a dozen bars had opened in town, in some cases just making public operations that had been busy for years in the back rooms. He began frequenting a couple of them in the evenings—Frank's on J Street and The Palms on Commercial—just to get out the house and be around people.

He'd sit at the bar alone, nursing a beer, looking more formidable than he felt. He was cordial enough with the other customers, but distant in the way he always was without trying to be. It seemed there was a thick wall of misunderstanding between him and the world, or perhaps not a wall but a moat, wide and deep and covered with a blanket of fog. He didn't understand the other men. They seemed perfectly content simply to work shit jobs all day—or not—and drink cheap booze all night, then to get up the next day and do it all over again; to be poor as dirt, living hand to mouth while their dirty kids ran shoeless in the streets and their wives looked as ragged as the Okie women out in the tent camps. Was this his future, too?

On a Wednesday night, a week before the Sheiks' first game, he sat at the bar in The Palms. It wasn't much of a place. Its centerpiece was a long oak bar, singed by cigarette burns. Tin ashtrays sat on the tables. Behind the bar were two beer taps, a row of whiskey bottles and a few brewers' advertisements from back in the teens that no one had ever bothered to remove. There was a big open area with a pool table, its surface stained and scarred by liquor and frustration. Hal liked it as well as any place.

Out of nowhere, Rex walked in. He had a woman with him. A pool game stopped abruptly, its players standing, their eyes big with wonder, turning as one toward the door. A table of loafers paused in their endless game of five-card draw. The bartender dropped a shot glass that bounced across the floor with a hollow ring.

Women did not frequent The Palms. As a rule they didn't enter any of the small dives and taverns that had sprung up around town. Yet here was one, and a looker at that. She was dark-skinned, taller than Rex by a half a head. She wore a green dress that fell almost to the floor; hardly the current style. Her face was a perfect oval and her eyes were almost as black as her hair, which was long, severely straight and neither covered nor tied. Her skin was as clear as a girl's, but she had the grace and bearing of a woman. She appeared neither uncomfortable nor shy, marching ahead of Rex to the bar, leaning across and asking in a clear, confident voice for two rye whiskies. The bartender mumbled "yes ma'am" and backed away as he might have from a talking scorpion.

"Your mother said we might find you here," said Rex.

Hal said nothing. His nemesis grinned. Rex was dressed in a jacket and striped tie, with a crisp new fedora on his bulldog head.

"I came up from the city with Warren," Rex volunteered. "He's over at your house with Vera. This here …" he nodded at the woman, "is my girl. Rose."

Hal bristled at the use of his mother's first name. He held out his hand.

"Pleased to meet you," he said woodenly. Rose slid onto the adjoining barstool and interrupted in a deep, melodious voice.

"Vera is so sweet. I can't imagine why your father would have left her."

Hal's jaw dropped open, then snapped shut.

"She speaks her mind, this one," Rex chuckled. "I told her plain out that your dad was a cheap bootlegger who got rode out of town in a box car full of debt. Right?"

Hal's eyes narrowed to slits.

"My father is away on business."

Rex continued as though Hal hadn't spoken.

"You're wondering what we want. We want you."

Rex had his hands on his knees, elbows akimbo, and looked at Rose. She cleared her throat and put her hand on Hal's arm.

"Rex has told me about you," she said. "You're a big part of the Plan, I gather."

She said *Plan* with a clear capital "P."

"We're to bring you back to the house so we can talk."

Hal looked around the bar. The men had gone back to their pool and drinking. The bartender stayed close by, eyeing the threesome suspiciously. Hal wanted to stand up and shout. He wanted to tell them that he had come to this dive for peace and quiet, not to be hunted down by Warren and the "Plan." He wanted to storm out the door like a cowboy in a matinee. Rose kept her wide eyes on him.

He signaled to the bartender, whose eyebrows shot up like popped toast.

"One more round," he said, then turned to Rex, "while you two tell me what you—what Warren—wants me to do. And you're buying."

They were ready to proceed, Rex explained; just a few more "logistic details" to be worked out, including the precise location of the dig and some of the excavation techniques, and, of course, the permit.

"We'd like to arrange a meeting," he said, "with you present."

"What good will I do?"

Rex pulled at one end of his moustache.

"Once Shaw knows you're with us he'll know we're serious."

"About blackmailing him, you mean."

Rex tugged his moustache on the other side, and turned his head away.

"And if I say no?" Hal asked.

"Warren says you won't."

Great, thought Hal; now he knows what I'm thinking. What's worse, he's right.

The scene back at the house was celebratory, as though Warren had guessed exactly how the meeting at The Palms would go. There was a store-bought cake on the table in the kitchen and porterhouse stakes wrapped in butcher paper, waiting for the frying pan. Several bottles of wine stood at attention on the coffee table in the living room, along with one, quite empty, that Warren and Vera had drunk while waiting. Vera's eyes gleamed when Hal walked in the door.

"Everything is going to be good again," she whispered thickly, standing on tiptoe to meet his embrace. "You'll see."

"Apart from the permit," Warren said, "what we need most is the map."

He turned to Rose.

"I'm still working on it," she said.

Warren assumed his speechifying voice.

"With the permit and the map we are unstoppable. And the world—not simply *our* world, my friends, but everything and everyone we know—will never be the same."

The party broke up abruptly. Mr. Martin hurried off without saying goodbye. Rex left with Rose on his arm. Hal watched his uncle curiously. Surely he intended to leave? It was a little after ten. Vera was flagging. She lifted an iron pan from the stove and moved toward the kitchen sink. Hal took it from her and steered her to a chair.

"Shall I walk you to the car?" he asked Warren.

"I can manage on my own," his uncle said. "It's good to see you looking after your mother. I'm sure your father would be proud of you."

CHAPTER EIGHT

HI-DE-HI

A MONG the Hopi it is understood that the world that we currently inhabit, *Túwachi*, is but the most recent in a series of four. Each of the previous three (*Tokpela, Tokpa* and *Kuskurza*) were destroyed by the Creator (*Taiowa*) when he became displeased with the failure of the People to sing his praises. The People were not themselves destroyed, but were permitted in each instance to emerge into the next world—from the World of Endless Space to that of the Dark Midnight, then to the Red World of Corruption, and lastly into the present World Complete.

Not in a million years would Hal have imagined that he should be learning the first thing about such things, let alone that his fortunes were said with all seriousness to be connected to them. What's more, that he would be hearing about them from his own mother.

"I'm still figuring out the details," said Vera, "but from what I can gather the lizard men were trying to go backwards, to a world they'd left behind. I'm not sure I get it all yet. That's why you need to meet Chief Greenleaf."

"Why don't *you* go?"

"These are the secrets of his people. He can't share them—well, with women."

"So much for suffrage."

"Don't joke. These are tribal mysteries. Chief Greenleaf is their custodian. Except that he's an outcast. It's taken Warren years to gain his confidence."

"And why does this Greenleaf character trust him?" Hal asked, rubbing his forehead. He felt as though he was swapping riddles with a precocious four-year old.

Vera sniffed and raised her chin.

"Because he's brilliant," she said.

They were sitting on the front steps in the morning sun. Today was the Sheik's first game against the Angels. Lucky himself would be by any minute to fetch him. Hal wore his uniform, gray flannel with blue piping and a red "S" on the chest.

"Here comes the car," he said. He hefted his duffel off the porch.

"Don't forget to wear a clean shirt and tie, if you do get to see him."

"Aren't you going to wish me luck?"

"Of course," said Vera, brightening suddenly. He bent for her kiss. "You're going to make me proud," she said. "Both of you."

"I meant at the game," he said. "I'm pitching."

"I'm sure you'll be fine," Vera said. "I mean, you'll win and all that."

Hal laughed in spite of himself.

"And all that. Sure."

Lucky had packed his old Ford full; three in the front and three in the back, the whole infield except for the catcher Payton. The boys were in rare form. No sooner had they made it to the highway than Lewis the first baseman pulled out a flask of gin. Lucky barked something about after the game, but Lewis whined that there wasn't "enough in this ol' bottle to get a bat boy bent." Hal didn't partake. No way was he was going to face a PCL team after drinking. He didn't mind the other fellows whooping it up. It was a welcome change from Vera and her rag-twisting worry. Timmy Cochran the shortstop started singing "Minnie the Moocher" in a hair-curling falsetto. The boys howled out the chorus—*Hi-de-hi-de-hi-de-hi!* Even Lucky joined in, jerking the wheel back and forth in time. They passed trough Camarillo and Thousand Oaks, the hills ranging from soft, green globes that Cochran swore looked "just like tits," to jagged rock outcrops. They drove past fields crowded with workers in turbans, weeding in the furrows and picking bugs off the new leaves. Lucky drove fast. Oxnard businesses liked to advertise that the town was "100 minutes from Hollywood Boulevard." He'd bet Payton that he could make it to the stadium in less than an hour and a half. Cochran started up another song. Hal joined in. To hell with lizard men. At least for today.

The game was at Wrigley Stadium, right downtown, a gem of a ball field built in imitation of Chicago's Wrigley, both brain-children of the chewing gum king himself. It occupied the corner of 42nd and Avalon; a colossal cathedral, white with a red tile roof and an office tower, of all things, sticking up at one end, adorned by a giant clock that was visible from the field. There were lights for night games, something Hal had never even heard of. He looked forward to pitching under them someday.

The "kranks" in L.A., as the fans were called, were accustomed to good baseball. They called their beloved Angels the "Yankees of the West," and stoked desperate rivalries between them, the Hollywood Stars and the Seals from San Francisco. They had superstar players, ex-major leaguers like first baseman Bunny Brief from St. Louis, and Jigger Statz, their center fielder, who had played for both the Giants and the Cubs. Being on a field with guys like that seemed to Hal as close as he'd ever get to the Big Show. He looked forward to it with that sense of confident terror that pitchers know best.

Wrigley had an actual visitor's clubhouse behind the first base dug-out, where Lucky's carload met the rest of the team with a couple of hours to kill before game time. The other boys had taken a few snorts too, and Lucky lost his cool for a minute. Payton told him not to blow his wig; that they'd all be fine in time for the first pitch. It amazed Hal how quickly they all acted like a pre-game dust-up with the manager in a PCL clubhouse was something that happened every day of the week; how the boys took it in stride, banging open lockers and getting into their uniforms. Hal felt a little foolish, arriving suited up. He stuffed his duffle in a locker and went upstairs to look at the park.

A double-decker concrete grandstand ran from foul pole to foul pole; seating for twenty thousand, somebody had said, and though Hal hadn't believed them then he sure did now. There were no left-field seats, just a towering, unpainted concrete wall with the beginnings of an ivy blanket creeping up it, meandering tendrils of pale, hopeful green. The grass was emerald, the outfield as flat and perfect as a new pool table. Hal felt butterflies in his bowels. He'd been waiting for this his whole life.

Tonight the Angels were throwing a new guy named Mosley, a pock-marked right hander with an un-hittable change-up that arrived at the plate with all the pizzazz of a sick dog on three legs. The Sheik batters looked awful for three innings trying to connect on him. For the next three innings they looked merely pathetic, and finally, as they began to pick up his timing in the seventh, they looked look simply bad, pepper-ing the infield with harmless two-hoppers and old-lady pop flies. The crowd laughed.

They didn't laugh when Hal was on the mound. When he threw his heat, Angel batters hardly had their bats off their shoulders before Pay-ton was tossing the ball back and the ump was yelling "STeeeeRIKE!"

like a drill sergeant. When they caught up to it at all they managed only harmless fouls, or (twice), a can of corn to the outfield, or (once) a dribbler to Cochran at short. Then Hal would toss his cutter and the batters would bail, leaving the box—and more than once their feet—at the prospects of being hit by that demonic white bullet before it snapped away from them, across the plate and into Payton's mitt. Big-names and no-names alike, it made no difference. Indeed the famous guys, Jigger Statz especially, went down hardest, desperately over-swinging in their fury at being upstaged by this towering unknown from the beet fields.

Soon the ninth was upon them. The Sheiks sat silent in the dugout while the Angels took the field. The Sheiks had to put a run up here. They were batting the bottom of their order; the seven, eight and nine hitters. Hal was hitting last not because he didn't have a good stick—it was one of the best on the team—but simply because Lucky favored the tradition of sticking the pitcher in the nine-hole.

Gibbs the third baseman fanned, swinging through a three-two fastball. But every Sheik on the bench saw something in the pitch sequence that scooted them forward on the bench: Mosley was flagging. His pitches were up in the zone, falling across at belt height instead of tumbling over the plate at the knees, and they had almost no juice at all.

Tompkins got a healthy piece of a pitch, though not quite all of it. The sight of the ball jumping off the bat (and sailing in a perfect arc directly into Jigger Statz' glove) electrified the crowd. They rose as one man with a roar, and then a gasp, a mixture of relief, disappointment, excitement and sheer love of the drama as Statz tossed the ball back in and Tompkins walked to the dugout shaking his head. They stayed on their feet as Hal walked over from the on deck circle.

Hal got Mosley's first offering off the end of the bat. If he'd hit it on the sweet spot, it may well have left not only the yard but the stadium. As it was he sliced a rope the other way, a fair ball down the first base line into the right field corner, where it rattled around like a Ballyhoo pinball before the Angels' right fielder got it back to the first baseman, by which time Hal was standing on third. Mosley stepped off the mound, circled it twice, returned to the rubber and tossed a fat one to Harris, who promptly ripped into the left field gap, scoring Hal. Cochran flied out, but it didn't matter. The Sheiks were up, 1-0. The game was all but in the bag.

Hal took the mound. The crowd still stood, dumb with excitement. He glanced up at the tower. Three o'clock on the nose. He took a breath, rubbed the ball on his pants and licked his lips. It was time to win a ballgame.

He still had his stuff. His shoulder, though sore, would hold up. Unfortunately the same could not be said of the Sheiks' defense. The first Angel batter hit an 0-2 fly ball to left field, where Tompkins dropped it, claiming later to have "lost it in the sun," a neat trick as the sun was behind him. Hal was disgusted. He struck out Bunny Brief on three pitches, the last of which was a nasty curve that Payton couldn't handle. It hit the dirt in front of his mitt and scooted all the way to the wall. Bunny made it to first without a throw.

Hal knew they would bunt. The batter was Joey Josephs, the Angel's third baseman. He squared off as Hal went into his windup and laid down a beaut, back towards the mound. The runners were off like jackrabbits. There was nothing Hal could do but charge the ball and try to nail the runner at first.

Barehanding was the key. Some guys would get flustered on a dribbler, scooping with their mitt a ball that was practically laying still. Then they'd have to transfer to their throwing hand, and the second that took could make the difference between an out and another runner on. Hal picked the ball off the grass and set himself in position, weight back, shoulder toward first, Josephs only halfway down the line and dead to rights.

Or at least he should have been. Hal's throw sailed about eight feet over Lewis's head, at something close to ninety miles an hour, past the first base coach, over the fence, all the way to the seventh row above the visitor's dugout, where it hit a man square on the nose. The poor bastard dropped like a stone. The crowd screamed; a collective, horrified yelp, then went silent. Hal, frozen in his follow-through, counted his own audible heartbeats: one, two, three, four, five. A voice rang out like a bugle:

"He's dead!"

Pandemonium ensued. Lucky rushed out of the visitors' dugout, and was met right away by the home-plate ump, who without his mask looked like a sunburned gorilla. The Angels spilled out on the field, pointing at the crowd and Hal in turn as the two runners easily scored. The game was over. Hal shook his head, rubbed the back of his palm across his nose. As he trudged to the dugout he heard the crowd.

"Freak show!"

"Wild man!"

"Murderer!"

"Nuts to you," he muttered. He hadn't meant to hit anyone. He tripped down the dugout steps and nearly knocked over Lucky coming up.

"Guess the boys let you down out there," he said.

"What do you mean? I'm the guy who killed a fan."

"There ought've been two outs," Lucky said. "No need for a bunt. Tompkins makes a catch, Payton blocks that ball, and we're heroes having a cold one."

"But ..."

"The point is you did the smart thing, staying out of the fray. I'll go up and talk to the family or friends or whoever."

Hal put his hand on Lucky's chest, impeding his progress up the stairs.

"I'll take care of it," said Hal.

Lucky shrugged.

"Don't be surprised if somebody takes a poke at you."

"I said I'll take care of it."

CHAPTER NINE

GOTTA KNOW THE SCORE

I SABELLE ROBINSON was leading Ralph Berlucci along. Ralph wasn't especially good looking, though it was clear he thought he was a handsome pip, with his slicked-back hair and his suit. But he had a little money, an income from his dad who owned a heavy-equipment company in the city. A little money was a rare enough commodity these days to get a girl's attention. So Isabelle had gone out with him a couple of times, always with a gang so far, just drinks or a movie, nothing romantic. It was becoming clear from the way he was starting to treat her that he had other plans. He'd take her arm when there was no need to, or pull her toward him if she started talking to another guy. He was starting to irritate her.

Normally, if a guy spent a few bucks on Isabelle, she didn't mind the odd grab or grope, especially after a few drinks, and if he was sweet and decent enough it might lead to, well, whatever it led to. But she was *not* a vamp, not at all, in spite of what some of the guys said. Simply because she went to bars and stayed out late there was bound to be talk, but Isabelle was "practically a virgin," as she insisted indignantly to her friend Betsy. In any case she was not loose, whatever Ralph might think. Today would be their last date. In the meantime she intended to have some fun.

There were four of them out on a Saturday afternoon. The other two were Betsy and her new fellow, a jazz drummer she had met at a club someplace. He *was* a bit of a dreamboat, Isabelle had to admit; the dark, mysterious type, made all the more exotic by being a musician. But he had nothing to say for himself, except occasional slang words that nobody used anymore, like "hooey" and "daddy-o."

Betsy wanted to go to a ballgame. She had read somewhere that the Angels were the hottest thing going. Jazzboy followed her lead, announcing that the idea was "the cat's meow." Ralph said he'd go, but he'd rather they went to the beach. "Football is my sport," he said. "A contest for men."

Isabelle smiled. Ralph hardly seemed the gridiron type.

"But I already got the tickets," Betsy said. "My brother got them from a guy he knows."

"Take me out to the ballgame," Isabelle sang out. Baseball meant little to her. She didn't even know the rules. But if Ralph didn't want to go, that was good enough for her. She suspected that all he wanted to see at the beach was her in a swimsuit. So she feigned enthusiasm, and off they went.

Her mother was working today, entertaining the wives of L.A. businessmen who gathered weekly to play cards and sort out the truths and otherwise in the stories their husbands brought home from downtown. Isabelle detested these Saturday sessions. She had not yet let go of the private kernel of hope that there was *something* genuine about her mother's "gift." Maybe not actual prescience, but something—a kind of sixth sense maybe, a way of telling a person things *important* about themselves that they already knew. With these L.A. ladies it was all incense and malarkey. Even when she had nowhere to go, she made sure she was out of the house when the matrons arrived.

Sometimes she went to the library, even when it was closed. There were few places she felt more at home. Her favorite spot was up on the third floor, in the corner where the drama section met the foreign languages—on a sunny bay window shelf, snuggled against a blue chintz cushion she'd brought from home. Or she would roam the stacks, breathing the sweet, bookish dust and tracing titles absently with her forefinger, pausing to knock a random spine backward into her waiting palm. She would flip the pages of a history or travel book, tasting with her eyes. Sometimes she would take the volume back to the window seat and not read it at all, but just lose herself for hours, staring down at the street below.

Come evening, she would seek more vigorous diversions. Jazz clubs were her favorite, with the cinema a close second. Lacking any of those a party would do just fine. Seldom did she stay home weekend nights. Life was always the same there, and out "in the world" life was always bound to be, well, at least different than yesterday. Isabelle liked surprises.

This day would be full of them.

Notwithstanding his professed scorn for baseball, once resigned to the plan Ralph turned in a wink from scoffer to booster. He knew the ballpark, the quickest route by bus, how to buy peanuts from the vendor outside for eight cents a bag instead of the dime they charged in the stands. He knew the players' names: Statz and Mosley and Bunny Brief (Isabelle giggled at that one), and he rattled off their batting averages without looking at the program.

"I thought you didn't like baseball," said Isabelle.

"I don't much," said Ralph. "But a guy's gotta know the score."

Jazzboy was of a different mind. To Isabelle's amazement he displayed a knowledge of the game even scantier than her own.

"What are the white squares for? What do they wear on their hands?"

"Oh, you big kidder," said Betsy, her face a comic mask of horror.

Below them the Sheiks took infield practice. Jazzboy thought it was the game.

"Go!" he yelled, leaping to his feet. "Catch it!"

"At least he has the idea," Betsy whispered to Isabelle.

"Just make him sit down," said Isabelle.

They had a bird's eye view of the visitor's bullpen.

"Hey," said Betsy "Get a load of that guy. That's one long tall drink of water."

Isabelle glanced in the direction she was pointing. The man throwing the ball was big for sure. He looked like an oversized choir boy, all cheeks, smiles and bright blue eyes. Except that choir boys were never so intense. This fellow threw a baseball like a preacher hurling prayers at the devil. Yet along with his fierceness there was worry in his eyes.

"What's he doing?"she asked Ralph in a sideways whisper.

"Warming up. I read about this guy someplace."

"He looks like he misses his mommy."

As the game progressed, Isabelle began to understand (with Ralph's help) that even though neither team had scored any runs, the big guy gradually was asserting an upper hand. The batters he faced seldom managed to get their bats anywhere near the ball. She wondered several times if they even saw it as it went by. With each new batter the big kid's features relaxed a bit and the worry went out of his face. Isabelle suspected that he was having the time of his life.

As the contest entered the ninth inning, the score was still tied at zero. Ralph told Isabelle about extra innings. She hoped they wouldn't happen. It was hot in the sun, and she was thirsty and cramped from sitting on the wooden bleacher. Jazzboy was sound asleep, but every other eye in the place was riveted on the duel between the pitcher—the

Angel's Mosley, stepping up on the mound—and the batter Gibbs, swinging his bat like an axe as he stepped into the box.

Gibbs struck out. A sigh rippled through the crowd. Ralph put his arm around Isabelle's back. She shook him off.

"This is exciting," she said

"I thought you didn't care about baseball."

"Shhh."

The next batter hit the ball hard, but it was caught by the right fielder. A cry of *"Jigger! Jigger!"* arose from the men around her. Jazzboy stirred, opened one eye and dropped off again. Isabelle laughed. When she looked back to the game, the big kid was stroking the ball into the right field corner. The crowd jumped to its feet, willing the ball to find a ready glove, but instead the kid reached third. The crowd groaned. When he scored, on the next pitch, groups throughout the stadium began to gather up their belongings and make for the exits.

"Where are they going?" Isabelle asked.

"Beating the crowds," said Ralph. "The way this guy has been throwing, the game's in the bag. Let's go."

"Not 'till it's over," said Isabelle.

The teams switched places. One of the Sheiks dropped a ball, and suddenly the Angels had a base runner. Then something happened that Isabelle didn't understand. The next batter struck out, only this time he ran to first base anyway, as though he'd gotten a hit. Ralph was explaining what had happened when suddenly the crowd roared and Isabelle looked to see the big guy hurrying off the mound toward a ball that was lying still in the grass halfway between him and the plate. The catcher had thrown off his mask and was standing with his hands on his hips, screaming *"ONE! ONE!"* The big kid turned and threw the ball, to Isabelle's astonishment, directly—well, almost—at her.

It hit Ralph between the eyes.

Blood. A lot of it. They found out later that only Ralph's nose was broken, but it looked at first as though his whole face had exploded. He emitted a pitiful, high-pitched wail that lasted as long as it took for him to slide off of the bleacher and onto the floor. Betsy screamed, startling Jazzboy awake. He blinked his eyes, shook his head and groped about him for balance. The first thing he saw was Ralph at his feet.

"He's dead!" he cried, breaking the shocked silence around them.

"Oh, no he's not," said Isabelle, for she could see Ralph bringing his hand to his face.

Betsy helped Ralph to his knees, which brought him—perhaps unfortunately—fully to his senses. He began to blubber and gasp, his eyes rolling madly in his head, his nostrils continuing to flow crimson down his chin and onto his sharkskin suit. For an instant his gaze fixed on Isabelle. It seemed to her wild with not only pain but accusation, as though he wanted to say *I told you we should leave,* except that at this moment he passed out.

Uniformed stretcher bearers arrived, shoving Isabelle out of the way. They loaded Ralph onto the stretcher and off they went, followed by Betsy and her date. Isabelle hesitated. Surely she should follow them? But what use could she be if she did? Better to join them later at the hospital, once the doctor had done whatever setting, patching, plastering or stitching was required. Then she'd bring him something—some flowers or some candy or a bottle of something. Or maybe the ball. It lay on the floor under the bench, just by her foot, where she bent to retrieve it. She studied it, turning it in her hand, feeling the smooth white leather and the tight, perfect stitching. It had a gray scuff mark on one side, and a pink smudge on the other. Yes, he'd want this as a souvenir. She would take it to him after the game.

Betsy reappeared and put her hand on Isabelle's arm.

"They took him to General," she said. "They don't think it's real serious. You want to catch a taxi with us?"

Isabelle hesitated. She had seen something out of the corner of her eye, and she glanced quickly to confirm it before answering with a quick shake of her head.

"You go on," she said. "I'm going to stay and have a word—you know, with the management. They ought to apologize or something. I'll come over in a bit."

"You sure, honey? You okay?"

She wished they would hurry.

"I'm fine. You two go ahead."

As Betsy and Jazzboy descended the stairs, Isabelle turned to meet Hal, coming up.

..

They had dinner at the Roosevelt on Hollywood, a ritzier place that either would otherwise have picked, but when Isabelle suggested it, Hal said "suits me" before it occurred to him that she might be joking, or at least half-joking, and then it was too late to do anything but go. A few of the Angels were at the bar. They treated Hal like a celebrity. Jigger bought a bottle of champagne, one of the other fellows bought a round of bourbons, and then the door opened and Mosley came in with gang of his own. When Mosley saw Hal he marched over and grabbed Hal's hand, pumped it up and down and told him he was the best god-damned pitcher he'd ever seen, excuse his goddamned French to the lady. Everybody laughed. Hal seemed more at ease in the company of other men, but Isabelle didn't feel left out. In fact she was soon in the thick of things, and she had them guffawing with her account of Ralph hitting the deck and Jazzboy waking up and all the rest. One of the Angels made a joke about how Ralph was the only guy all day that had made any solid contact with Hal's fastball.

Suddenly Isabelle squealed as she remembered what was in her purse. She took the ball out and held it in the air.

"Voila!"

Now she was *really* the center of attention. Everybody wanted to hold it and toss it up and down and smack it against their palms, as if they'd never seen a baseball before. Pretty soon they were all passing around a fountain pen and covering the ball so thoroughly in signatures that Mosley, the last guy to get it, couldn't even find a place to put his name, so he just scrawled a fat "M" on top of the Spalding logo and presented it to Isabelle with a flourish.

"Ma'am, here's a souvenir that'll last, in case the big fellow don't stick around."

Another laugh, and Hal and Isabelle were shown to their table.

Isabelle looked over the top of her menu at Hal, who was grinning and shaking his head. Hers felt pretty light with the champagne and whiskey. Hal winked when the waiter approached, all formal and stiff, lighting a single white taper in a cut glass vase and presenting Hal with a wine list. Hal made a show of looking it up and down. Isabelle didn't imagine that a baseball player would know the first thing about spirits other than beer. As the thought crossed her mind she giggled: *A baseball player! I'm out to dinner with a baseball player!* Hal giggled back, and she wondered if he was thinking something similar about her. She'd told him she worked at a library, but not much else.

"I'm pretty hungry," he said, nodding at the menu.

"You're a growing boy," she teased.

"Killing fans takes it out of a guy."

"So why didn't you go back to Ventura with your team?"

"Because I was going to have dinner with you," he said.

She blushed.

"You sound like my mother. Everything is pre-ordained."

"Pre-ordained? Do you always talk like a librarian?"

"No, when I'm really bent I talk like a baseball player."

"This I want to see."

Hal ordered wine and dinner for both of them; steaks and oysters and lobster salad and mashed potatoes, as though he ate in places like the Roosevelt five nights a week. He turned back to her.

"So why do I sound like your mother?"

She told him about Edith. To her delight he listened attentively, without suggesting that her mother was either nuts or a con-artist; in fact he nodded a few times as she talked, as though she was walking him through a familiar landscape. Then he told her a little about his family. He simply said his father had been in the "delivery business," and that he "traveled a lot." He made Vera out to be just a tad less touched than he feared she was. He said that had an Uncle in the city who was providing him with a business opportunity, but he didn't give any more details. Indeed, he didn't want to think about the details. He hadn't given much consideration to the Plan all day. It was easy not to think about anything other than being here, at this table, with this girl.

Hal had little experience with women. Toward the end of the boot-legging days Charlie had gotten them into a few parties where there were tarts for hire, and though Hal hadn't asked for it a couple had taken him up to their rooms, whether out of curiosity about the big man or on somebody else's nickel (his father's, he reckoned), he never knew. He went along, glad enough to learn whatever they had to teach him, which wasn't much, he figured—a beginner's course at best. As for reg-ular dates with girls he actually knew, well, there'd been few enough to count on one hand: A classmate in high school he took to the pictures. A counter-girl from Poggi's who accompanied him to a band concert at Plaza Park. A double date with a guy on the school team. They drove down to the beach with a bottle. The other guy's girl got sick so they went home. That was pretty much it.

This Isabelle, though. Hal had not looked at anyone before quite like he found himself looking at her. There was her chin, for instance. Or not so much her chin but her chin and her throat together, the way the one pointed at you and the other fell away as though it was taking your heart for a walk, down her neck to where her blouse opened at the second button. And it wasn't just the chin and the throat. There was so much else here that he'd never noticed in any other woman. Her collar bone, of all things; the way it opened up beneath the soft white fabric of her blouse toward her shoulders, still and taking flight both at once, like the wings of a bird you've just startled at the beach. And her voice. Clear but throaty too, like she was just waking up, except when she laughed so loud that the diners at adjoining tables turned to look.

"So tell me again," she was saying, "what you're going to be doing in L.A.?"

Hal ate a bite of steak.

"Mining," he said as he chewed. "My uncle is a geologist."

"What are you mining for?"

For half a heartbeat Hal wanted to tell her everything. Instead he had a gulp of wine and said:

"Minerals."

"What kind of minerals?"

"Expensive ones. That's what they tell me. I'm only the help."

Isabelle squinted at him, and it seemed to Hal that she knew she was hearing less than the whole truth. Again he stopped his blabbermouth with a swallow of wine. He let her talk next.

"Baseball and prospecting. An interesting combination. Which do you prefer?"

"I hope I'm better at baseball."

"You never know," she said.

CHAPTER TEN

CITY OF ANGELS

H AL wasn't scheduled to meet Uncle Warren until dinner time on Sunday, so he had an entire day in the city to himself. He was staying at a guesthouse on Hope Street, and the first thing he did after a cup of coffee was call Isabelle. She had given him her number when he walked her to her taxi after midnight. Alone in his own cab, having helped to close the Roosevelt with a rowdy chorus of "Shine on Harvest Moon" (with Mosley on the Jew's harp), Hal pretended to plan his day off—a trip to the beach, to the Olvera Street Market, to the Olympic Village, to Universal Studios where they made the talking pictures. He knew all along what he really would do, and though Isabelle and he had not discussed it he suspected that she knew too.

The phone was answered by a woman he assumed was her mother. He caught himself nearly asking for "Isabelle," and instead managed "Is Miss Robinson available, please?" Then he heard her laughter and his knees turned to rubber beneath him so that he had to sink onto a guest house sofa.

"Took you long enough," she said.

"It's not even eight," Hal answered. "How early do you get up on a Sunday?"

"Depends if I have plans."

"And do you?" he said, his heart in his throat.

"I'm meeting you at nine, at the corner of Whittier and Dufee in Pico."

"Whittier and Dufee. Got it. What are we going to do?"

"Sightseeing. Don't be late."

So it was that Hal found himself at an intersection in the little town of Pico, leaning against a lamppost beneath a faded Carnation Milk sign, smelling the overpowering sweetness of orange blossoms from the groves surrounding the town on every side, watching a high white cloud bank roll east across a deep blue sky, wondering what corner his life might turn next. He'd taken a taxi, and when the Mexican driver asked him "what's for you in Pico?" he'd answered "a friend," which had earned him a wink and the single word: *chica. Am I that obvious?* thought Hal. But then where else would he be going at that time in the morning except to church? Especially dressed in the suit he'd brought for the meeting downtown tomorrow, for what else did a guy wear to meet a girl on a Sunday morning?

Isabelle arrived on foot. She explained that her mother's house was only a half-mile away, but that they didn't want to go there, not yet at least, for both her mother and her brother were home. He was a "bit of a bimbo," she said; mean with his mouth and quick with his fists, and no fan of her suitors.

They walked the orange groves all the way to the San Gabriel, along the dusty paths the workers used, vacant and still this morning apart from the sounds of their footsteps and the low drone of honeybees. They heard the bells of St. Mary's on the other side of the river, and the distant bass lowing of a cow, anxious for its tardy Sunday milking. Hal took long strides and Isabelle kept up with him, two steps to his one, their footfalls tapping out a quick waltz rhythm on the rich, packed earth. They didn't talk much. That was fine with Hal. As delighted as he was by her company, the scenery, the sounds and the day in general, he couldn't stop himself from looking ahead, somewhat grimly, to tomorrow.

"Why the long face?" said Isabelle.

At the sound of her voice he cheered immediately, but she was looking at him with real concern. He edged as close to the truth as he thought wise.

"Worrying about the job, I guess. But I shouldn't let it spoil such a pretty day."

"Where would you most like to be right now?" she asked. "Anywhere in the whole world. What's your favorite place?"

Hal stopped on the path and looked about him. He hadn't been that many places really; nowhere exotic at least. Where had he been happiest? He thought of his kitchen in Oxnard, sitting at the table in the kitchen while Sarah did her homework, watching his mother at the stove—but that was another life, and he couldn't bear to go there again. He thought of the highway, the wind blowing his hair, Charlie or Abe beside him telling bad jokes and giving worse directions—but that wasn't something he could return to, either. He thought of the shoe factory in Oxnard; of hurling his fast ball at the chalked-in strike zone while the first evening bats swooped figure-eights above him in the purpling sky. He thought of taking the mound yesterday in front of twenty thousand people; the smell of grass and leather and dust. Where *did* he want to be? He thought of the restaurant last night—the candles and the waiter and the winking, rowdy men. He thought of right here, right now. He didn't know what to say.

"You go first," he said. "What's *your* favorite place?"

"We're on our way there."

She took him to the library. It was closed for Sunday but she had a key. It felt like breaking in to Hal, but Isabelle said not to worry. She made a joke as she unlocked the door, about how maybe a baseball player like him had never seen the inside of a library, and he almost protested, telling her what a good student he'd been, or about the books they'd had at home; the fat volumes of history and anthropology that sat piled on every level surface after one of Uncle Warren's visits. But he decided not to protest. She'd agreed to spend the day with him, after all. He simply told her she might be better read but he bet she couldn't make heads or tails of a box score.

"What's a box score?" she asked.

"See? I told you." He said as they went in.

Even though they were alone Hal didn't raise his voice above a library whisper, which echoed like a cymbal off the shiny oak floors and shelves. Isabelle giggled and answered in a normal tone. Hal shushed her, which set her off laughing harder.

"Where do you work?" he asked.

"All over," she said. "Behind the desks, in the stacks, sometimes down in the basement store room, but that's not a very nice place. I've seen mice down there."

"I don't like basements much," he said. "Pick out a book for me."

"I bet you like mysteries."

"It depends."

She led him through the first floor, up and down the stacks of fiction, biographies, and reference books; fat encyclopedias and dictionaries that crowded the wooden shelves. There were tables here for working, each with a folded paper card imploring *Quiet Please*, surrounded by hard-backed chairs. There were cut glass ashtrays and a fat Bible on a stand of carved black ebony. "From Africa," Isabelle told him. "A gift to some missionaries from the tribe they converted." There were racks of newspapers and magazines from as far away as London, and rows of cabinets with flat drawers holding maps of places Hal had never heard of and Warren probably had been to.

He touched things—book spines, the card catalogue, the ink-wells in the tables—but he said little. He followed her upstairs to a second floor of history and science books, engineering and mathematics, with fewer tables and many empty shelves up high, and a big bay window occupied by a life-sized plaster copy of a marble sculpture, a mostly unclothed woman holding a bow, with a quiver of arrows on her back.

"Diana," said Isabelle. "We talk to her when there aren't any readers around."

Hal bowed before the statue.

"Does she talk back?"

The third floor was sparsely furnished, with fewer shelves and wider spaces between them. Here was poetry, Isabelle told him, and plays, and the foreign language section, mostly books in Spanish. Here also were travel books, geographies and books about the customs of foreign places—books that Isabelle said made her want to travel; to see a world that wasn't California—a world of surprises.

"I'd like to see New York," Hal said, and it seemed to him that she frowned, so he added: "And Alaska."

"And India? And Australia? And Spain?"

"Sure," he said. "One of each."

This was the best floor, she said. She was the one talking quietly now, and though he had let his voice rise to normal volume he lowered it and bent down to hear her as she drifted around the room to its bay window, a seat with a big cozy pillow striped with a shaft of morning sunlight. Isabelle sat down with the cushion behind her back, and patted the seat next to her.

"This is the spot," she said. "My favorite place."

They sat without speaking, warmed by the sun. There were no street noises below them, but Hal heard the St. Mary's bells strike eleven, the shriek of a seagull passing the window and the rhythm in his ears of his own heartbeat, quick and urgent, almost like fear though that made no sense. Surely there could be nothing frightening about this girl sitting next to him with her feet tucked up beneath her, her eyes closed and an expression on her face of such complete satisfaction that it was all Hal could do not to lay his head down in her lap and bask in her contentment. Instead, and without thinking, he took her hand in his. She did not resist his grasp, but scooted sideways toward him on the seat without turning her head or opening her eyes. She laced her fingers through his and ran her thumb along the top of his hand. Hal shivered at the contact, and responded with a pressure of his own. She leaned closer against him so that their shoulders were touching, hers in a blouse of peach-cream silk and his in his only suit. He inhaled the smell of her hair and skin, and made an involuntary noise in his throat, like the first part of a hiccup.

"What?" she said. Her voice was barely a whisper.

"Nothing," he managed.

He knew he ought to kiss her. Yet he didn't want what was happening now to end, or even change. After all, this was a sure thing, and who knew what would happen if he upset the balance? She might not want to be kissed, or worse she might not want to be kissed by him, or at least not now, or she might want to be and then he might kiss her poorly, and the moment would be ruined. If only, he thought, he might have just a glimpse of her thoughts, just for a second …

Suddenly the question was moot. With a single, fluid motion, as though expertly mounting a horse, Isabelle swung one leg up and over Hal's knee and landed straddling his lap. His expression—shock, delight and a dash of terror—made her laugh. Her skirt had ridden up around her thighs, most unladylike, yet she made no move to fix it. Hal held her around her waist and then higher up, his hands fumbling for whatever yielding softness they could find. She took the lapels of his jacket in her hands and pulled him close. The kissing decision was made for him. So were a number of others, or at least that is how it seemed, for things were happening quickly now, far more quickly than Hal's experience had prepared him for, though he did his best to keep up.

He gained confidence as they progressed.

When noon rang out at St. Mary's, Hal and Isabelle were sleeping, tangled in one another's warm limbs and cast-off clothes, still on the window ledge. Hal opened one eye to the sound of the chimes. Isabelle's head lay on his bare chest. She was breathing evenly, and did not stir at the twelve steady bells. He looked down the length of her back to her legs and marveled at their perfection. At her perfection. He laughed softly to himself, and this time she shifted slightly and pressed against him—an acknowledgement, conscious or not, of his pleasure. He stroked her hair.

..

Hal was to meet his uncle at six, at a bar near the studio apartment Warren had rented just off Figueroa Street. He tore himself away from Isabelle at five, dashed by taxi back to his place to bathe and change, and was fifteen minutes late for the rendezvous.

Warren wasn't happy with his tardiness. His lecture was brief but stern. He reminded Hal that, Charlie Gates' son or not, he was an employee, and that he would be expected to behave like one. Hal was only partly paying attention.

"I told you I was sorry," he said. "I got lost."

"Very well," said Warren. "Apology accepted." But he was looking at his nephew funny, and Hal squirmed a little, wondering if he saw something new.

From a worn leather map case beneath the table Warren pulled a sheaf of drawings with which he intended to impress tomorrow's audience. The Board had heard the gist of the Plan but this would be their first exposure to its nuts and bolts. There were diagrams of the X-ray machine, and of the equipment that would be used to bore the shaft. There were maps of the City, covered with dotted lines like the tentacles of a mutant octopus; the putative outline of the treasure tunnels far below.

"So you've gotten the map?" Hal asked.

"I've had a glance at it. I've reproduced here what I saw as best as I could from memory. The map itself is with Chief Greenleaf. We are still negotiating."

"You mean he wants a cut," said Hal.

"He wants to make certain the job is done properly," Warren said sharply. "We are dabbling in sacred matters. This map is quite precious to him, as you might imagine. He has it from his great-grandfather, who had it from a shaman who was said to be nearly two hundred years old himself. It is itself a copy of a much older document. I believe that it will corroborate what the X-ray has revealed."

"Can we find the gold without it?"

"I believe we can," Warren said. "But it will make our job much easier. And it would go a long way to silencing the skeptics."

Including me, thought Hal.

"As for you, young man," his uncle continued, "it seems you may be even more valuable to the Plan than I imagined."

"How so?"

"You've met Mr. McCreery's paramour. She came to dinner at your mother's."

Hal was confused for a minute. Who on earth was Mr. McCreery? Oh yes: Rex. Hal had trouble thinking of him as a "mister." And his "paramour" must be the mysteriously insolent woman who had been with him at The Palms.

"Sure," he said. "Rose, isn't it? Wasn't the map supposed to be her job?"

"She has been working on it. I don't suppose you know who she is?"

"You just said. She's Rex's girlfriend."

"She is also the daughter of Chief Greenleaf."

Hal's eyes grew wide.

"Her relationship with her father has been somewhat strained. Her romantic interests, for one thing, have not been to his liking. Including her current one. The Chief seems to think that Mr. McCreery is ..." he paused and tapped his water glass. "Let's say a little unpolished for a young woman he considers to be a princess of her people. Bluntly put, the Chief does not trust him."

"I can't imagine why not," Hal deadpanned. His uncle smiled.

"There is no question that he has his rough edges. His value to the project, though, is inestimable. He knows Los Angeles, and he knows mining. In any event he is one of us now, as is Miss Rose. We need to restore her father's confidence."

"And so I fit in exactly where?" Hal said.

Warren smiled conspiratorially.

"Let us imagine that Rex, as you call him, were to be replaced in Miss Rose's affections. Let us say that her new suitor presented a different image to the Chief: More genteel. More trustworthy. More respectful. Even more, shall we say, robust."

Hal felt the blood rise in his face.

"She's not really my type," he said, hoping Warren might let the matter drop. "And I hardly seem to be hers."

"Don't sell yourself short. It seemed to me that she was watching you closely at dinner. I notice these things."

"But it's not my game," Hal protested. "Courting and all. And even if I asked her out—I mean, it could take weeks. Months. Rex wouldn't be happy, either."

For a moment his little speech seemed effective. Warren frowned and nodded, looking down at the table. When he looked up he was smiling again.

"I tell you what: Let's get tomorrow out of the way. Then in the evening we'll all have dinner together, Rose too. Just the three of us; a little get-acquainted party. I suspect things will proceed more quickly than you imagine. And I wouldn't worry about Mr. McCreery. All's fair, as the old saying goes."

Hal resolved to say no more on the subject, but to consider it a bullet dodged. Warren's idea was preposterous of course, but then what should he expect from the author of the Plan? Once they had the permit in hand, Rose surely could persuade her father on her own. The only courting Hal intended to do had nothing to do with her.

A waiter appeared. Warren ordered a bottle of wine, and porterhouse steaks for both of them. Hal had no appetite. He liked nothing he'd heard so far tonight, and they hadn't even gotten to the real reason for getting together. But there wasn't much to discuss, Warren said, about the meeting. All he required was Hal's presence. Mr. Shaw would be there himself, though he had not attended the previous sessions.

"You just do your best to look forthright and big," he told Hal. "Should Mr. Shaw question you directly—well, we've been over that. You know what to say."

Hal wondered what would happen if he simply said no. The word was always available to him, always dancing on the tip of his tongue, always the first and most sensible response that came to mind. But he knew what stopped him. It was the thought of Vera; of her simple, crackpot faith; her hope that the Plan would spare them somehow from the shadow of failure that Charlie's departure still cast. It was her confidence in him; a mother's abject reliance; the strongest shackle a man can bear. He would swallow his "no" once more, at least for the time being, and go through with it. With the Plan. With tomorrow. With another fat slice of Houdini Pie.

Warren offered Hal a ride back to the guest house. When they arrived Hal had to will his legs to lift him out of the passenger seat, and he nearly stumbled stepping onto the curb. He was weak and slack, hardly able to hold up his head. He breathed deeply of the fresh air. It helped, but only a little.

"A little more wine than was needful, perhaps?" Warren joked through the window. "I'd have thought the offspring of Charlie Gates could soak it up like the Sahara in a storm."

"It's been a long day."

"I suggest you get some rest. You'll be needing your strength."

It was hot in his little room. There was only one other boarder in the house, the landlady had told him; an elderly bachelor in the back corner on the first floor. Hal could pick whatever room he liked. He'd chosen one facing west, hoping for evening breezes off the ocean. She'd left a basket of fruit on the dresser next to the wash basin and a folded towel. Hal ignored them and threw himself on the bed, pausing only to turn off the light and drop his clothes in a heap in the middle of the floor.

He began dreaming at once, messily and randomly, as the stored-up imagery of not only the day, but of months and years reaching back beyond memory rearranged itself into a madcap, whimsical newsreel: A baseball field by an ocean shore, him at the plate, facing Charlie Gates who stood on a mound as tall as a sand dune, hurling not baseballs but bottles that turned to geodes in mid-air, that Hal smashed with swings of a bat made of beet greens, then turning heel and running across a field of burning barns, the air filled with shotgun blasts. Then he was in a library, following a woman in a bouncing skirt down endless aisles of leather bound books, her laughter echoing. Then she stopped and turned, he took her in his arms, and the dream was simply, deliciously memory—the kisses, the groping, the shyness, the absence of shyness; all as fresh as the real thing had been just hours before.

And all at once he knew that he wasn't alone in his rented room. There was someone else in the bed. It was not Isabelle, neither her scent nor her skin pressing his in the darkness. Still, as if acting on someone else's will, he responded. The line between dream and reality blurred, then vanished as this unknown flesh yielded to an urgency he had never known before, not even on the window seat. His mind was blank. His body was anything but.

When his passion was spent he rolled on his back, his animal satisfaction giving way to a very human fear. A sliver of the rising moon found a gap in the curtains above the bed and offered him a little light as he turned to his side, to confront the mysterious manifestation of his dreams.

"Hello darling," said Rose. "Welcome to the City of Angels."

CHAPTER ELEVEN

AN HONEST MAN

T HE Los Angeles County Board of Supervisors was concluding the strangest session in its history. Its members, along with Mayor Frank Shaw and Timothy Gavin, his personal lawyer, sat silently; each waiting for another to speak, or maybe just repeating in their minds the outlines of the astonishing presentation they had witnessed. The presenters—a bald engineer and his giant nephew—had but recently said their good-byes in a flurry of handshakes and assurances of certain success. But how could success be assured when its object was impossible? Lizard men, they had said. Treasure. Cataclysms. X-rays. Sheer, stark, raving madness.

Of course they had done some checking. Shaw's lawyer had his "sources," as he called them. He'd tracked down the bald guy's diplomas, his jobs, a few of the adventures to which he'd alluded. He was on the up-and-up, Gavin concluded; as much as anyone was these days. As for this machine of his, Gavin had looked into that as well. A couple of professors at the University had seen it in action. The damned gadget could *find* things. Break a china plate, hide one half on the beach and give the other half to the bald guy and by damn if he couldn't locate its mate, lickity-split. Same thing with a chunk of pyrite, or feldspar, or sulfur. One fellow had seen him snip a man's neck-scarf in two, then locate half of the cloth that a skeptical colleague had tossed into a trash bin behind the building.

But if there's gold down there, the men asked, why not dig for it ourselves? That's where Shaw stepped in. First, he explained, because it would be too complicated: the publicity, the bids, the awards, the inquiries, the contracts, the insurance, the press, the public. Not to mention the cost. The City wouldn't stand for it; not after the debacle of the Olympics, which had left a nasty taste in the public mouth. There would be no patience for such shenanigans in an official capacity. Let Mr. X-ray take the risk, and the criticism, while we stand benevolently by.

And if there really is something? That, Shaw explained, is when things might get delicate. There would be a rush, and there was no controlling a rush. Control was everything. While the bald engineer might know about deep-rock mining, it wasn't likely that he knew squat about the consequences of success. That which was granted—permits, for example—could be revoked. Mining was dangerous, particularly in the middle of a city. There might be signs of flooding, for instance. Or of the site caving in on itself if the soil was not stable enough to sustain the hole—"subsidence," they called it. At the first report of success the Board would step in. Clearly the operation was not sophisticated. The skinny engineer, the young giant, and a surly gorilla who'd attended an earlier meeting—they weren't a very formidable group. If they failed, it would hardly be news. If they got lucky, well, then it would be time for the entire enterprise to fall into more responsible hands. Several Board members worried privately that he was as crazy as the bald guy. But when the Mayor was behind something, it was futile to stand in his way. So they acquiesced. Let the little man dig. What could it hurt?

..

Hal spent Monday in a state of bewilderment. What had happened, exactly, at the guesthouse? Or not *what*—for that was clear enough—but *why*? Rose hadn't stayed around long enough to explain. Not that she'd grabbed her clothes and run, exactly. She'd lingered a while; a warm, whispering presence that convinced Hal more than once that he was still dreaming. But when he'd awoken in the morning—alone, thank God—he felt awful, disgusted, filthy, sated and (oddly) ravenous all in the space of time it took him to sit up straight, look around his empty room and let out a howl of baffled anguish that brought his fat landlady huffing up the stairs. She burst through his unlocked door to find Hal completely naked in the middle of the room, his arms open to some invisible, imagined embrace. The landlady froze.

"Do you need something?" she said.

Her head was turned to one side, and she was appraising him frankly. Hal rushed to the bed and pulled a sheet up in front of him. Here was the third woman in twenty-four hours to see his private parts. What was happening to him?

"I'm fine," he said. "I'll be … I'll be wanting some coffee in a few minutes. If you have some. After I wash up. Thank you."

She didn't move for a moment, and when she left she shook her head and clucked her tongue, whether in disapproval or regret, Hal did not care to speculate.

Warren arranged a dinner with him and Rose on Monday evening. At first Hal was not able to meet her gaze. It was as if he'd merely dreamed the guesthouse episode, and was fearful that his glance might betray his subconscious. But he bore the marks of her nails on his back and a purple bite-mark, the size of a dime, in a place he had never been bitten before. After a glass of wine he began to make eye contact with her. She was lovely, but not in the way that Isabelle was lovely. Isabelle was beautiful like a flower, like the dawn, like the sound of a church bell in the still, clear air. And she was young. Rose was a grown woman, whose age Hal could not even venture to guess. Thirty? Forty? She was beautiful like a thunderstorm. Like a forest fire. Her eyes bored into him as though his thoughts were readable just beneath his skin.

"When did you talk to him?" Warren was saying. "What did he tell you?"

Hal shook himself out of his reverie. He hadn't been listening to a word his uncle was saying. Thankfully the question wasn't directed to him.

"I went to his room yesterday morning," Rose said. "He told me that he'd had a dream. That voices from below sang to him. They told him that this was not the time."

"Damn it," said Warren. He leaned forward slightly, waiting for her to continue.

"I told him that our fortunes had turned," she continued. "He didn't speak for the longest time. I thought he was angry. Finally he said that I should come back again."

"Did he say when?"

"He never does. Time doesn't work for him like it does for the rest of us. I could not show up for three years and he'd greet me as if I'd gone out for a walk around the block. I know. I've done it before."

"You're talking about your father?" Hal interrupted. "About the Chief?"

Warren turned toward him with what seemed to be mild annoyance.

"Precisely," he said. "Rose made an effort to obtain the map. She was not successful. It looks like we're going to need to pay the old man another visit after all."

Hal did not like the sound of that "we." Rose was looking at him again.

"Don't worry," she said. "I told him all about you."

Oh great, thought Hal.

"Would he see us tonight?" said Warren.

The restaurant had emptied but for the three of them. Surely they wouldn't visit an old man so late?

"He'll see us whenever we arrive," said Rose.

"Then let's not waste time," said Warren, rising quickly and signaling the waiter.

"But …" Hal sputtered, rising as well. "But where?"

"Not far," Warren said. "Come on."

They drove in the Studebaker to Hal's boarding house. Hal was mystified. He followed Warren and Rose up the steps he had come down a few hours before. The landlady opened the door. She led the way to a door in the far east wing of the house. One more boarder, she'd said. An elderly bachelor. Of course.

Rose knocked.

"Father?"

Her voice was soft, with an unexpected sweetness. She pushed the door open slowly. The room was lit by candles: one on a battered desk, one on a window ledge and one in a cup on the floor, next to which sat the silhouette of a man, cross-legged, his head bowed. He was wearing a floppy felt hat and smoking a cigarette. When he inhaled its tip briefly illuminated a face of advanced old age, as gnarled as sycamore bark, with a hooked nose, a wide forehead and a pair of round, dark glasses, the kind Hal had seen only on the blind. Except for that long, slow, drag on his smoke, the old man neither answered nor acknowledged their entrance.

Rose fumbled with her hand along the door frame and flipped on an overhead light; a single, dim bulb that hardly dented the gloom, but the old man—Chief Greenleaf, Hal assumed—flinched and drew a hand up in front of his eyes. He was wearing a shirt that had once been white and a pair of black pants with saucer-sized holes at the knees. He was barefoot. His toes were long, their nails hooked like claws. Above the glasses sprouted weedy eyebrows that twitched as he surveyed the intruders. He smelled of sweat and piss.

He sat on a sort of perch made of old sacks and blankets. Next to the candle was an ashtray full of knobby butts. The rest of the room was vacant but for the desk, a straight-backed chair in the corner by the window, and a couple of bundles stacked against the wall. The old man held his cigarette in one hand. In the other he clutched an unrolled, weathered page, the size of a sheet of newsprint, covered with lines and inscrutable symbols. The map, Hal assumed. As he bent forward for a better look, the Chief rolled it shut with a surprisingly fluid flip of his bony wrist. Then he spoke in a voice hardly that of a fossil, as Hal expected, but as strong as a man in his prime.

"So you are the Little Giant," he said with a toothless smile. "Please come in."

Hal entered slowly, propelled by Warren's hand on the small of his back. Rose brought the straight-backed chair and set it facing her father. She motioned to Hal that he should sit, which he did, bewildered but unable to think why he should protest. *Little Giant?* He hadn't heard that name since grammar school. Chief Greenleaf was following him with his head, and Hal assumed that he must see something through those black lenses, but once seated he noted that the old man appeared to be staring past him to the vacant wall behind. Rose and Warren stood to either side of the rag pile, waiting for something, though Hal had no idea what.

The Chief stood. There was nothing feeble or awkward about the act; indeed he did not even use his arms for balance, but simply popped upright like a Jack-in-the-Box. His brown hand shot forward and grabbed Hal by the chin, freezing him in his place, left buttock off his seat, right hand thrown in the air for balance, head snapped back in astonishment, eyes wide and unblinking.

"Be still," the old fellow commanded.

Hal obeyed. He managed to scoot his bottom back onto the chair and lower his hands to his sides. With his free hand (where had the cigarette gone? and the map?) the Chief lay three splayed fingers in the center of Hal's forehead. His touch was firm and sure. The fingers traced Hal's head, eye sockets, nose, cheeks, ears, chin and neck, all slowly and methodically. Hal tried hard not to move. When the old man apparently was satisfied things got stranger still, for he brought his craggy head close to Hal's and sniffed him; hardly different, thought Hal, than one dog might smell another passing in the road. Then the old man spoke.

"I have not heard your voice," he said. Hal looked at Rose and Warren in turn. No help from them was forthcoming.

"Well, I ..." began Hal, his voice cracking with nerves. What should he say?

"I am very, um, glad to meet you," he ventured. "I, ahhh ..." He could think of nothing. Out of the corner of his eye he saw that Rose was smiling.

"Tell me a story," said the Chief. He sat back on his pile of rags, and waited.

What in the dickens was Rose smiling at? Hal didn't appreciate being the subject of her derision. A story my eye, he thought. I ought to tell this guy exactly what his daughter gets up to while he's up here marinating in his bedclothes. But still he didn't know what he would actually say.

"Tell me," said Greenleaf, "about your birth. There was something propitious about it, I believe."

Hal exhaled sharply. *Now* what? His mother? His birth? Whose idea was that? Damned sure there was a story there; one he had heard a hundred times. All right, then. He'd tell the story of the Stardust Pills. He'd make it short and sweet. And then, by God, it would be time for the Chief to tell a story or two of his own.

"Well," he began. "Of course I wasn't there. I mean, I was, but you know—not so I'd remember anything. Though my Uncle Warren here was. In fact some of this I learned from him. I was born during a comet. A big one. We lived up in Oxnard. Still do. Everybody was running around thinking it was going to be the end of the world ..."

The Chief cut him off.

"Enough, enough," he said. "I knew it was a special moment. A child of the comet is a truth-teller. Now we know for certain that you are that child. I approve."

He half turned to his daughter, then to Warren. Each of them nodded in turn.

"What about the map?" Hal blurted. Wasn't that why they were here?

The old man smiled, an expression Hal found vaguely grotesque. The rolled-up parchment lay amongst the rags. The Chief picked it up and tapped it on his knee.

"Of course I know that is why you are here. But this map does not give up its secrets easily. If I let you walk away with it, you would be disappointed. It is nothing without knowledge. More knowledge than you have, and still less than you may need."

He smiled again.

"I will tell you something of what you desire. Not everything, of course. Even I do not know everything. But I'll tell you some things that maybe some of you have not heard before. And then we'll see."

Rose and Warren moved forward. The candle on the floor had sputtered out, and the one on the dresser was smoking fitfully. Only the flame on the window sill still burned, uselessly, in the gloomy light from the overhead bulb. The old man's voice got soft. There was a sadness to it.

"You dream of gold," he began, "and yet gold is not the story. The story is of the People, and how they fled the surface of this world and did not return. When their world was threatened with destruction, they escaped. You would do the same. Perhaps some day you will.

"They were of the Lizard race. In those days the People took many shapes. The Lizards were large and strong, and they were rulers. The world has not since known their kind."

Ah, thought Hal. The lizards. So Warren had not invented that, at least.

"Catastrophe threatened," the old Chief continued. "Great earthquakes; fires and floods. The Elders knew the portents. Councils were held. A plan was presented. Some thought it foolish, but the Elders' word was law. They brewed a liquor so potent it could melt the rock beneath their feet. They tunneled deep, beneath the dens and caves of animals, deeper than the wells you drill for your precious oil. When the fires and floods came the last of the People slipped beneath the surface. They were spared."

The old man paused. Hal looked at Warren. His uncle's neck muscles were straining, the veins in his temples pulsing. Rose's eyes smoldered like hot coals as she sat coiled on the floor. They believed, thought Hal. They actually believed.

The Chief was watching him. Hal knew that his distrust—which must be evident from his expression—was being held against him. Hell's bell's, he thought—what does it matter what I think of the scheme? Then he remembered Warren at the restaurant: *We need to restore her father's confidence.* He nodded, hoping he looked sincere.

"So what happened?" he asked. "Are the, um, People still down there?"

Warren shot him a look that Hal couldn't interpret. The Chief answered in a voice even softer and sadder than before.

"The earth betrayed them," he said. "At first the air was sweet. The Wise Ones had tunneled passages all the way to the ocean, to gather the breezes that blew in off shore. But the earth held its secrets. It had taken a breath when the digging began, and as the People settled—over many years, mind you, for the ways of the earth are slow—it exhaled. Its breath was poison. Children sickened. The old began to wither. Mothers made no milk for their babies. Finally the last of the People passed on. A great cycle had been broken. No one remained to mourn."

"If nobody survived, how do you know what happened?"

The Chief lowered his eyes.

"Some of the Elders ascended just before the end. They did not flee, as some accused them. They sought escape for all. They saw that the waters were receding and that life was reborn. But when they tried to return below the earth heaved and shook itself one last time. The passages were sealed. They were trapped above. No one has returned since to the world they made."

The old man's shoulders slumped. He sighed deeply, and his head drooped to his chest. Rose put her finger to her lips. She tiptoed to the door and beckoned. They didn't speak until they'd passed back through the kitchen to the main hallway, where she led them through a closed door into a sitting room that Hal had not been in before. She and Warren sat in separate chairs on either side of a cold fireplace. Hal stood by the door.

"It's all so preposterous," he said. "Like the Three Bears or the Man in the Moon. And he never answered me about the map. It *is* what we came for, after all. Why didn't anyone talk about it?"

"Have patience, Little Giant," Rose answered. "The map was the most important thing to us, maybe, but not necessarily to him. You told him a story, remember? And so he told you one in return. He has a lot to think about, now. And so do you."

CHAPTER TWELVE

THE STRETCH

EDITH ROBINSON was not a baseball fan. As far as she knew neither was her daughter. So she was surprised when Isabelle insisted that they attend a game together up in Ventura, where Edith had planned to pay a visit to her old school friend, Clara, a widow who kept three rooms for travelers in the house her husband had left her on the coast road. When Isabelle offered to accompany her mother on the bus ride north, Edith knew that something was afoot.

"That sounds wonderful," she said. "My first baseball game. Is there anything special I should wear?"

"Nothing too causal," Isabelle said, "In case we go out after, you know."

"Go out where?"

"Just wherever," Isabelle answered airily. "In case something comes up."

They took a Thursday bus that put them in Ventura around dusk. Normally on these visits Edith would porch-sit and gossip with Clara late into the evening. But Isabelle's presence threw the older women off—their usual lazy rhythm of small talk and gossip was upset by her torrent of squeaky, nervous energy. Clara was amused. She gave Edith a wink when Isabelle was in another room.

"Who's the fella?" she asked.

Edith threw her hands up with an exaggerated shrug. There was always a fella, it seemed—on the phone or on the porch or pulling away in a rattletrap car after midnight. But no boy had ever affected Isabelle like this.

Isabelle told her to be sure she was ready by ten the next morning.

"The game starts at noon," she said. "I want to be there early for batting practice."

Batting practice? Where did this lingo come from? Edith had to laugh. Something was up for sure.

When the taxi dropped them off at the park Isabelle led them confidently to the ticket counter, through the turnstile, and up the steps into the bleachers. The ballpark was small by ballpark standards; fewer than four thousand seats, but to Edith it seemed enormous. The playing field was a vast carpet of grass so green it seemed painted. The ball players, in gray or white flannel uniforms, stalked its perimeter. Some swung bats at imaginary pitches; others played catch, a few made quick, sprinting forays onto the field, a dozen steps forward then back, retrieved on invisible leashes. Isabelle's excitement was infectious as she pointed things out—the drink and peanut hawkers beginning their descents into the stands; the grounds crew laying down the white chalk lines, the black-suited umpires clustered behind home plate like a coven of fat witches.

The sun was brassy and hot. Isabelle stood on her toes, shading her eyes with a program.

"Looking for somebody special?" Edith said.

She was staring down what she'd told Edith was the first-base line, bent slightly at the waist, her eyes squinted tight, biting her lower lip.

"There he is! Hal! HAL!"

Edith shielded her own eyes and followed her daughter's gaze. Lord knew who she was looking at. How she could distinguish anyone among the milling spectators was beyond Edith; it was like trying to identify one ant among a marching swarm. Isabelle was practically hopping now, waving her program above her head like a semaphore.

"HAAAAAAAAAL!"

Edith laughed.

"Who is it, dear? Who on earth are you waving at?"

Whoever it was, he either didn't notice or was too far away. Isabelle flew off along the bleacher aisle, down the steps and into the crowd. Now it was Edith on her tiptoes, trying to pick out her daughter among the spectators clustered at the railing. The boisterous crowd was calling for autographs, shouting advice and heaping good-natured abuse on the last players emerging from the dugout. There was the coach, she supposed; an older man in uniform, talking earnestly to one of the umpires. Farther down, in what Isabelle had called the "bullpen," an enormous man was stepping off a mound of dirt, wiping his forehead with the back of his arm. And suddenly there was Isabelle, next to him, her hand on the big mans arm.

"Isa ..." Edith began to call, as if her voice would reach them. Just as the name died on her lips she saw the giant bend down and kiss her daughter on the top of the head. Then he ran off to the dugout with his teammates, and Isabelle disappeared again.

A rag-tag brass band was huffing out a sour version of the "Star Spangled Banner" when she came panting back down the aisle.

"So that's Hal," Edith said.

"That's him," said Isabelle. "Hal Gates. Look."

She picked her program off the ground and proudly pointed out Hal's name, listed among the players as Gates, Halley, Number 6, Pitcher, BR, TR.

"That means he bats right and throws right. Handed, they mean."

"Mmmmm," said Edith.

It seemed that Hal was not simply a pitcher, but a damned fine one. As little as Edith knew about the game, she recognized (with the considerable help of non-stop commentary from her daughter) that the young man displayed an uncanny talent for throwing a baseball in such a way that a man with a bat could not possibly hit it. Hal's team had a lot more luck against the opposing hurler. The Sheiks put up an 8-0 lead by the fifth inning. Isabelle beamed and talked to Edith like a girlfriend: Hal this, Hal that, Hal everything. The crowd didn't seem to mind that their boys were losing—indeed, they cheered for Hal's strikeouts, rooting him on as though he was a local.

There was a break in the seventh inning after the Sheiks' turn at bat. "The stretch," Isabelle called it. Vendors passed through the crowd, hawking their drinks and snacks. Two clowns cavorted around second base, juggling inflated baseballs the size of pumpkins, until they were chased away by another clown swinging an oversized bat. No one paid them much attention.

Isabelle scanned the players, most of whom were clustered around the dugouts. A few meandered along the rail in front of the front-row seats, signing an autograph here, accepting a snort of whisky there, backslapping and handshaking like politicians. Edith started to ask her daughter if she would like another lemonade.

The look on Isabelle's face froze Edith's question on her lips. She followed the girl's gaze down to where Hal stood towering over his teammates. He was as tall as many of the fans who were elevated above the field on the first bleacher step. He was ignoring them. His attentions were commanded by a woman at the end of the first row. She was dark-eyed and obviously beautiful, even from a distance, dolled up like some exotic princess from a travel magazine—a long red dress, a blue dangling sash, large loop earrings, a half-dozen necklaces of brilliant beads. It was not an autograph she was after.

She leaned over the rail toward him, and he leaned toward her. She brought her right hand up and touched his face; she put the flat of her hand on his chest. He said something, pulling away, and she pulled him back by his sleeve. He appeared to resist, and she laughed. He took hold of her wrist and lowered it to the rail. She turned away. Hal ran back onto the field, where the players were taking their positions again.

Isabelle made a noise in her throat.

"Oh my dear girl," said Edith.

Her daughter sat down, biting her bottom lip.

"I say we get out of here right now," said Edith.

"No," Isabelle replied evenly. "I want to see the game."

Edith sat down slowly and frowned.

"Very well," she said. "We'll stay."

Unbelievably, the Sheiks managed to lose. After the incident with the mysterious woman, Hal's prowess on the mound evaporated like fog in a morning sun. He hit several batters, walked a few more (Edith was learning the lingo, roughly) and served up a long series of hits in the seventh—bloopers, line drives, three home runs—leading the Sheiks to a 12-11 loss.

At the end of the game Isabelle rose wordlessly and made for the steps. Edith followed. She went not to the front gate, where they might hail one of the taxis that were already lined up along Telegraph Road, but around to the players' entrance on the south side of the park.

"Oh, dear," said Edith. "Oh dear, dear, dear."

Just outside the gate they found Hal alone on a concrete step, his head in his hands. When Isabelle approached he groaned and stood up.

"Who is she?" said Isabelle.

Hal stood slowly, dropping his hands to his sides.

"I really stunk it up out there," he said miserably.

"I said, who is she?"

"Who is who?"

A bad liar, Edith noted. This, at least, was a good thing.

"The gypsy woman, or whatever she is. The one who ruined your game."

Hal's eyes got wide. Apparently the notion hadn't occurred to him. He had a nice face, Edith thought—boyish, given the size of him. He looked baffled.

"She's an Indian," he said. "My boss knows her father. I have to be, um, nice to her. She's sort of unusual. But you don't think …"

"You were winning until she touched you."

The big guy blushed furiously. Yet another good sign.

"I guess she rattled my concentration."

"That's the understatement of the century," Isabelle said with a smirk. "You couldn't have hit the side of a freight train."

They walked without speaking for a moment, around the stadium toward the entrance. Edith found herself wanting to believe this over-grown boy, and to protect her daughter at the same time.

"She did something to you. Don't you see?" Isabelle said finally.

Hal shrugged and held up his palms. Isabelle stood aside.

"This is my mother," she said. "Edith Robinson."

Hal stepped forward and took her hand.

"Very pleased to meet you ma'am."

"Can you join us for dinner?" Isabelle asked. Edith was surprised—they'd discussed nothing like this, and it was quite forward of a woman to ask a man on a date, even with her mother present. But Hal shook his head.

"I'd better go with the team," he said. "Lucky—he's the manager—he got us a bus from a tour guy he knows in L.A. He's going to drop the team in Oxnard and drive me and a couple of other guys back to the city."

He and Isabelle stared at each other for a moment. Edith cleared her throat. Isabelle gave her a sideways look.

"Call me," she said softly to Hal.

The crowd was steaming out of the exits. They were jubilant with the unexpected win. A sodden trio of men in rumpled brown suits and crushed gray fedoras recognized Hal and insulted him cheerfully. They staggered, slapped their knees and leaned against each other, lurching toward Hal like a three-headed cartoon creature. From around the east side of the stadium came the honking and chuffing of the Sheiks' big bus. Lucky swung the vehicle inexpertly in a wide arc, cutting Hal, Isabelle and Edith off from the onlookers. The heads of a half-dozen ballplayers were thrust through the open windows as Hal's teammates took in the commotion, hurled a few insults themselves and motioned for him to get on board.

"Kiss her goodbye and let's go!" Lucky shouted.

Hal tossed his glove into an open window, took Isabelle in both his arms and planted a movie-star kiss on her lips. The players broke into wild applause as he released her and leaped up the steps. Isabelle, blushing furiously, waved a vigorous goodbye through a cloud of stinking diesel smoke. When the bus reached the road and turned right, Edith saw Hal leaning from an open window. She scanned the crowd for the Gypsy woman, but could not find her.

Not until the bus was out of sight did Isabelle approach her mother.

"Let's get a taxi," she said.

··

"Hey, Gates. You want a snort?"

Payton leaned across the aisle, a pint of Canadian in his outstretched hand. Hal took the bottle, took a polite little gulp and handed it back. The catcher's concern seemed sincere. None of the Sheiks were giving Hal a hard time about the loss. They were ballplayers. Things happened.

Yet this loss needled him. Isabelle really thought it was Rose's fault. Christ was she mad. Not that she didn't have every reason to be. Talk about bad timing. But where the hell had Rose come from? When she emerged from the crowd along the rail, he'd felt like he was dreaming— like he couldn't summon the good sense to wave and smile and get the hell into the dugout where she couldn't follow him. She beckoned and he came. Had she really done something to him? The idea was ridiculous. But still.

He thought of her in the boarding house. He thought of Isabelle waving goodbye as the bus pulled away. He shifted in his seat and gestured to Payton.

"Anything left in that bottle?"

Payton tossed it to him—there were maybe six swallows left—and dug in the canvas bag at his feet for another one.

"Keep it," he said. "You've had a hell of day."

Hal raised it in the air and nodded his thanks. He didn't want to think anymore about Isabelle or Rose. Seeing them hadn't even been the weirdest thing about this trip. Last night, after the Sheiks had gotten into town, he'd borrowed a car from Tad Lewis, a back-up outfielder whose family lived in Ventura. He'd left the team in a flop house on Victoria Avenue and driven down to Oxnard.

Over the past few weeks he had spent the odd night in his own bed, between road games with the Sheiks and trips to the city. Vera usually was asleep when he got in, and when he left. He had called last night to tell her he was coming. She would wait up for him that way.

She was lying on the sofa when he'd arrived, her back propped up by pillows. She had an unopened book on her lap. She wore a faded nightgown buttoned to the neck. Her graying hair was tied in a blue scarf. Her eyes, though open, were unfocused, fixed vaguely on the ceiling above the kitchen doorway.

"Here I am," he said, coming through the back door. He'd picked up a bunch of flowers for her, and a few groceries. When she didn't answer he unloaded his purchases on the table and approached through the dining room. She swung her legs around and patted the cushion next to her.

"Sit down and let me have a look at you," she said. "My boy."

He settled down beside her after a perfunctory kiss on the cheek. She smelled nicer than usual—some kind of perfume, maybe.

"Found any treasure yet?" she said. "Or have they locked up your uncle for a nut-case?"

Hal squinted at her. This was not the way his mother talked about the Plan.

"We got the permit," he said. "We start digging Monday."

Vera's eyebrows went up a little. She giggled—a sound Hal couldn't remember hearing, at least not in years.

"Well then," she said. "The gold ought to start rolling in any day now."

And so began the oddest evening Hal had ever spent with his mother. She cooked him dinner, and opened a bottle of whiskey. She had a drink herself. She turned on the radio while he ate, filling the kitchen with crooning harmonies and plunking guitars. She laughed often and at just about anything. Hal tried to ask what was going on, but she deftly teased her way out of any direct conversation about herself. She didn't even talk about the Plan. If he mentioned Uncle Warren she made a little *"pffft"* sound, wrinkling her nose and waving a hand in dismissal. If he persisted she turned the subject on a dime.

"Are you eating enough? You look thin."

"Didn't you ever get yourself an automobile?"

"Where did you get that shirt? I don't remember it."

"So how are things with the girls? Is there anyone special?"

The last was a question he dodged himself, asking instead how the garden was doing, and how construction was coming on the new boat dock on Marine Drive. Their conversation resembled a game of chess—a game Hal had never been good at. After an hour he conceded defeat.

"I suppose I'll be getting along," he said, declining another glass of whiskey. "I have to pitch tomorrow. I'd better get some sleep."

Vera didn't say a thing about him staying. Indeed, when she looked at the clock she seemed to get flustered, and agreed that yes he'd better be getting along. She would see him soon, she said. She might even come to a game one of these days.

"Really?" She'd never seen him play, even in high school.

"One of these days," she repeated. She handed him his hat and stood on tiptoe to kiss his cheek. That smell again. Like flowers. He shook his head.

"You sure you're okay?"

"Fine," she chirped. "You get some sleep."

"I'll call," he said.

Something troubled him as he circled the house on his way out to the street. It nagged him as he drove back up to Ventura, and needled him as he undressed at the flophouse, trying to be quiet in a room he shared with the snoring Payton. He tossed and turned as it tugged at his memory, and the more he tried to ignore it the farther it kept him from sleep. It wasn't just Vera. Not just her elusive conversation or peculiar demeanor, or that the house was clean, and the larder stocked, and that she didn't smell like old bedclothes since the last time he could recall. Well, it *was* all that, but it was something else as well. Something peripheral. Something he noticed without noticing it. Something ...

He sat upright with a grunt, blinked three times and shook his head so hard the bedsprings squeaked. Peripheral, indeed. In the dark bedroom he saw clearly in his mind's eye the image that had dogged him since he left his mother's. On the back porch, off to the side, clearly visible in the light from the kitchen widow, in view so plain he'd almost missed them: A pair of men's boots. Intricately tooled. Worn but well-cared for. Looking like they'd walked a million miles.

CHAPTER THIRTEEN

MUSCLE AND BONE

O N a hot Monday morning on a residential street in downtown Los Angeles, Hal stood in a circle with a half–dozen other men, including Warren and Rex (and Rose as well), next to two flat bed trucks overloaded with equipment, staring at a roped-off square that looked remarkably like a boxing ring. Missing from the entourage was Mr. Martin, the third partner. Warren said he'd been called back east on business. Hal wondered if he'd simply had an attack of good sense.

"Gentlemen," said Warren. "And our charming young lady. This is an occasion auspicious beyond our wildest dreams. We are on a mission that may alter history."

Of course Warren would speechify. Not that anyone was paying attention. The assembled men were laborers except for Rex. One ate something brown from a can with a pocketknife. Two appeared to be asleep on their feet. The other two whispered in Spanish. Rose tapped her foot with an air of exaggerated boredom.

Warren did have an attentive audience of one. He'd chosen for the excavation a vacant lot on North Hill Street, behind the imposing wall of the Hall of Justice. There were modest houses scattered up and down the street. The site overlooked Sunset Boulevard and Spring Street to the north, where Warren's studies—and his few peeks at Chief Greenleaf's map—convinced him that a maze of tunnels stretched all the way up Broadway to Lookout Street. Directly across North Hill from where the flatbeds were parked stood a tiny frame cottage not much bigger than a garden shed. Its façade was something a preschooler might draw and call "house." On either side of a torn screen door were two four-paned windows, and a black stovepipe elbowed out of the middle of the crumbling slate roof. The place seemed oddly insubstantial, as if it *had* been drawn there, and might be erased by a stiff wind. Inside one window stood a shirtless fellow about Hal's age. He had dark eyes, prominent ribs and greasy black hair. A cigarette dangled from his mouth. He stared at the assemblage and scratched his belly.

Warren reached an oratorical crescendo. "Forever and more," he said, "When this day is lost in history, our discoveries—our *revelations*—will reverberate. Our deeds will outlive us. Our destiny lies beneath us."

Rose stifled a yawn. Warren produced a champagne bottle that he had been holding behind his back. The hired men brightened at the sight of it, but their expressions turned to horror when Warren raised it over his head and smashed it in the center of their little ring. Someone groaned. The ground at their feet was dry and bare but for a few scattered blades of grass and a single dandelion stalk gone to seed. Within a few seconds nothing remained but broken glass and a damp spot on the earth.

"Let us commence," said Warren, "to dig."

..

The sinking of a mine shaft, Hal soon learned, was neither complex nor mysterious. It was simply back-breaking, dangerous, unpleasant work. To his dismay he was expected to be right in the filthy middle of it. He could see very little difference between the hired men and himself in terms of duties. If anything he worked harder than they did, for Warren whispered to him during a break that Hal was to "set a good example." Of course his uncle did not get dirty himself. He spent the morning hovering around the equipment trucks and the X-ray machine, still hidden beneath its tarp, which he would lift occasionally for a reassuring peek. There had been talk of a reporter from the *Times* coming by. Frequently he walked up and down Front Street, shielding his eyes with his hat and peering into the distance. But aside from the man in the window the work proceeded unheralded and unobserved.

At first they simply dug. All day, into the evening, and for the long week thereafter. No drilling, no blasting, no special equipment. Just shovel and pick, muscle and bone. The idea was to excavate deep enough to encounter bedrock, into which they would drill and plant dynamite charges. Then, after blasting (Rex's department, apparently), they would go back in the hole, haul out loose rock and dirt by the bucketful, then dig, drill and blast again. Warren had sketches that he'd worked up from his last round of readings. They would proceed as vertically as possible for at least 600 feet—the very shallowest, according to Warren, that there would be hope of encountering anything "significant"—by which he meant not a main tunnel or chamber but, at best, an auxiliary passage. If they didn't find anything they would dig some more.

A trio of workers wielded long-handled picks and shovels while the others stood by with wheelbarrows that they filled with dirt and rock and hauled to a spoils pile at the corner of the property. Through each long day the hole grew, the pile grew, the shadows grew, and Hal's belief that this was all sheer lunacy grew most of all. The earth beneath their tools was tough and nasty; layers of dense, chocolate-brown clay interspersed with rocks of all sizes, from fists to bowling balls, all stubborn and unyielding. They snapped shovel blades and pick handles at least hourly, and Hal would fetch a replacement from one of the trucks.

They were down perhaps twenty feet now. Climbing in and out of the hole required a ladder. Only two men at a time could work safely in the shaft. They bumped, poked and jostled as they went, sweating so profusely that the earth turned to mud beneath their feet. At breaks they sought the meager shade of the trucks. Warren allowed only water for refreshment, though when his back was turned one or another of the men would produce a fruit jar filled with some clear, potent homebrew. Hal could hardly begrudge them a couple of belts. Indeed he took a few himself. They called him *el monstruo*; first behind his back, then to his face. It was a compliment, after all.

Waking, sleeping, digging or hauling, Hal thought about those boots on the porch. The possibilities they raised were too far-fetched to believe. He'd had a few whiskeys that night. A million memories lived in that house. A fellow's mind could play tricks. But he knew better. He'd seen them as clearly as he saw the mattock in his hands.

He had tried to phone Vera the morning before the game. No answer. He'd tried again from the city. No answer. He'd tried every night this week. No answer. Her behavior at the house made sense now. Charlie was back. He had to be.

Warren announced that they would begin blasting the following week. The Pit had narrowed as it deepened, and it was more difficult to maneuver in. There were so many bruised ribs and cut hands that Hal doubled as a field-nurse, dousing wounds with carbolic acid and wrapping them in gauze. Warren put two of the men to work building a wooden structure somewhere between an outhouse and a garage in size, as well as a skeletal framework of four-by-fours topped by a crude hand-crank winch. The little building was to be a blacksmith shop—a skill that Rex apparently had picked up in his travels. The winch was for bringing up dirt, rocks and—eventually—artifacts from the shaft. There were also a couple of smaller equipment sheds, two canvas Army tents and a hurricane fence around the entire lot. The Pit itself was enclosed by a smaller pine board fence with a gate that opened out toward Front Street. Every time it did Hal caught a glimpse of the skinny man, always shirtless and always smoking, watching from his window as though he could see right through the boards.

..

He had a game that evening after work, about fifteen minutes south of the city. The ballpark was a run-down, third-rate heap built behind an asparagus cannery, the powerful odor from which hit them like a wave as the bus pulled into the gravel lot. Payton stumbled off the bus, sniffed the air and threw up on Hal's shoes.

"I hate fucking asparagus," he mumbled, then staggered away.

They were a long way from the Pacific Coast League. The outfield doubled as a cow pasture. The grandstand consisted of two rows of bleachers, five seats high. The clubhouses were house trailers set on concrete blocks—the home team's a little bigger than the visitors', with a fresher coat of paint. There were perhaps fifty spectators. The cannery team leaned against their trailer, passing a bottle of whisky. Hal hoped the game would be short.

Instead it was interminable. Lucky started a new kid named Samuels on the mound, and the Sheiks lost, 13-0. Hal played left field and didn't even manage a single. Lucky mercifully pulled him in the seventh. The fans jeered and taunted the visitor's bench. The Sheiks' section of the bleachers was empty but for a lone couple in the third row that paid more attention to each other than to the game. A woman Hal could barely see, way down the first base line, was sitting alone. She wore a long skirt and a buckskin jacket. Her was face hidden under a cowboy hat. It looked like Rose, but at this distance he couldn't be certain. He held up one hand in a half-hearted wave. Whoever it was did not acknowledge him. He buried his head in his towel.

He glanced up once in the ninth inning, when he heard a roar of approval from his own team. They were waving wildly and slapping each other on the backs. The Giant's infield was applauding. Walt Garber, the back-up catcher, had just gotten the first Sheik hit of the game—indeed, his first of the season. The buckskin woman was gone. Hal picked up his mitt and went to the trailer, where he found Lucky snoring loudly on an army cot. He changed into his street clothes and walked alone to the bus. He could not stop thinking about those boots.

Lucky dropped the team near Union Station. Most of the boys headed off for drinks. Hal took a taxi to his guesthouse. He was surprised when the landlady held up a folded sheet of hotel stationary and waved it at him like a hanky.

"Message for you, Mr. Gates," she said. "Marked 'urgent.'"

Hal thought immediately of Vera, that something may have happened to her, then just as quickly of his father. The old fox. Could it be? He was apprehensive as he unfolded the page under a gooseneck lamp.

Hal: Can we meet after your game? (I hope you won!) I am waiting in the bar at the Majestic Hotel. Join me as soon as you can. Isabelle.

He felt his heartbeat quicken. He folded the note into his pocket, took his gear bag upstairs, changed quickly into a clean shirt and tie and headed back out. To hell with Charlie, he thought. At least for a couple of hours.

CHAPTER FOURTEEN

THE WORST THING THAT CAN HAPPEN

TIMOTHY GAVIN sat in a windowless ante room in Los Angeles City Hall, smoking his fourth cigarette in a half hour. He was nervous, but in an excited, not a fearful, way. He was waiting to see Mayor Shaw, who had summoned him. That might just mean good news. Every mayor had his back room boys. What people didn't talk about so much was that every one of those back rooms had its own back room. That's the room that interested Gavin. Shaw *needed* him. Surely that was something to feel swell about.

A buzzer sounded. The receptionist smiled at him in a practiced way.

"Mr. Shaw will see you now."

Gavin snapped to attention, shot his cuffs, tightened the knot in his tie, opened the door and walked right in. Shaw sat behind a table, coatless, his own tie undone and his sleeves rolled up over arms that looked like hairy pillows. A file of papers lay open before him. He had an unlit cigar between his teeth.

"Don't you know how to knock?" he growled.

"Sorry, sir. The receptionist said—"

"She said I'd see you, not that you have the run of my fucking office. Sit down."

This was hardly the greeting Gavin had anticipated. He sat on a leather couch near the door, and regretted his choice at once. The entire office lay between them. He felt distant and insignificant. Under his jacket his underarms were becoming damp.

Shaw took the cigar from his teeth and exhaled deeply.

"Remember that crazy bastard with the X-ray gadget?"

Gavin sat up straighter.

"Yes sir. They're out there digging now."

Shaw looked up sharply.

"How the hell do you know?"

"I drive by sometimes," Gavin said. "It's over on Fort Moore Hill. They've got a bunch of equipment. Trucks go in and out. Has something happened?"

Beads of perspiration tickled his forehead. Shaw glanced at his file and sat back.

"Yeah, they're digging," he said. "I have somebody keeping an eye on them. But it's getting weirder. We've got another application here for an excavation permit. Same deal: hidden treasure, ancient Indians. Even the Lizard guys. Different group of nuts. Guy named Pike came to see me. Squirrely fucker in a big hat. They want to open a hole about a half mile from the one they got going."

"They have an X-ray?"

"No. But supposedly they have a map."

Gavin sat back on the sofa. Shaw pulled something from a lower desk drawer: a rolled piece of paper; yellowed and crinkled, as if it had come out of an attic.

"I thought Baldy had the map," he said. "The old Indian, all that."

Shaw smiled.

"Funny how bullshit comes in twos. All I know is this guy leaves a package all wrapped up like a dozen long-stems in a box. He's got a letter in here, and a permit application, and this. He swore it's a handmade copy of an authentic map depicting the location of the tunnels of the ancient Lizard clan of the Hopi tribe. Says it shows the treasure rooms, and—here's the killer—the entrances. Guy claims he can locate one right off Aurora Street. Wants to start next week. Says he can have the gold by Christmas. And the City gets two-thirds."

Gavin squinted. So where did he fit in? Shaw continued as if he'd spoken aloud.

"I need help with this, damn it. I can't have this nonsense going on. People keep digging their damned holes around here, the press is going to get too interested. Dolores already had a call from some yo-yo from the *Times*. She told him she had no idea what he was talking about; sent him off to talk to a County engineer whose name she made up on the spot. It'll confound him for a couple of days, but he'll be back. I can't risk shit like this my first few months in office. And I sure as hell can't risk letting this slip out of control if there is anything to it, as crazy as it seems."

"So what do you ... ?"

"Take all this crap off my hands. Find out if there's anything to it. I'll sign another permit; you send it to this guy and tell him you're acting on my behalf. We'll have a gentlemen's side contract, off the books—your regular rate plus ten percent. Let me know if anything happens that I ought to give a rat's ass about."

Gavin held his breath. This wasn't the back room, but it might be close. He screwed his face into his best imitation of a man carefully weighing the pros and cons. He would take the assignment, of course. But first he would prove himself to be shrewd and canny customer. He exhaled slowly and fixed Shaw with his steeliest gaze.

"Fifteen percent," he said. "And a share of the gold, if there is any."

Shaw's eyes flared open, and he sat back as though someone had punched him. Then he laughed—a lusty, full-chested laugh that rolled plump, shiny tears down his puffy cheeks. The receptionist stuck her head in the door. He waved her away. When he finally composed himself Gavin was laughing too—laughing along, he thought; a man's laugh, at life, at Fate, at the whole ridiculous situation. Then Shaw spoke:

"Do you ever take the cake. My lame-brained, dog-bite lawyer waltzes into my office and talks to me like he's Al Capone. Tell you what: you ever try to nickel and dime me again and I'll snap you in two like a pencil. I offered you a job. You want it?"

"Of ... of ... I ... of course," Gavin managed. "Naturally. That thing I said about the money? I was only kidding. I mean ..."

Shaw slammed a fat palm on the table. Gavin shut up.

"Here's the map and the letter," said Shaw, holding them out. "Call Dolores if you learn anything."

Dolores? The receptionist? He wasn't even going to see Shaw himself? Gavin opened his mouth to protest, then shut it. He rose and crossed the room, trying to appear neither overly eager nor terrified, though he was sure his trembling hands gave him away. When he'd accepted the folder, Shaw put his cigar back between his teeth and turned to another stack of papers on his desk. Gavin stood for a moment, waiting for the big man to speak, but it was clear that the interview was over. He backed his way to the door, opened it and slipped out into the waiting area. Dolores gave him a little smile that looked to Gavin like a smirk. He rode the elevator down to the street, hailed a taxi and told the driver to take him home. After two blocks he leaned over the seat.

"Take a left," he said. "We're going to Pico Rivera."

••

Hal's restaurant meeting with Isabelle brought a new surprise. She was excited, even breathless. To his relief she spoke to him as bright-eyed and openly as she ever had, with no mention of Rose. It seemed she'd been doing a little eavesdropping—inadvertently, she claimed—and had heard something that she had to tell him. Her mother had a customer on Thursday, a little shifty-eyed lawyer whose name Isabelle hadn't caught.

"I know it was wrong but I had to listen," said Isabelle. "Most of my mother's customers are nuts, if you ask me—or they wouldn't come to her in the first place. But there was something about this guy. He was breathing hard, and his face was flushed, and I thought he might be drunk but it wasn't that. I had to know what his hurry was. So I waited till the door was closed and listened from the other side."

Hal leaned across the table. Isabelle was even lovelier than he remembered. He hoped she would agree to follow him back to the guest-house when she was finished her story. He'd ordered drinks for them, whiskeys with tonic water and lemon, but both glasses sat untouched. Isabelle lowered her voice. Hal bent forward.

"It turns out this guy is some sort of bigwig downtown. What he said popped my eyes out: The City is digging for buried treasure. Indian gold of some kind. I couldn't hear every word because he talked really fast and he was half-whispering at that. Something about tunnels. There are two different crews out there digging, he said. This guy wants to figure out who is going to get there first. He says he plans on becoming a wealthy man, and he wants to know whose side he should be on. If Mother can help him out she will be 'handsomely rewarded.' It's the screwiest thing I've ever heard."

Hal's throat went dry. His heart beat so hard he wondered how she could not hear it. He lifted his glass, then set it down again.

"Tunnels?" he managed.

"That's what he said. He wants Mother to help him see what these all characters are doing. He thinks she's psychic."

"Isn't she?"

Isabelle let loose a little giggle.

"I don't think she has ever had a vision any clearer than what next month's water bill will look like. She's a practical woman. It's not that all her powers are fake. They're more like common sense. So when this creepy guy pulls out a map ..."

"He had a *map?*"

Hal didn't mean to yell. There were only four other tables occupied at the restaurant, a dozen customers all told. They all looked over as if he'd rung a big brass gong. Isabelle sat back, her head cocked.

"He did. I saw it rolled up when he left. Why is that so exciting?"

Hal cleared his throat and shrugged.

"It's not, really," he said. "It's just—I mean, a map of what, anyway? Why did he show it to her? What did she say? That's all I meant, I mean ..."

Hal took a gulp of whiskey that drained his glass. Isabelle watched him with a bemused expression. It was impossible to lie to her. Nor was it possible to tell her the truth. He kept his eyes fixed on the tablecloth.

"He didn't say where it came from," she answered slowly. "He just said it was old. Remember, I was hearing this all through a closed door."

"Wild," Hal said. "What a nut case."

Up until now he had imagined dimly that he would tell Isabelle some day about the Plan, in the past tense because it finally had fumbled and failed. He would feign a kind of retrospective incredulity, even indignation; certainly *he* didn't know what his crazy uncle was up to, he thought they were just digging for minerals, and so on. In rare moments of optimism he allowed himself to imagine revealing the caper to her as a surprise, after they'd found, well, whatever—not a treasure of gold, not hardly, but whatever evidence or artifact might somehow vindicate Warren's vision. Neither option was viable now. Either he confessed, thereby infuriating her—for what possible reason could he have had for hiding it?—or he continued to play dumb, which meant forever. This approach also bore the risk of discovery. One way or the other he was doomed.

"Either a nut case or a genius," Isabelle said.

Hal looked up sharply. Her eyes were sparkling. Hal had seen such a sparkle before. In Warren's eyes. In Vera's. Goodness, in Charlie's. In the eyes of a thousand men at the morning labor lines, as rumors flew of new fields and factories, of deals and chances. It was the sparkle of willful delusion, the belief that something could be had from nothing.

"But you can't ..." he began. He wanted her to be smarter than them. Than him.

"I don't know what to believe," she said. "He had some kind of map. He mentioned the mayor. There must be *something* to it. People have found ancient treasures before. The Egyptians. The Aztecs. That guy who dug the pyramids probably got called a nut case too."

Hal toyed with his empty glass. He was certain of very little at this moment, but it seemed that he was in love with this woman. How could he lie to her? And if she loved him in return, wouldn't she forgive him if he simply told the truth? *You're not going to believe this*, he would begin, and it would all just tumble out like water from a spigot. Later, back in his room, they would laugh.

But the fellow had a map. What was up with that?

"So what do you want to do?" he asked. And with that question he squandered his chance for redemption.

"Well," said Isabelle, "I don't feel so good about spying on my mother any more. She's going to want to talk to somebody about this, and I'm her daughter after all. And I think we ought to have a look at this map. What's the worst thing that can happen? It's not like we're going to get caught doing something wrong. I mean, if the City is in on it and everything. So I'm going to have it out with her. You want to come along?"

"Might as well."

··

So it was that Hal Gates met Edith Robinson again, this time for tea, cakes and sherry. He was terrified. He'd been brought up as a liar, one way or another, or at least as a dissembler, a con man, a sneak. But that was lying to the law, or to suppliers, or to half-drunk customers, and it had never been his idea. He was not so much a liar as a liar's son. But no longer. And this was no fat cop he was deceiving. This was a girlfriend. His *first* girlfriend. Lying to your girlfriend was bad. Lying to your girlfriend's mother? Sure, there were times a regular guy might have to, but certainly not about the same things you weren't telling your sweetheart. The whole thing made him sick.

"It's the most fascinating thing, Mrs. Robinson," he heard himself saying. "My mother is a student of Indian lore. She would be delighted by a story like this."

Mrs. Robinson smiled.

"Where does she live?"

"Up in Oxnard. This is exactly her, ah, cup of tea."

He raised his own cup, smiling sheepishly. The women laughed politely.

"Have you studied the Indians as well?" Mrs. Robinson asked.

"Me? No, I ..." he faltered. "I've not really studied, I mean, not the way ..."

"He studies baseball," Isabelle said. "It's a bigger topic than you'd think."

Mrs. Robinson laughed. Hal felt his shoulders relax a little.

"I'm well aware of your prowess," she said. "I've seen you pitch, remember."

"Hopefully not at my best."

"Bad luck. How's the season going otherwise?"

"Not very well," he said with his best rueful smile. "We're a better team than the way we play."

"One would think," Edith said.

"Mother," Isabelle said reprovingly.

Hal felt like a goldfish in a bowl.

"We have an exhibition game tomorrow," he said. "Some kind of charity deal. You want to come?"

He looked beseechingly at Isabelle.

"I have to go to a birthday party," she said. "Next game, I promise."

"And I need an evening of rest," said Edith. "I have appointments all weekend. This Gavin among them. Perhaps he'll clear this all up for us."

"I sure hope so," he said.

CHAPTER FIFTEEN

EVERYTHING UNDER CONTROL

CHARLIE itched. His whole body sometimes, but his feet without fail, no matter how clean they (rarely) were. And his hands. Even his knuckles. He would stomp his feet to ease it, or clap his hands or both, at which times he would look like some kind of jitter-bugger on dope. There were days when he itched from head to toe; days it got so bad he couldn't stomp or even stand. He would wrap himself naked in a wool blanket, a bottle at his elbow, and curse the minutes into hours until sleep brought some relief.

This was just a foot-itching day, it seemed, after a hell of a wool-blanket night. At least the bed was his own; his *actual* own, not some flop house or flat car or ten-by-ten cell, but his genuine four poster in his bedroom on Downing Street, a bed that more than once he'd given up on the notion of ever sleeping in again. His head hurt, his breath stank, and his stomach felt like he'd swallowed a box of nails. But he was home.

The door opened slowly, like a cage to a man-eating tiger. Vera's head appeared first, then an arm, then finally all of her spindly self. Her eyes were shining.

"It's nearly noon," she said.

Charlie grunted. He truly was fond of this woman. But she could be so goddamned dingy. Waking a man, for instance. He needed his sleep whenever he could get it. He'd told her so. She had tried to wake him last night. He knew what the hell she wanted. Hal was coming over. He had not seen his son in *ages*, she'd crooned, as though he wasn't aware to the goddamned day, hour and minute when he'd last seen the kid, and not only when he'd last talked to him, ages to be sure, but every time he'd watched him from a distance, which had been a damned sight more often and recently than she knew. He'd seen Hal in the beet fields; he'd seen him in the labor lines; he'd seen him baby sitting that sorry bunch of spics up at Fort Moore. Christ he'd even seen him pitch once, and though Charlie didn't know the first thing about baseball he'd heard that the boy was supposed to be damned good, even if he'd lost a few more games than he'd won so far. Charlie figured that baseball had its up and downs, just like life. He was looking forward to a few more ups.

"I know what time it is," he growled.

He spoke more roughly than he needed to. He was fond of her, yes. But he was still pretty ticked about Warren. Clearly his old buddy had been too damned attentive in his absence. So he continued, more or less reflexively, to play the role of the possibly wronged husband. Did he recognize no symmetry in his own abandonment of her? Not especially. That had not been his fault, after all. He had not intended to be away so long. He'd gotten caught up in stuff out of his control. He was getting control back now. That's what was important.

"Aren't you going to get up?" she asked.

"Looks like I've got no damned choice."

He threw off the blanket and swung his legs over the side of the bed, resting his feet on the cold wooden planks. There was no modesty in his posture. She was his wife after all.

"I made coffee," she said. "Strong the way you like it."

He grunted again, but he couldn't suppress a smile. When was the last time anybody had made him anything "the way he liked it?"

"I could drink a gallon," he said. "I've gotta see some people later. And then I'm back down to the city. Couple of days. Maybe a week."

Vera made a face.

"Can't it wait?"

Charlie rolled his eyes and moved toward the door, shaking his head. Since the night he'd returned—almost a week now—she'd acted like a stranded puppy every time he tried to leave the house for anything—a pack of smokes, a bottle of booze, a walk around the block. She was scared, she said, that he wouldn't come back. *Don't make it like before,* she whined. *Don't go away again.* Well, hell's bells. A guy can't sit around cooped up inside a house all day. Did she think he'd come home to curl up and die?

"Pack a bag," he said. "Come down with me for a few days. Do you good."

"All that way? I couldn't."

Even back when times were good, Vera had been a homebody. Now she was really overdoing it. She acted as though the fresh air might blow her away. All these years cooped up like this. What the hell did she do all day? The old crystal radio was on the davenport end table when he'd first come home. Houdini Pie again. At night while he writhed in his blanket he could hear her downstairs, humming and chanting words. Once he got his business squared he was going to have to work on his wife.

"You won't be gone long?" she asked.

They were at the kitchen table. She had made him toast, opened a jar of marmalade and soft-boiled three eggs. Charlie ate like a starving man.

"A week tops. I've got some things to arrange."

"What things? What are you doing down there? Where have you been? What's going on? Why won't you see Hal? What have you gotten yourself involved in? You're not going to leave me again? You're really coming back? Aren't you?"

Charlie chewed his toast. That was a hell of a lot of questions, one right after another. He replayed them in his mind, seeing if there were any he was prepared to answer just now. It wasn't that he mistrusted Vera especially; it was that he'd learned to keep his own counsel. Sure he was up to something, and as far as he was concerned too many damned people knew about it already. When the time was right, he'd tell her. Hal too. But not a minute before.

She'd asked about Abe, of course, the poor son of a gun. Charlie wished he knew what to tell her. His old friend hadn't left Oxnard with him; he'd stayed behind to take care of some loose ends, actually some bad business with a swell down in L.A. that Charlie had gotten them into and couldn't quite get out of. Abe had been mad about that, but he'd stayed loyal as usual. There had been that incident where he and Hal had got shot at—by the swell's thugs, unfortunately—and Abe had high-tailed it out himself, three days behind Charlie on the road, catching up with him at a flop house in Salinas. A few weeks later they had an argument in Oakland and Abe headed off. The fight had been over something stupid, as most fights are; in this case which of them had finished a bottle of hooch they'd bought to share under a railroad bridge. They'd polished off half of it and fallen asleep, then awoke to find it empty, each accusing the other of having hogged it while the other dozed. Abe took a half-hearted swing at him, and Charlie took a poke in return, but instead of coming to serious blows Abe suddenly had grabbed his duffel and marched away into the night. Charlie figured he was only going to burn off steam. It wasn't till later that he realized his partner wasn't coming back—about the same time he remembered that he'd kicked the bottle over himself, staggering off to pee while Abe had slept. Charlie hadn't seen Abe since.

As for where he'd been? Hell, where *hadn't* he been in the past year? He'd given her the bare bones: Some time up in Seattle. A couple of trips east. St. Louis. Chicago. Then Seattle again, and Vancouver, and part of the winter in San Francisco. Mexico a few times. L.A. a few times. (And a trip or two through Oxnard, though he didn't mention them.) San Diego. La Jolla. Out to Denver.

Weeks here, weeks there. The long and short was, there was no simple answer to "where have you been?" "What's been going on?" had an even harder answer. Lots and very little all at once. He'd been on the run a great deal of the time, from one thing or another. There was no point in rehashing it all now.

The bit about seeing Hal, well, that brought things right up to the present, and that was a matter of some delicacy. If he tried to explain his business to her now, or even worse to Hal, things would get too damned complicated. So far, this new thing seemed to be working out more or less okay, and damned if he was going to take any chances. He knew it drove her nuts, not knowing. That was just how it had to be for the time being.

The last two questions, though—about leaving again, and coming back—those he could answer after a fashion. He fixed her helpless gaze with a level stare and spoke as sincerely as he knew how.

"I've got some business down south. You're welcome to come along. Of course I'm coming back. I'm home now, Vera. The bad times are behind us."

"I'm glad, Charlie," she said.

It was a nice moment, and he hated to ruin it. But he had to be careful. He reached for her hand.

"Like I said, Vera. You've got to get used to not calling me Charlie. Not for a while, anyway. You'll understand why soon enough. I'm using my other name—have been for almost a year now. It ain't that uncommon, you know, for a man to have a spare name or two in his pocket for emergencies. My new name is Jackson Pike, and I'm your cousin from Seattle. Just until everything is under control. Understand?"

Vera laughed the way she used to when he teased her. It was good to hear.

"Whatever you say, Mr. Pike. As long as you're here to stay."

He squeezed her hand tighter.

"That's my girl," he said.

··

Charlie took the bus to L.A. He didn't mind the bus. It beat the hell out of hoboing. Getting caught hoboing was no fun. Charlie had been kicked off a few trains in his time, but he'd always found a way to get where he was going. He'd heard stories about guys who weren't so lucky; guys who baked to death in the Arizona sun or froze solid as firewood on a Montana plateau. Guys who died of starvation. Guys who ate them. Guys who went crazy. Everywhere he traveled, he met guys who had gone crazy, one way or another. The craziest so far had ended up changing his life.

He had met the fellow in—where else?—the tank. There had been a small altercation at a card house in Seattle; a place on Pike Street, which was where Charlie picked up half his fake name. He liked the sound of it: "Pike." Slight but powerful. It seemed to suit him. There was a "Jackson" street in Seattle too, but Charlie already had been using it, as the name had been Abe's idea.

"Like that old President," Abe had said, surprising Charlie that he knew of any presidents prior to Teddy Roosevelt.

In Seattle he'd been roughly escorted to a twelve-by-twenty foot room with a dozen other men, mostly vagrants and drunks, none of whom had been involved in the card house fracas, as the cops had taken to heart the assurances of the other incarcerates that if Jackson was put in with them they'd kill him barehanded. At first Charlie resented the segregation. He had not been badly hurt in the fight, and he was still bubbling over with spit and vinegar. He banged on the bars a few times, answering the abuse of the men down the hall, but the cops and his cell mates ignored him, so he slumped to the ground in the only vacant spot he could find with a stretch of concrete wall to lean against. The only light source in the cell was from a high dirty window at street level, and outside it was well past midnight, the streetlamps long since extinguished. He drew his knees up to his chest and surveyed the slumping shadows around him with a sneer of disgust.

"I don't suppose one of you girls has a smoke?" he asked.

No answer. He might as well have been speaking in a tomb. He shook his head, closed his eyes, stretched his legs and arched his back. It would be a long night, but at least it would be quiet. He'd spent nights in jail before, God knew. With luck he would manage some sleep.

A match struck in the darkness, as profound as a gunshot. Charlie's eyes popped open. He sat up straight. The light burned steadily for several seconds on the other side of the cell, then went out. Another took its place. Charlie blinked and tried to focus, but there was nothing to focus on. Just the flicker of flame, like a beacon in the fog. Well, he thought, it's got to be a man holding the match, and a man with a match in the pokey is likely a man with a smoke to share, sell or sacrifice. He pushed himself off the wall and made his way on hands and knees toward the light.

A third match was burning by the time he got there.

Words came from behind the flame:

"You're not like the others."

Charlie squinted. The flame went out. He waited for another light. None came.

"So, you got a smoke? Or did you invite me over 'cause I'm handsome?"

A flashlight beam passed perfunctorily across the bars, then clicked off. In that instant of light he glimpsed his man: wrinkled forehead, scraggly hair, beaked nose and eyes as black as shadows in a well. Then all returned to darkness. The man spoke again.

"Where did you come by those boots?"

Before Charlie could think of a comeback another match was struck, and twin glowing tips appeared simultaneously. One made its way in Charlie's direction. He reached for it greedily, found the cigarette, brought it to his mouth and inhaled. In the ensuing glow he saw the man's features again: weathered, old and mischievously smiling. The eyes reflected nothing. Charlie held the sweet smoke in his lungs as those leathery features melted back into the night, then exhaled. When he'd caught his breath again, he answered in a wheezy whisper.

"What the hell do you care about my boots?"

The reply came quickly.

"More than you do."

"They're only a pair of boots."

"No they're not."

Charlie rolled his eyes. Okay, so the guy was nuts. But he wasn't drunk, and he didn't seem doped. His *boots*? He took another hard draw off the cigarette and looked for a glimpse in the glow. The old fellow was still smiling.

"I got the boots from a friend," said Charlie. "He got 'em down south. Now give me another smoke."

The old guy started talking. Just like that—another puff, a slow sigh, and then the blabbing started. Sometimes to Charlie directly, sometimes to himself, as if there was no one else there. The rest of the damned night the man gave Charlie smokes and talked, until the dirty window showed the dismal gray of another rainy Seattle morning. Nothing the fellow said made sense, but Charlie found himself chewing up every word.

He talked about the four ancient worlds of his people. How the sun created the original world out of nothing, and how "Grandmother Spider" led the beings of the first world to the caves and tunnels of the second and the third, changing their shapes as they went, from animal, insect, bird and reptile to human, and back again. To Charlie it was like hearing the Bible stories his mother used to tell him to frighten him into tolerable behavior. They never made sense but he loved to hear them—everything grand, thunderous, mixed-up and larger-than-life. Only this fellow's stories were as much about critters as people, and instead of Noah and a boat, every time the going got tough it seemed like everybody headed for a hole in the ground. Charlie got pretty confused. But that had been true of the Bible yarns too.

At last the old man talked about the boots. It seemed there were a couple of chiefs. They were brothers of some kind, but it was hard to tell if they were actual relatives or just close buddies. It seemed that these two brothers were rivals for a woman's affections. Charlie liked a yarn about a good fight, and a fight over a woman was the kind any guy could understand. It seemed that Grandmother Spider (her again) didn't approve of fighting, so she packed the brothers off to the desert to have it out.

"One brother won," he said. "But even in the pride of victory, the defeat of his kinsman hurt his heart. He took his brother's skin ..."

"He took his *what*?" Charlie said. The old guy ignored him and continued.

"And with this skin fashioned a pair of sturdy boots. Then he set off for his people, with the vanquished body across his shoulders. He did not reach his home. Many ages later the Elders discovered two skulls and a pair of boots, as supple as the day they were made, in the sands beneath a high red cliff. The rocks were alive with lizards, their tails as thick as a grown man's arm. It is a holy place now, though few can find it."

Charlie let out a long, low whistle and shook his head.

"Hell that's a mighty good story. Sure helped pass the night. Now if I could trouble you for one more of those smokes, we can see about getting out of here."

"Ah," said the old man. "But the story is not over."

"'Fraid I'm going to have to wait for the to-be-continued," said Charlie.

But something in the old fellow's gaze held him in place. The next words came in a whisper that Charlie had to lean forward to hear.

"The boots are on your stinking feet. Where did you get them?"

"I told you," Charlie said. "Somebody gave them to me. I don't know where he got them. Arizona or some such. He was just being, you know—"

"He was just taking his life in his hands. If it happens that he stole them—"

The cell door opened. A bull-dick guard stood there, all attitude and B.O.

"Clear the hell out," he said.

"Give us a minute. C'mon, pops."

The old man gathered up a blanket and a worn leather pouch on which he'd been sitting. He moved with surprising suppleness. The guard held the door open, tapping his foot, chucking his head toward the hall.

"Been a pleasure," said Charlie. "See you again soon."

They walked to a slop house on Yesler Avenue; a cavernous room with long wooden tables, low benches and a narrow window to the kitchen, through which red-faced women passed mugs of steaming coffee and bowls of something the color and texture of topsoil. A fat man in a bowler hat sat on a stool at the door. He held a cigar box open on his knees.

"Ten cents," he growled. To Charlie's amazement, the Indian dug two bits from out of his pouch and tossed the coin into the box.

"Keep the change," he said.

Everybody seemed to know the Indian. The red-faced ladies grinned at him; a couple of hobos nodded amicably; a toothless Mexican tipped his sombrero and made room at the end of one of the tables. Charlie took a seat across from his companion and concentrated on his meal. He waited for a pause between spoonfuls to ask one of the dozens of questions that were taking shape inside his aching head.

"So why," he said, "were you in the pokey? You ain't flat broke, and you don't look like much of a threat if you know what I mean."

The Indian nodded.

"I had to ask them for the lock-up," he said. "They said no at first, so I kicked a sergeant between the legs. That changed their minds."

"You *wanted* to be in that shit-hole? So which were you—drunk or doped?"

The old man took a sip of coffee.

"Neither. I just wanted to make sure I got behind bars."

"You mind telling me why?"

"I was looking for you."

CHAPTER SIXTEEN

THE BOOTS HAVE CHOSEN

W ITH all that was going on—working at the dig, worrying about Isabelle, the weirdness with Rose, the question of Charlie, this new strange business with Gavin—Hal had no energy or concentration left for baseball. So naturally he went out and pitched his best game since high school, and against a good team, too; the new Padres from San Diego. They had a couple of big sluggers in their lineup, including a guy named Noble who supposedly was going to sign any day with St. Louis. But they might as well have been school girls for all they laid a bat on Hal. Despite his victory, he was in no mood for painting the town with the boys, so he high-tailed it out the exit before anybody had a chance to collar him.

He stood on Avalon Street in the dwindling post-game crowd, wondering whether to walk a bit or hail a taxi right away. Out to Pico, maybe? But it was too late to be barging in on the Robinsons. A couple of fans slapped him on the back, and he signed an autograph for a little kid in short pants and a grey fedora that came down over his ears. He made up his mind to walk. He tossed his equipment bag over his shoulder, took three steps and ran into Rose.

"Quite a performance," she said.

"Thanks," said Hal, blinking hard. He was not surprised to see her, which in itself surprised him. She looked lovely and dangerous as usual, dressed simply in a belted navy dress with a long, deep-purple scarf of some material that shimmered in the streetlight. She wore a broad-brimmed hat, tipped at an angle, and her hair was pulled back. The overall look was more glamour girl than Indian princess, but she pulled it off easily and was still unmistakably Rose. Her eyes locked onto Hal's and held his gaze. It was as if the city around them dimmed and faded out of focus as she spoke.

"I seem to be turning into quite the baseball fan," she said. "You sure had some stuff tonight. You made some believers out there."

She took his arm lightly in her own. They walked in silence. The air was balmy, and fresher than normal for L.A. Hal was on his guard, but he wasn't sure why. There was no particular mystery or drama to Rose tonight. She was just a girl—a woman—on his arm, going for a stroll.

She'd sought out his company, and paid him a compliment. It seemed to him that he should say something.

"So, um," he began. "How is, you know … your father? Still in town?"

Rose laughed.

"Oh, he's around somewhere I'm sure. He always is. Sometimes months go by without my knowing where, but he always shows up eventually."

So far so good, thought Hal. A question, an answer. He tried another.

"Did you grow up here?"

"I grew up all over," she replied. "Mostly in the desert. My mother died when I was born so I've pretty much followed my father wherever he decided to move."

"Where do you call home now?"

Rose shrugged.

"Wherever he is. Mostly in the city lately, which is fine with me. I like the bustle. I like the feeling that something big is always about to happen."

They were headed west, away from the stadium and toward downtown on residential streets with low, hacienda-style houses and only one gas lamp on each long block, so that they moved through the night from pool to pool of fitful yellow light. Rose still held his arm. When they reached the next pool she gave it a little tug.

"What about your father?" she asked. "Do you see him much?"

Hal felt himself go cold. There was something in her voice—something taut and wary, not quite in tune with the casual chat he'd been starting to enjoy. But she leaned her head against his arm and let the question dangle, not pressing for an answer. He was imagining things. They were just talking, after all. He shrugged.

"Haven't seen him for ages," he said quietly.

"I'm sorry to hear that," she said, glancing up at him.

Hal cleared his throat.

"It's not a big deal. We were never especially close."

He looked away, and was surprised by what he saw. They were in the neighborhood of his rooming house, just a few doors away around the corner. She had brought him through back streets he never could have found on his own. He felt his pulse begin to race and a sense of light-headedness that seemed to come from his toes. Would he send her off now, alone in the night? He was deeply unsure what to do next.

"You are working tomorrow?" she asked. "At the dig? I understand it is going very slowly. My father says that the treasure may not want to be found. "

As she spoke her hand dropped down and settled in his. She was smiling openly now. She took a half step toward him. An image of Isabelle's face took shape in his mind, and then dissolved, leaving nothing in its place. He pulled Rose to him, cradled the back of her head in his free hand and bent to kiss her. For an instant she yielded to him. Then quicker than thought he felt three things at once: cold air beneath his lips, a burst of pain in his groin and a vicious slap across his cheek, trailing fingernails as sharp as thorns. He winced and dropped to his knees on the sidewalk, his cry of protest frozen in his throat as she hissed at him in the dark.

"Who do you think you are? What do you think I am?"

When he opened his eyes she was gone. No sign, no footsteps, no fleeing figure in the shadows. All he retained was the sting on his face, the pain in his nether regions and the odor of her, sweet and musky, with a trace of something bitter that he could not name. Her questions echoed in his head. He couldn't answer either of them.

..

The old Indian had a name now, which was good. Greenleaf, he had said it was, and "Chief" Greenleaf at that, which made perfect sense to Charlie as the old guy was suddenly a pretty big person in his life. Big people in your life needed names. Abe, Vera, Sarah, Hal … it was funny how few there had been, even after so many years. And Warren, of course. It was because of Warren that he was on a bus headed south. Because of Warren, because of Greenleaf, because of Hal and because of that bastard Frank Shaw. If anyone had connected those names together in that stinking Seattle cell, he'd have considered them crazier even than the old man.

He'd traveled with Greenleaf for six weeks after their meeting in Seattle, hopping freights, hitchhiking, even buying a few legitimate tickets along the way, on Greenleaf's money, of which the old guy had sporadic, mysterious reserves. They'd traveled generally south, through Oregon and California, backtracking now and then for this reason or that; rumor of a card game, or a free meal, or a famous whorehouse, or as much as Charlie dreaded it a few hours of labor for some farmer who wasn't picky about his hired hands. Greenleaf could turn out a hell of day's work, if he had to. Charlie would have been put to shame, if he cared about such things.

The Chief kept his stories up night and day; weird tales about talking critters and the People and the Wise Ones and perilous journeys from one world to another. Charlie couldn't follow them, even when he tried. He had some doozies to tell about the present, too. This business about how he'd been "looking for" Charlie, for instance. It turned out that it had to do with a scheme that Greenleaf had been hatching for some time. A hair-brained scheme it was, but it seemed genuine; something the old man had cooked up carefully, and now, as unlikely as it seemed, wanted Charlie to be a part of.

Greenleaf was looking for gold. No, it was better than that. Greenleaf was certain that he'd *found* gold. A lot of it. A buried treasure, Charlie understood, smack in the middle of L.A., under the streets, stacked in vaults and chambers like a regular Fort Knox. The trick was getting it out of the ground. Greenleaf had a plan. He'd found some crackpot to do his dirty work—a scientist of some kind who had a machine that could smell gold the way a bloodhound smells a rabbit. The crackpot— Greenleaf referred to him only as "my Digger"—had a little money, and a crew, and permission from "big men" in the city to sink a hole to try to find the treasure and bring it to the surface. Fair enough.

But it got better (and crazier) still. The Digger wasn't going to find beans. He was just a diversion. Oh yes, he'd sniffed something out all right with his contraption, and with that Greenleaf seemed modestly impressed, but the chances of him hitting the treasure dead-on with a four-foot vertical shaft were about as likely, he said, as a drunk China-man pissing through a keyhole in the dark. There was a quicker way to the treasure. The Indian had a map. He was vague about where and how he got it, but he claimed he could locate entrances only a few feet underground that led to tunnels through the very rock the poor Digger was trying to drill. The idea, the Indian explained, was to let the Digger dig, to make the big noise, and to keep the swells looking one way while somebody else snuck in the back way and grabbed the treasure.

"The big men must cooperate," Greenleaf said.

"Why should they?"

"Greed."

"Why don't they just dig themselves?"

"Fear. The idea is mad, after all. You think so yourself."

He had a point.

Greenleaf spun the scheme out so slowly, a bit here, a bit there, that it was only in the last few days of their journey south that Charlie began to grasp that he was being taken in as an accomplice. He still didn't know what his role was to be.

"Why me?" he said.

"But I've told you," Greenleaf said. "It is because of the boots."

"Oh, for crying out loud," said Charlie. "Not the damned boots again."

Greenleaf had not mentioned them in several hundred miles, and Charlie had given little more thought to the fanciful tale he'd told in the cell.

"The boots," Greenleaf answered, "are a part of the story you cannot escape."

"What story?"

"The one we are in together," said Greenleaf. "The boots have chosen you."

Charlie snorted.

"Houdini fucking pie," he muttered, shaking his head.

Greenleaf raised a bushy eyebrow.

"Never mind," Charlie said. "What do you want me to do?"

They were drinking at Heinhold's in Oakland, a ramshackle watering hole near the water with a sawdust floor so crooked that Charlie felt drunk before they'd finished their first snort. Greenleaf had just told him that they'd be parting ways for a while.

"Business calls me," he said, "your business as well as mine, but I must tend to it alone for a while. We will meet again soon."

The old man was looking at him with more than even his usual intensity. He had taken from his pouch a folded sheet of paper, which he said were Charlie's instructions.

"You will go to Los Angeles and write a letter," said Greenleaf. "Its content is here. You may use your own words, but use them well. You must be persuasive. You are going to approach one of the big men. He is the man who will give us permission. He is a fool, but he is powerful. His name is Shaw."

"Frank Shaw? That son-of-a-bitch?"

Greenleaf's eyes opened slightly in surprise, which Charlie found gratifying. It wasn't often he caught the old Indian off-guard.

"You know this man?"

"Hell yes," said Charlie. "He's a double-crossing skunk. He nearly had me killed a while back. He's a lot of the reason I left L.A."

He told Greenleaf how Shaw and his friends had organized a business venture, based on fixing public contracts for hospital commissaries all over southern California. Shaw tapped into Charlie's distribution network to haul the goods. When Shaw caught Charlie skimming a percentage of his customers' fees Shaw decided to make an example out of Charlie: he would torch a bunch of inventory, blame it on Charlie and have him arrested red-handed. But Shaw's henchmen bungled the job, killing an innocent farmer in the fire and nearly taking out Hal when they turned their guns on Abe's car. Charlie decided that he needed to make himself scarce for a while. Abe had followed soon after, and Charlie thought he'd heard the end of Shaw.

Chief Greenleaf's expression made it clear that he suspected he was hearing less than all the facts. His next comment caught Charlie off guard.

"You have told me very little about your son," he said.

The old Indian beckoned the barkeep for refills.

"He's still down south," Charlie answered. "Oxnard. He's okay. Big boy. He was born during that comet, back in 'ought ten. Named after it, too. Halley. His mother always said that's what gave him his size."

Greenleaf smiled.

"She's right, I expect," he said.

Charlie snorted.

"Oh, you'd get along real well with Vera," he said. "Birds of a god-damned feather." He patted the folded papers that Greenleaf had given him. "But hell, I like you anyway. We're partners. Right?"

The old man took Charlie's hand. His grip was a strong as a longshoreman's.

"To the end, Jackson Pike," he said.

He walked across the crooked floor to the door with easy confidence, and didn't look back. Charlie was the only customer left. The bartender looked at him inquiringly. Charlie shook his head. He had no money to speak of. The drinks had been on Greenleaf. What little cash he had left would have to last him the rest of the way to Los Angeles, if that indeed was where he was going. The Chief's instructions lay folded on the table beside his empty glass. Charlie unfolded them, and out fell a stack of greenbacks—two hundred dollars, in new twenties. That rascal, thought Charlie. He laughed out loud. He's had me under his spell since Seattle, and now he's disappeared, and I'm still on the end of his chain. I'm not his partner, I'm his hired man. He fanned the bills out before him.

The bartender was still eyeing him. Charlie waved a twenty in the air.

"Set me up," he said. "Don't this place ever get any livelier?"

"Around midnight. Sailor crowd, mostly. And the girls out looking for them."

The clock above the door read ten minutes after ten.

"I'll just hunker in and wait," said Charlie. "Being especially partial to the company of sailors."

He laughed again.

He was still laughing five weeks later, on the bus from Oxnard to Los Angeles. On his first visit to the city he'd done just what Greenleaf had told him to do. Not only did he contact Shaw, who was now the goddamned mayor, Charlie actually went to see him, in disguise of course. He took the paper and the copy of a map that Greenleaf had delivered to his rooming house, and he'd had a good time yakking with hizzoner in a mischievous sort of way, with no fear of being recognized, as he was sporting a bushy paste-on beard, a big straw *sombrero* and a pair of little round glasses that he'd lifted from a pawn shop on Figueroa Street. His own mother would not have recognized him.

Nor did Warren, who was coming out of Shaw's office just as Charlie was going in. Charlie nearly shouted when he saw him, but managed to keep his cool. Greenleaf hadn't told him the name of his "Digger," or much less that Hal was working for him. A couple of nice little omissions, those. Had the Chief known that they were Charlie's oldest friend and his flesh-and-blood son? Charlie was sure he had, but he couldn't think for the life of him why the old rascal would keep it a secret. So he wasn't ready yet to reveal himself to anybody. Not until he knew what Greenleaf was up to.

It hadn't been hard to find out about Hal and the dig. An off-duty cop in a bar on Broadway showed Charlie a spot in the *Times*, a column inch buried back on page thirteen: "Search Continues for Ancient Hoard."

"You read about that ballplayer from Oxnard?" the cop said. "The big mothering pitcher for the Sheiks? He works up there at this lizard dig. Shit, I seen him, whippin' them wetbacks into shape. Sounds crazy if you ask me. Ancient gold and fuckin' reptiles. He must think it's a surer bet than making the Big Leagues. But hell he can pitch, that kid."

A "big mothering pitcher" from Oxnard? There was only one fellow that could be. Charlie kept the newspaper and bought the cop a whiskey. The weirdest thing he'd ever heard had just gotten ten times weirder.

After having his own secret look at Hal and his "wetbacks," Charlie went to Downing Street to rest and brood. He got another wad of bills and a letter from Greenleaf summoning him back to the city. And now he sat in the bumpy back seat of the Number 624, gagging on dust and diesel fuel, squinting out a dirty window at the sun-baked hills and wriggling his itchy feet inside his lizard-skin boots. He patted the money in his shirt pocket, tucked next to three new cigars from Poggi's. One thing was certain: nobody double-crossed Charlie Gates. Maybe soon he'd have some secrets of his own.

CHAPTER SEVENTEEN

MAYBE

WHAT a funny little man this Gavin was. There he sat, again, just talking and talking and sweating. There were beads of perspiration along his hat line; occasionally one would break free and scamper toward his eyebrows or his cheeks like a tiny crystal bug. As soon as he came in Edith had offered to open a window. "No, no," he insisted; "I'm fine, I won't be long." But he was.

"I've been studying the map," he said, rolling it out on the table between them. It was only a copy, he explained again; not as old as it looked, though to Edith it looked old enough. Gavin wanted to know if it was "real"—that is, if it "seemed right" to her. "Could you get a feel for it," he asked, "if I left you alone with it a while? Isn't that the sort of thing you do?" That wasn't all. He'd been to the "big dig," as he called it; the operation up on North Hill Street, and he'd been to the new site too—there wasn't anything there yet but a wooden post with a red flag driven into a weedy lot adjacent to a school yard. He wanted Edith to visit both places with him. He began talking faster, drumming his fingers on the side of the table.

"We'd only drive by at first, maybe. Not even get out of the car. There's often a little crowd up at Fort Moore. Sometimes the big fellow who acts as the foreman comes out and tells everybody go home, there's nothing to see. Some of the gee-gawkers are there mostly to see him, more than likely—strapping, good looking kid. He's the head guy's nephew, and he's some kind of semi-famous ballplayer. He looks like an athlete. Hell, he looks like two. Anyway, we'd just, you know, get a feel for the place. Then maybe go back at night. Wouldn't it be better at night? For vibrations or whatever?"

"A ballplayer?" Edith asked.

"That's what they say. I would've pegged him as a fullback, but he's got a reputation as a hurler. Of course that doesn't pay the rent unless a guy makes the Big Leagues. So he digs for lizard gold as a day job. The things a guy will do for money, huh?" He laughed his little nervous laugh. "Times are hard everyplace. Brother can you spare a dime, and all that."

A big fellow. A ball player. Good looking. A pitcher. Surely any number of men in Los Angeles met that description? But Edith knew with sick and sudden certainty who this one was.

The map showed what appeared to be a maze of interconnected pathways, interspersed with empty circles and misshapen squares, like a clumsy child's maze. There was writing that Edith couldn't read—part recognizable letters, part meaningless symbols, and there were black arrows pointing here and there, drawn in a much firmer hand than the squiggles they pointed to. At the left hand edge was a row of wavy scribbles obviously meant to show the sea. Gavin was certain that the maze depicted tunnels, and that the empty shapes were treasure rooms. A circle marked the location of the new project Shaw had approved. An "X" showed the dig in progress, where the big fellow worked.

The big fellow. Edith tried to smile.

"I'm still not sure how you think I can help you. I mean, normally my clients …"

"Just go with me," he pleaded. "I'll pay your fee plus fifty percent."

How desperate he looked, like a hungry child. His eyes were wide. His necktie was undone. Edith sensed that there was nothing to do but give in, at least for now, if only to find out what Hal was up to. She sighed.

"I will come with you," she agreed. "Just once. If you think it will help."

He said he would come back on Tuesday to escort her downtown. Finally he got his coat and left. Now Edith sat alone. This new bit of news was just a bit too much; a puzzle piece she hadn't expected and didn't know where to fit. She closed her eyes, trying to clear her mind, so that she could put the pieces back in some kind of order, some kind of sense. She was not looking forward to having this out with Isabelle.

The front door slammed. Edith jumped to her feet and ran to the hallway. But when she reached the door, she saw that it was not her daughter at all. It was Reggie, looking as though he had been in the fight of his life.

..

Could there be an activity more opposite to that of pitching a baseball, thought Hal, than working in a mine shaft? He wouldn't have disputed the notion that the pit was some manner of divine payback, for what he couldn't be sure, though he certainly had a growing list of transgressions from which to choose. But what on earth might his co-workers have done to deserve their days underground? Surely they didn't all have rum-running pasts and two-timing presents? Or maybe they did. If Hal was learning one hard lesson about the world, it was that nothing was at it seemed.

The shaft was getting deeper—alarmingly so, from the point of view of the men who had to labor in it. They had measured one hundred seventy-two feet from ground surface last Saturday at quitting time. That was far deeper in the earth, in Hal's view, than a man should be. The shaft had narrowed too much for the work to be done efficiently by two men side-by-side, so trips below were solo. Hal could not fully extend his hands without running into the sides of the hole, walls of which were starting to feel damp. Warren said they wouldn't hit any real water on the way down, just "pockets" here and there, but there were pumps at the ready in one of the equipment sheds, just in case. The *hombres* at the shaft entrance spoke in murmurs of gushers and floods, words they'd heard from other laborers who'd worked the mines up and down the coast. And of course there was the constant fear of cave-ins; unfounded in a vertical shaft like theirs Warren claimed, and in the material through which they were blasting. Hal's faith in Warren's judgment was less than complete. When the drop line played out and his feet hit the crumbly bottom of the hole he felt every bit of the panicked claustrophobia of his greenest laborer, but he knew he must not show it.

He had talked to his mother, finally. She'd answered the telephone on Wednesday evening after work. He got right to the point:

"Have you seen Dad?" he asked her.

She was quiet for a few seconds, then laughed a laugh that didn't sound like her.

"Of course not," she said. "How could I?"

"You've heard from him, then.

"Hal, dear, where do you ever get such wild ideas?"

"You thought this was him calling, didn't you?"

"Well, darling—" this was a name she hadn't called him in years—"if you're so certain your father is here, then why would he be calling me?"

"Don't be cute, Ma. What's going on?"

"There's the doorbell," she said, though all was quiet in the background. "Try to visit soon."

She left Hal holding the dead receiver, feeling angry and stupid. But angry and stupid were better than crazy. It had been Charlie. He knew it for sure now. Next came the little matter of why.

It gave him something to think about in the hole. His stints weren't long. Hal wouldn't let anybody stay down more than a half-hour tops, and that included himself. But a half hour with a hydraulic drill, a sledge hammer or a shovel, or even just a ten-minute inspection by the meager light of a lantern, felt like a week. It was so cold and lonely down there that the men talked to themselves. Hal was no exception.

"Maybe he didn't run away. Maybe he was kidnapped, or arrested, or beat up all to hell. Maybe he got into some trouble worse than bootlegging. Maybe he needs help. Maybe he's a two-timing cowardly son-of-a-bitch who I never want to lay eyes on again. Maybe my mother is in cahoots with him. Maybe he's spooked her into not telling me he's back. Maybe he's threatened her. Maybe I'll make him wish he hadn't. Maybe Warren knows something. Maybe he's the last person I'd ask."

On Friday at two-thirty, Warren announced that they'd had their most productive week since breaking ground in April. They would knock off early, and there would be no more digging until Monday. There was mumbled relief from the crew. The temperature was over a hundred without a whiff of breeze. Dust from the morning's blasts hung in the air. There was no group of onlookers. Even the guy in the house across the street was absent. Warren passed out pay envelopes. Hal stepped forward last, wiping his face with a dirty towel, but when he reached for his envelope he got Warren's handshake instead.

"I think this week calls for a special celebration," he said. "Why don't you join me for a drink? Rex is coming. It's time we all had a meeting."

"I have dinner plans," Hal said.

"This won't take long."

They went to Callahan's, on Figueroa Street. Rex was already there. Hal's skin and clothes were still covered with dust that stuck in his throat like a dry sock. The dim, cool bar was an instant relief when they passed through the door and out of the white sidewalk heat. It was nearly empty, a surprise on a Friday afternoon. Hal figured it was too hot for most fellows even to drink. As soon as they sat down the bartender brought them three cold beers, locked the door and vanished into a back room.

"The place is all ours," Warren said. "There are ears everywhere."

"No kidding," said Rex. Hal squinted at him across the table. He looked terrible. One eye was swollen, the skin around it a greenish purple. There was a crust of dried blood on his lower lip. On his neck beneath his left ear he wore a dirty bandage, its tape peeling off his reddened skin.

"What happened to your face?" Hal asked.

"Me and a fellow had a difference of opinion."

Hal looked from Rex to Warren and back again.

"We've got competition," Warren said.

"For what?" Hal asked, as casually as possible.

"What do you think?" said Rex. "We got other gold diggers on our tail. They've been spying on us. They're trying to beat us to the treasure."

Hal took a swallow of beer. Rex's words hung in the air unanswered. Hal certainly wasn't going to let on that he knew about this "competition."

"Who?" he asked.

Rex said nothing. His lip curled again, and then he looked away. Hal turned to address his uncle, and suddenly Rose was there too. He hadn't seen where she came from—through the locked front door? From the back? Or had she been waiting in a dark corner all the while? She took a seat and acknowledged neither Warren nor Rex, but instead fixed Hal with a steady stare

"Your daddy is back," she said.

It seemed that Rose had spotted Charlie first—several times within a couple of weeks, though it had taken some time for her suspicions about him to grow. First she had seen him at the site itself. She'd gone there after dark, for what reason she didn't say.

"I saw a guy lurking around," she said. "He'd gotten over the fence, and he was checking out the hole, the gear, the shop, the works. Skinny guy, not young, wearing boots and fake beard and a sombrero way too big for him. Finally he climbed back out onto the street and wandered away."

Hal swirled an ounce of warming beer in the bottom of his bottle. Skinny. Boots. Not young. So? It could have been any vagrant. Lord knew there were enough of them.

"Next time I saw him was in broad daylight. It was at your game last week. He sat behind the plate, on the third-base side. About five rows up. Never left his seat; just sat like a statue and watched you."

Hal thought back to the game. He recalled a man off to his right, with a big hat and a beard. But surely this was just the power of Rose's suggestion? He never paid attention to the crowd when pitching; never saw anything but the catcher's fat mitt and the look of fake bravado in the batters' eyes. *Had* there been such a man up there? A man who smoked one cigarette after another, who never clapped or cheered? A man, now that Hal thought about it, who seemed completely out of place?

"It got so I could hardly avoid him," Rose went on. "A couple of times on the street. Once in a bar on Broadway. Once over on Second, in a school yard with a group of Negroes, unloading equipment from a flatbed truck. He was still wearing the hat."

It was hard enough accepting that Charlie had returned. Imagining that he had anything to do with the dig defied imagination. Hal needed a change of subject; a chance to break Rose's spell. He turned to Rex.

"So who beat you up?"

"Tell him," said Rose.

Rex sighed deeply. He didn't lift his head.

"I been seeing your daddy around too," he began. "I followed him yesterday. He walked up Sunset to a restaurant and went inside. I waited a half hour and he came out. Then he walked back to Second off Aurora, to the lot where Rose saw him. I read the paper, sitting against a lamppost, minding my own business. All of a sudden your dad crosses over to me. He's got a cigarette in his mouth. He asks me for a match; I dig one out and he strikes it on his shoe and lights up. He's looking at me real hard. I don't like being stared at like that, not by an old geezer in a sombrero. So I walk past him, and I give him a little shove."

"And?" said Hal.

Rex lifted his head and glared.

"And we had us a tussle. Bastard fights dirty."

Hal sat back. *Charlie* had done that to Rex? Suddenly he was starting to warm to the idea that the man they'd been following was indeed his father.

"I saw him too," said Warren softly. "It was at Shaw's office. I went to ask, well, for money. An advance of sorts. Our resources are a bit stretched. We no longer have the backing of Mr. Martin—you remember him?"

Hal nodded. The quiet guy. His name had not come up in ages.

"When he found out about the competition, he pulled his assets out of the project. It is a considerable setback. I was hoping that Mr. Shaw might see his way clear to a small loan. He was unreceptive to my proposal, and dismissed me abruptly. I went out into the anteroom, and that's where I saw Charlie in his disguise. Had he been a passing acquaintance I might not have given him a second glance. But you must remember that he was once my closet friend. Our eyes met and he looked away."

The clock above the bar read ten after four. Hal wanted time to think, not to mention bathe, before seeing Isabelle. Above the table a ceiling fan turned sluggishly in a sudden breeze from the front door transom.

"Maybe," said Rose, "it's time for a little father-son reunion."

"But I don't know where he is," said Hal. "You all might be trailing him like bloodhounds, but I haven't laid eyes on him since sometime last year."

"He took the nine o'clock bus this morning to Oxnard," said Rose.

"Well then he's there now," said Hal, "and I'm here."

"Mr. McCreery can drive you tonight," said Warren.

"Tonight?"

"Your mother will be delighted to see you," Warren said.

Hal took a deep breath. They were all staring at him. He was to meet Isabelle for dinner at six-thirty. And he had a game in Irvine tomorrow.

"No," he said.

Warren's expression was one he might have used with a child who has just thrown a public tantrum.

"You have time to pack a bag," he said.

Hal ran his hands through his hair and shook his head.

"I said no. Tomorrow there's a game and tonight I'm ... I'm busy. If my father really is involved, then he'll need to come back to L.A. You seem to know his whereabouts. You can talk to him yourself."

He wondered if anyone noticed the quaver in his voice. He stood up.

"Thanks for the beer."

He nodded to each of them in turn, and hurried out to the street. He'd just said no to his uncle for the first time. It felt good. Now there was something else he had to do that he'd been afraid of. What the consequences would be of either act, he couldn't imagine.

CHAPTER EIGHTEEN

MADNESS

H AL was late for his date. He barely had time for a quick wash and change before he sprinted two blocks to meet Isabelle at the front door of Gleason's on Macy Street. He got right to the point. Indeed he'd hardly said hello before he was spilling out his tale, all mixed and jumbled as he tried to choose what to say in what order, watching the expression on her face turn from peeved to curious to bemused to worried.

He tried to include everything: stories of Warren, of his mother, of Charlie and Abe; of his life as a bootlegger. He talked about the dig, the X-ray machine, and the session at City Hall. He even told her about Rose—well, not everything; he concentrated on the first meeting in the bar, and on the trip to see her father, and the little session he had just come from. He tried to make her sound just exotic enough that her rather familiar behavior at the ballgame wouldn't need further explanation. When he finally paused for a drink of water she spoke. Her first concern was not about his deceit, or even about his own involvement. She was worried about her mother.

"That Gavin guy is at the house now," she said. "Up until now I thought he was just crazy. But maybe he's dangerous too."

"What makes you think that?"

"Because there must be something down there."

"There must be what?"

"Something," she said. "Down there."

Hal leaned forward. He lowered his voice to a whisper.

"You can't imagine there's anything to all this. Gavin is nuts like the rest of them. It's like a disease, spreading from one guy to another. If there is really anything underground—I mean, if the X-ray even works, and if it picked up anything, it's probably just a cave. An underground lake. Maybe some ore deposits. Even if Warren gets half of southern California to follow him it won't make any of it real."

Isabelle fixed him with a look every bit as hypnotic as Rose's, only this was one of affection, and (he hoped) of fond exasperation.

"If it's all madness," she said, "then what are you doing two hundred feet down in a hole? You're no dummy. You must think there's a chance …"

Hal shook his head vehemently, searching for the right words.

"You'd have to know my mother," he said, his voice still low. "She made me promise I'd see this through. I know it sounds silly. But it's like I told you. We had to stick together. So I said I'd do this, and now I'm doing it."

"You wouldn't be out there every day if some part of you didn't believe it."

Hal sat back in the booth. What *did* he believe about Warren's chances—hell, anybody's chances who had gotten mixed up in this? Could they really *all* be crazy?

Belief was a funny thing. Charlie believed in opportunity, and when it didn't come his way he tried to invent it. Vera believed in spirits. All those nights with her crystal radio, looking for Sarah on the other side. Isabelle, apparently, believed in him, or else she wouldn't be sitting here, knowing she'd been deceived. Apparently belief made you stubborn. Two hundred feet. If that wasn't stubborn, what was? Was he really doing it all because of his promise?

Isabelle reached for his hand.

"If there is something down there," she said, "we have to get to it first."

Hal blinked. *We?* Did she think he was going to bring her on board with Warren and the rest? Or did she mean the two of them?

"I'll find out everything Gavin told my mother," she went on. "We've got to make him think he's one of us."

"But … but he's not," Hal sputtered. "And neither are you. There isn't an 'us' to be one of. I just turned Warren down. Walked out on him. They won't let me on the site Monday, I'm sure. I'll be lucky if I get my last paycheck."

Isabelle shook her head. "You stood up to your uncle for once, that's all. He'll think better of you for it. You'll go up to see your mother next week like you promised. All will be forgiven. You know too much now—he can't risk cutting you loose. Not with your dad slinking around. You might go work for him, after all. They can't take a chance on that."

"But …"

"No 'buts.' I'm going home. You need your rest—you've got a game tomorrow. You'll sleep better now that your conscience is clear."

She gathered up her purse and scooted toward the edge of the booth.

"But ..." Hal said again. "What about our date?"

Isabelle gestured for him to rise. He did, and though he towered over her he felt about two feet tall in her presence.

"I'll see you at the game tomorrow," she said. "We'll get a bite after. I should know more by then. Come on."

They found a taxi outside the restaurant. Hal told the driver to take them out to Pico first, then back to his place—an expensive trip home, but he wanted as much time with Isabelle as possible. She was quiet on the ride. That worried Hal, for it meant she was plotting. When they arrived at her mother's place he kept her in the car for a moment for a kiss goodbye, which she cut short. She ran up the drive like a school kid on a Friday afternoon. Hal shook his head. For better of worse, he'd confessed. Whatever happened now, at least he would have Isabelle to tell.

As the taxi eased away from curb Hal noticed a familiar car across the street.

"Hold on a minute," he said.

The driver braked. Hal rolled down the window and stuck his head out. It was a beat-up Model A, just like the one Rex had parked outside Callahan's that afternoon. Surely there were dozens of cars like it in town. Hal pulled his head back in, slid across the seat and looked out the opposite window at Isabelle's house. There were lights on downstairs, and in one upstairs window. Isabelle's room faced the back, he knew. The only other person who lived here was her brother Reggie. He was usually traveling, she'd mentioned. That was about all that she'd said about him. Hal didn't know what he did for a living or what he looked like, even. Or perhaps he did. He pictured Isabelle's face, and Edith's face, and Rex's face, and suddenly he knew for sure. Holy good Christ. He slid to the middle of the seat, hunkered down and shut his eyes.

"Let's get the hell out of here," he said.

··

Isabelle wanted to talk about Lizard men. Edith wanted to talk about Reggie.

"He got in a fight," she said. "He wouldn't talk about it."

"He's been in a lot of fights," Isabelle answered. "He never talks about it."

"He doesn't usually lose them."

"No matter how big you are there's always somebody bigger."

"This wasn't just one of his fights," Edith insisted. "His face looks like a slab of meat. He came in here and ate a sandwich and mumbled to himself the whole time, ignoring me. All I caught was 'goddamned bootlegger.' I hope he hasn't gotten himself mixed up with some bootlegger. Something's going on, I'm telling you."

Goddamned bootlegger? Isabelle knew only one bootlegger, and she'd only known him as a bootlegger for about two hours. And she knew as well about a man with a swollen face, from the story Hal had just told her. Rex, he'd called him. Of course. It was a nickname Reggie had in grammar school. She hadn't thought of it in years. Considering the events of the last few hours, this new news hardly surprised her. How it fit into everything else going on was the question; one she would like some time to think about before she said any more. She went to the kitchen to make some tea.

"He probably just lost a poker game or something," she called back over her shoulder. "I wouldn't worry."

"Not worry?" Edith was close to shouting, which was rare—even unheard of. "He's my son and your brother, and if he's in trouble I'm not going to shrug my shoulders, and neither are you! There's more going on here than you've been telling me, Isabelle. I'm not as dumb as you think I am."

Isabelle sighed. This was no time for secrets. If Hal could fess up, well so could she. This was her mother, after all.

"Come on in here," she said. "And have some tea."

··

Hal left Tuesday morning for Oxnard. His refusal was forgiven, if not forgotten, by Monday morning when he arrived at work, ready for confrontation, and found everything depressingly as he had left it, with a misty, dirty rain to make a miserable job that much more miserable. He called Isabelle after work to tell her he was headed north in the morning, on Warren's orders, and she approved.

"Let's take control of this thing before it takes control of us."

She had met him as she'd promised after his Saturday game in Irvine. They went to the Roosevelt for a drink. Hal seemed relieved when she explained that she had learned of her brother's involvement with the dig only last night. She giggled when Hal called him "Rex."

"It's a name they used to tease him with," she said. "Even when you said it I didn't put two and two together."

"Seems like it hardly makes four anyway, these days."

"At least he's on our side," said Isabelle. "I'd hate to be in competition with my own brother."

"You might have to get used to the idea."

"What do you mean?"

Hal wished he didn't have to talk about Rex. But what choice was here?

"Look," he said. "I know he's your brother, but … well, we don't get along. We've almost fought more than once. I don't know why Warren keeps him on. He's a hell of worker, but I guess I figure somehow he's out for himself, first and last. That's whose side he's on. Maybe someday he ought to know about you and me. But not now."

Isabelle bit her bottom lip and tapped her glass with her index finger.

"What do you know about this Rose?" she asked. "Aren't she and my brother a couple? Wouldn't that make him practically the Chief's son-in-law?"

Hal shrugged.

"They're a couple of funny ones," he said. "I don't know where my uncle came up with either of them. Can't we talk about something else for a while?"

"Maybe for a while."

..

Gavin came to Pico on Tuesday night an hour after dinner. He wore a cream-colored suit and a red bow tie. His face looked vigorously scrubbed.

"There's a bar convention downtown tonight that gives me an excuse to be out of the house," he explained to Edith when she remarked on his natty appearance. "That's where my wife thinks I am. I'll stop for a belt on the way home so she can smell my breath and think that's where I was."

"She doesn't know what you're up to?" Edith asked.

"I don't tell her about anything I don't want her to be in charge of," Gavin laughed. "There are already too many cooks in this kitchen."

He objected strongly to Isabelle accompanying them. Edith held her ground.

"If she doesn't go I don't either. It's a matter of prudence."

"We're not going anyplace dangerous," Gavin argued. "A rainy Tuesday in the city? We won't encounter a soul."

"Still," said Edith. "She comes."

"Too many cooks," Gavin muttered, straightening his tie. "I'm telling you." But he held an umbrella for both of them as he ushered them to his car.

Their first stop was the dig on North Hill Street. The site was dark. Gavin stopped the car at the corner of the lot. Isabelle could just make out the silhouettes of the tents and the blacksmith shop, the spoils pile, the equipment sheds, a flatbed truck, and in the middle of it all the plank fencing behind which was the shaft that led to Lord knew what. Across the street stood a tiny frame house with a light on in one of the windows. "Want to look around?" said Gavin.

"What's to look at?" Isabelle asked. "I assume the gate is locked."

"I have a key."

"Where in the world did you get a key?"

"Mr. Shaw insisted on the City having one."

He hurried around to open Edith's door.

"You just keep those channels open. Here we go."

The rain had nearly let up. Gavin walked briskly toward the fence as though it was his own front gate. Edith followed. Isabelle nearly had to run to keep up. In the corner of her eye she saw a dark shape cross the lighted window of the cottage. When she looked again it was gone. She heard the rattle of a key in the lock.

"Hurry up now, little lady," came Gavin's voice in the dark. "You were so insistent on coming. You don't want to miss anything."

Even up close the structures inside the fence remained mere shapes in the darkness. She watched her mother lean forward as though scrutinizing everything. Maybe she's humoring him, she thought.

But Isabelle was not seeing what her mother saw:

First there were men. Naked men, their muscles rippling like waves. Men in columns, hauling and pulling, working and straining. And women, their faces painted black and white, their shoulders bent under burdens, some carrying children pressed to bare breasts. They moved around and through each other, their bodies shifting transparencies. Then there was fire everywhere, flames leaping, the men and women vanishing in the smoke. Edith could feel the searing heat, smell charred wood and flesh, and hear shouts and wails and the roar of flames.

The scene shifted, and she saw the forms of other men—modern men—digging and shouting and swearing. These were the men who worked here, she knew. She even spied the figure of Isabelle's beau, moving like a giant among the others. She looked back to her daughter, wanting the reassurance of her face, and without warning the vision changed. Isabelle was still there, her features lost in the darkness, but behind her was a wall of green water, as big as the sky. Edith's mouth opened, but no sound came forth. She spun back toward Gavin, who was yammering on, and then again to Isabelle, and the wave was gone. She closed her eyes. Madness? It had to be. Plain and simple.

"Over here," she heard Gavin say, "is the hole."

He led her to the wooden slat fence with its crude, padlocked door. He fumbled in his suit coat packet.

"You have a key for this too?" Isabelle asked.

"In a manner of speaking," the lawyer replied. He pulled forth a squat pair of bolt cutters and snapped the lock shackle.

"Seems they neglected to close up proper tonight," Gavin said.

He pushed the door open. Isabelle saw the shape of the windlass; its heavy legs and cross beams, its fat coil of rope. It straddled the yawning blackness of the shaft, from which wafted a cold, moist air. She walked toward the hole in tiny, shuffling steps, attracted and apprehensive at the same time. The enormity—and perhaps folly—of what Hal's uncle and crew had accomplished overwhelmed her. She inched still closer, peering over the lip which was edged by rough-hewn timbers stacked log-cabin style as high as her waist. The darkness of the shaft sucked at her vision; she felt as though her pupils were being tugged from their sockets. She forced herself to step back and straighten up. Treasure or no treasure, there was nothing to see.

Edith moved in beside her daughter. As soon as the damp air rose and touched her face, another vision began. Madness again, but compelling beyond any power to resist. She knew now why Gavin had brought her. For this vision was one she almost understood. She closed her eyes and let it come clearly into focus.

She saw the tunnels. They stretched and fingered out before her as plainly as they had been drawn on Gavin's map, deep in the earth, revealed as though the shaft were a plate glass window into another world. They snaked off north to the right, south to the left, and before her, through miles of earth and rock, toward the sea. There were twists and cubbies, caves and narrow tubes, some passages wide enough for men to walk freely, others too small for a house cat. She shook her head in resignation. Madness, then, with a purpose. There was something down there after all. She had no doubt. She stepped away and opened her eyes.

"Mother …" she heard Isabelle begin, but Gavin interrupted.

"So? Did you pick up anything?" His face was illuminated briefly as he lit a cigarette and flicked the match into the pit. Who was this man? Why should she trust him? She felt Isabelle's hand again, coaxing her away.

"We've had our fill," her daughter said. "We need to go."

Edith looked again at the blackness beneath the windlass. This time she saw nothing. As real as her apparition had appeared, it now seemed ridiculous. She closed her eyes. Nothing at all. These were not visions she could command. She was not going to try to explain them to this greedy stranger.

"I've seen enough," she said. "It's only a hole in the ground."

Gavin sighed and took a drag off his cigarette. Its red tip glowed.

"Let's head over to Second," he said "Maybe something is happening there."

They returned to the car. Across the street, the light in the little house went off.

CHAPTER NINETEEN

LUCKY DAY

C HARLIE knew damned well when he was being followed. The life he'd led gave a guy instincts about that sort of thing. His pursuer was not hard to spot. He first noticed the guy hanging around City Hall when he came out of his meeting with Frank Shaw. A swarthy, mean-looking S.O.B., built like a water tank, with little bead eyes and moustache. Charlie recognized the type; an "enforcer" of some sort, stupid enough to take a risk on somebody else's dime, not smart enough to be in charge of anything other than his fists. When Charlie walked away up Spring Street the water tank put his hands in his pockets and followed a hundred feet behind, whistling a tune with all the idle ease of someone who never has whistled a tune before. Charlie kept walking, not too slowly, not too quickly, taking an abrupt right onto Temple to see if the guy would trail him. He did.

Most likely the sudden presence of this Dick Tracy on his trail had something to do with Shaw. After another half-block he looked back again. His follower remained in pursuit, still whistling. Then a Ford pulled up alongside the guy and slowed down, matching his pace down the sidewalk, until the passenger door swung open, the fellow got in, and the car accelerated past Charlie to the intersection at Main, where it made a right turn and sped off. Charlie spotted a woman behind the wheel.

His business sent him here and there on errands dictated by Green-leaf via instructions left with the proprietress of the rooming house where the Chief had arranged for him to stay. The purpose of some of the errands seemed straightforward enough: apart from his visit to Shaw, he was to arrange for equipment, labor and supplies, all for the dig on Second Street, which was nothing yet but a red cloth kerchief on a wooden stake stuck in the dusty earth by a schoolyard. It was on one of these trips, just a few days ago, that he'd had another encounter with his beefy pursuer. It left him chuckling still. When Charlie saw him slouching across the street, pretending to read the paper, he decided that he'd had enough. He crossed the street and asked him for a light, and after he got it the big fellow gave him a shove out of nowhere.

Something inside Charlie snapped. The fight was quick and mean. He depended on surprise to make up for his smaller stature. Life on the road had taught him a few things about using his fists—and his feet. He got the gorilla between the legs with the toe of his right boot, and he doubled up with a yowl as Charlie followed with a roundhouse left that caught him under the eye and set him on his butt in the sidewalk. After that it was just a matter of not letting him up to take a swing. He'd left the monster semi-conscious on the grass, face down, arms splayed at his sides. Charlie enjoyed the drubbing. It felt oddly like revenge for something, though he still had no clue who the hell the goon was.

Greenleaf was supposed to have joined Charlie by now, but over a week had passed with nothing but messages, including a terse order to return to Oxnard at once, on the morning bus if possible. Charlie had laughed. It was *possible*, all right, but he sat in bed for a half-hour smoking, scratching, drinking his coffee and wondering if it was after all *desirable* to hightail it out of the city again just as he was getting settled in. He had never much liked following orders. Still, he didn't know enough of what was going on to start taking independent action. Apart from missing an opportunity to go see Hal play ball this weekend (he'd checked the Sheiks' schedule in the *Times*), he had no objection to getting home for a few days and sleeping in his own bed. He stuffed his few belongings into his worn canvass duffle, put on his boots and hat and headed for the bus station.

He grabbed the back seat of a nearly empty coach, hoping that if it stayed vacant he could stretch out and sleep. The morning sun grew hot. Charlie swung his boots up on the seat, put his duffle behind his head and let his sombrero fall over his eyes. The message hadn't said that Greenleaf would be in Oxnard; it said simply to come at once, and to be at the Golden Pearl—a tavern by the public marina—no later then dinner time. Charlie assumed that he was being summoned to meet somebody. He hoped that whoever it was would have some cash to share. He folded his hands on his stomach and slept like a baby.

The driver woke him in Oxnard. The sky had become overcast while he slept. There was no breeze. The bus station was deserted except for a couple of old Chinamen asleep in the sidewalk shade by the door. Charlie thought about where to go first—there were still several hours to kill until his rendezvous at the Pearl. Should he drop in at the house? He was feeling a little too restless for an afternoon with Vera. But he could think of nowhere else to spend the afternoon. He hoisted the duffle over his shoulder and set off down C Street.

He hadn't walked three blocks before he knew again that he was being followed. He turned slowly as he walked. The streets were deserted, the parked cars empty, the shop doors vacant. He cut across Plaza Park. It was empty as well; not even an errant schoolboy playing hooky in the heat. He peered behind palm trees, looked into the pagoda, stood in the middle of the park and turned again, a full 360 degrees, shielding his eyes salute-style. Nothing. Despite the heat he felt goose bumps prickling his arms. He shook himself and walked on, willing himself not to look over his shoulder. He did anyway, several times. Still nothing.

He walked a roundabout way, winding and doubling back on side streets, partly to kill time, partly to throw off any pursuer who might have divined his destination. The duffle strap rubbed his shoulder raw. His shirt dampened with sweat. His feet started to itch badly, like he'd been buck dancing in a nettle patch. He stomped each boot twice, mopped his face with a torn bandana and trudged on.

His twisted route took him past the old shoe factory. He couldn't resist a peek. While the rest of Oxnard was growing and changing like everything else, even in the clutches of the Depression, the factory was the same—broken down and deserted. The path off the street was exactly as he remembered it, only the weeds were taller and thicker, some now the height of trees. The building loomed in front of him, dark and decrepit, the last remains of windows long since shattered by slingshots. A few glass shards glinted on the ground, reflecting the filtered sunshine. Charlie dropped his duffel and stood motionless. He could hear nothing but his own labored breathing and a sinister hum from a hornet's nest up in the crumbling brick of the second story. He peered inside the entrance, to where he and Abe once had installed a trapdoor leading to their stash, snug in the chambers that Hal had dug the summer he'd turned—thirteen, was it? It seemed a lifetime ago. Now the door was gone and the entrance crumbled. Someone had done considerable violence to their little warehouse. Charlie didn't care. There was no money in bootlegging now.

He felt them again: Eyes. The hum above him grew louder. He took a few steps forward, pushing his duffel ahead of him with one booted foot, seeking relief in the building's shade. No doubt it had become a hobo shelter over the years. It obviously had done duty as a lavatory. Charlie wrinkled his nose and peered into the shadows. The slight relief from the heat didn't make up for the stink. *To hell with this*, thought Charlie; *why did I come here anyway? I'll go see Vera, maybe have a nap, then I'll go to the Pearl.* He hoisted his duffle and turned around. His way was blocked by a woman.

She didn't even startle him especially, which was damned strange when he thought about it later. She looked at him as if she had been with him all day and had just stepped away for a moment; a look that seemed to say, what next? He recognized her as the companion of his swarthy pursuer. Her skin was dark, her eyes nearly black, her hair long and straight. She was wearing a dress the color of dried blood. She was smiling.

"I've seen you," Charlie said.

The woman raised her thick eyebrows.

"That's not likely," she said. "Since I didn't want to be seen."

"I don't mean here," he said. "Down in the city. In a Ford. Picking up a fellow—a mean-looking grunt. I know it was you."

The woman laughed.

"Well then you did see me," she said. "You have a good memory."

"Us old guys got to have good memories," he said. "We got a lot to remember."

"You don't even know old," she said.

Charlie pulled the duffle off his shoulder.

"All I know is that I want a bit of shade, a place to drop this damned luggage and for you to tell me why the hell you're following me."

"Well then it may just be your lucky day. What's your name, anyway?"

"Char … Um, Jackson Pike. From Seattle."

He held out his hand. She took it one of hers; cool, soft and smooth.

"I'm pleased to know you."

"Yeah?" he said. "Why?"

"All kinds of people would be pleased to know you," she said. "You'd be surprised.".

"Maybe. I'm kind of a pleasing fellow."

"And what brings you to Oxnard?"

Charlie tilted back his sombrero and scratched his head. He figured if he kept talking, maybe eventually she'd tell him something, instead of the other way around. It was worth a try. But couldn't they go do it over a nice cold one someplace?

"Well," he said, "It's kind of a long story. Maybe we could find some shade and answer each other's questions a little bit more leisurely."

"Now that's a fine idea," she said. "And I know just the place."

She led him away from the doorway, back onto the path. He was so mesmerized by her that he almost forgot his duffle, and she laughed when he had to go back for it. She walked out of the factory grounds, back along the street, with Charlie a few steps behind her. She didn't say anything else, and neither did he. He walked as though in a dream—as if he was *watching* himself walk; like he was in both a moving picture and its audience at the same time. He followed her as she took a right, then another block and a left, then another block, another right, and he realized with a chuckle that they were on Downing Street. She was taking him home.

··

There wasn't much to see at the new site. Gavin was disappointed. The whole block was empty, the schoolyard deserted, the vacant lot as vacant as could be. A single street lamp lit the scene. A stake had been pounded into the earth. From it dangled a strip of cloth, motionless in the damp, still air. There was a pile of junk a few yards away—a rusted, rolled wire fence, some timbers, a coil of rope, a wheel barrow with a broken handle. A distant big shadow was the school building itself; a smaller shadow was a ramshackle shack. Gavin clucked his tongue.

"I thought they'd have something going by now," he said

Isabelle turned toward the car. Edith did not move.

"Mother?" said Isabelle.

Edith was having yet another vision. Nothing as dramatic as on North Hill Street; no floods or fires or naked men. Not even tunnels, or at least not predominantly tunnels—she had more of a sense than a sight of them; a notion that had begun on the drive over in Gavin's car, an acute awareness of the deep labyrinth that spread below them. But there was something she did see clearly, off in the field, behind the stake, near the shack: a round door in the ground, with a ring in its center. It lay not far beneath the surface, and it seemed to move and shimmer, appearing now here, now a few yards away, so that she couldn't fix its location exactly. She blinked, and it was gone.

"Mother?" Isabelle asked again.

"What it is? You got something?" Gavin hurried to her side.

She felt him at her elbow. Was this not exactly what he was after? Exactly what he'd hoped she would see? A portal in the ground; an easy entrance to the world below? Should she share her vision? What if she was wrong? She felt simultaneously light in the head and heavy in her body, as though the earth was tugging at her, pulling her to her knees. Her resistance was melting away. She had to tell someone what was happening. She stumbled a couple of steps, and felt Gavin's hand on her arm.

"You saw something, didn't you?"

His skin was flushed, his eyes afire. His breath came in little fetid gasps. He was the very picture of greed. Isabelle was reaching for her, concern and wonder in her eyes.

"Yes," Edith said. "Damn it. Yes."

Isabelle caught her as she fell.

..

Hal borrowed Lucky's car, promising to have it—and himself—back from Oxnard in plenty of time for Thursday's game. He drove straight to Downing Street. Of course Vera was home. In fact she was exactly as he imagined she would be: curled up on the sofa in a ratty pink housecoat, her hair uncombed, her old crystal radio on her lap, not listening to it but simply holding it, a far-away look in her eyes. She smiled when Hal walked in.

"I've been expecting you."

"How did you know I was coming?"

"Mothers know these things." She sounded chipper enough.

"Right."

She set the radio aside and began smoothing out her housecoat, preparing to stand. Hal made a staying motion with his hand. His words tumbled out as fast as he could think them.

"Charlie is back. I know he is. He's been here and he's been to the city and you've seen him and didn't tell me. He's mixed up in something again and you know all about it. What's the story?"

Vera didn't flinch.

"Yes he's home," she said calmly. "Not at the moment—he's gone down to the city like you said. But yes, he's back."

"So why didn't you tell me?"

"I didn't have to tell you. You already knew."

She stood up. Lord, she was tiny. She approached Hal as if to give him a hug, but then stopped a couple of steps shy of him and simply stood, with her wild hair and her quirky smile.

"I have both my boys back now," she said.

Hal gave her a kiss on the cheek. She was useless, but she was still his mother.

"I'm going to go lie down upstairs in my room," he said. "We'll talk more when I come down. We're going to fix you up and take you out this afternoon. Buy you a new dress and some things. You need to get out of this house."

To Hal's surprise his old room was neat and clean, the bed newly made. A pitcher of water, a porcelain basin, and a clean towel were on the bureau. So she *had* been expecting him. Atop the bureau stood a row of his books, and the old Babe Ruth baseball Warren had given him. There was no sign of Charlie.

He took off his shirt and flopped down on the bed. He would find no help here. He was on his own. That was nothing new.

When he stirred again more than an hour later, it took him a moment to recall where he was, and why, and another moment to realize what had awakened him: voices. Familiar voices. He leapt off the bed, splashed a handful of water on his face, rubbed it briskly with a towel and started down the steps, pulling on his shirt as he went. When he reached the landing he could peer around the corner, and what he saw nearly dropped him to his knees. Vera was in her usual position on the sofa. His father, essentially unchanged, was seated in one of the over-stuffed chairs, wearing his boots and a big straw hat. Standing at the bottom of the steps with a smile as big as tomorrow was Rose.

"Come join us," she said. "Your mother is just brewing some fresh coffee, bless her. I believe you know Mr. Pike?"

CHAPTER TWENTY

TOGETHER AGAIN

F RANK SHAW was tired of his lawyer. He didn't like lawyers in any case, and this Gavin fellow was proving to be more much trouble than he was worth. But the problem wasn't only him, it was these damned lunatics and their holes in the ground. There were two groups of crackpots digging holes in downtown Los Angeles and Gavin in charge of figuring out what they were up to. And now it was looking like Gavin was trying to outsmart him. What a dumbshit.

Shaw had been suspicious from the moment that joker tried to bargain with him, asking for a cut of the pie like he was something besides a hired shyster. He'd thought about having Gavin followed, but how the hell many guys did he need out there trailing each other? He already had that little spook Lucas, a cousin of Dolores'. (The poor sucker had something wrong upstairs, couldn't read a word or add up two and two but he had eyes as sharp as a vulture and a memory so good that he could tell you what he'd had for breakfast on some random Tuesday ten years ago.) He'd put him up in a little shack across from where Crackpot Number One had his wetbacks down in the pit. He got reports every Friday. Yesterday Dorothy brought Lucas himself into Shaw's office. Seems Gavin had been to the North Hill dig the night before, and he'd been accompanied by two women. Shaw had said nothing to Gavin about enlisting any help, and Gavin had said nothing about any ladies. So it appeared there was a problem.

It got worse. Lucas had shown an extra bit of independent initiative that Shaw would have to reward in some way; a steak dinner at Mc-Grath's, or maybe a night with one of the Wilshire girls. He'd gotten on his bicycle and trailed Gavin to the new site on Second, where something seemed to have happened to the older of the two dames.

Shaw summoned Gavin first thing the next morning; he was due in a few minutes. If Shaw didn't like what he heard—and he couldn't imagine how he would—then the question was whether to give him another chance, or to can his ass right there. Canning would be easier, but he didn't want a pair of loose lips out on the street, and he didn't feel like going through the hassle of finding another spy.

Dolores's voice came on the squawk box, saying the lawyer had arrived. Shaw told her to send him in. He'd thought to play a little cat-and-mouse, just for the fun of it, but he changed his mind and got right to the point:

"Where the hell were you last night?"

"I was—I was on the job. Checking things out."

The lawyer's smile was so phony it must have hurt his face.

"You weren't alone."

"How—I mean, well. No, sir. I wasn't. But how—?"

"What were you doing?"

Shaw nodded to the guest chair and Gavin sat quickly, dabbing his brow with a handkerchief.

"Well?"

"I—ah, yes, sir. I was going to come in and tell you, as soon as—as soon as I'd tracked down just a few more facts. I have—that is, I believe I'm in the process of—what I mean is, there's something remarkable going on here. I have made an important discovery. I believe I am—or rather, that we are—onto something rather, um, big. Yes, sir. Something truly extraordinary."

Gavin's eyes were shining with excitement that almost masked his fear—not a good sign. What Shaw wanted from him was a simple, terrified explanation and apology. What he was getting was more breathless enthusiasm. Hell, he probably wanted a permit of his own.

"Go on," he said.

"I have employed the services of a psychic," Gavin said. "A fortune-teller, if you will. Hear me out, please. This woman is well-regarded and professional. She agreed to accompany me to the sites of the two projects. Just to see if her extraordinary powers of perception—I mean, not that I subscribe completely to the idea—"

"A *psychic?*"

"I had hoped that she might be able to provide insight …"

"I didn't hire you to provide insight," Shaw said evenly. "I hired you to keep an eye on the new nut case. Not to become a third one."

"I understand. But please. This woman had a vision, sir. Something that could be very important. She has had an intimation that suggests that the map-holder—well, that he may well be onto something. You remember how the letter mentioned a door ..."

"No."

"Excuse me?"

Shaw stood up. He didn't want to hear another word. There was some kind of group hysteria afoot; some contagion or vapor or virus or Lord knew what. He'd had his fill of it.

"You're fired, Gavin. I'm revoking the permits. This bullshit has gone overboard. I wanted facts, not visions. I never should have let that professor and his gadget into City Hall, and I'm going to make damned sure it doesn't come back. You can pick up a check from Dolores next week for everything I owe you and an extra week besides. You're to stay the hell away from Fort Moore Hill, and you're not to say a word about any of this to anybody. Understood? Anybody asks about holes in the ground you tell them the City is digging a sewer line. Or you'll find yourself digging one in person."

Gavin's puppy eyes were so pathetic that Shaw nearly laughed aloud.

"I got work to do. Now scram."

The lawyer backpedaled out. Shaw shook his head. He was letting Gavin off easy, compared to others who'd crossed him. At least he could leave under his own power.

Shaw would deal with the gold diggers later. He'd have stop-work notices posted on the weekend; maybe send over a couple of off-duty guards while they got their equipment out. He'd have the big hole boarded over for now and wait a few weeks to fill it in, in case anybody was paying too close attention. People had short memories. As for what he'd tell the treasure hounds themselves, he'd think of something. Some technicality, some violation, some fatal fine print in a statute that had been "brought to his attention." Maybe he'd have Gavin draft something up. Throw the loser a bone.

A pile of papers sat in front of him: forms, letters, petitions, budgets, approvals, requisitions. He'd had Dolores put them in order of priority. She knew his affairs nearly as well as he did. He pushed a button on his phone and leaned toward the speaker.

"What's left today? No more lawyers, I hope. Or lizard-men. Not that there's much difference."

He chuckled, pleased with his little joke. He heard Dorothy laughing dutifully along, and the sound of pages rattling.

"Just your appointment tonight," she said, "with the Police Chief."

"Oh shit I'd forgotten." Shaw was in no mood for the Chief of Police. Still, he needed the Chief's support. The Department was a critical partner for a new mayor. He punched the button again. "Where are we meeting?"

"He's taking you to a baseball game. Your car will pick you up at six."

··

Isabelle answered the phone. She knew who it would be, and was tempted to ignore it, but Edith had come into the living room, and Isabelle wanted to spare her any more stress. She rolled her eyes and mouthed "Gavin" for her mother's benefit.

"We have to do something right away." The lawyer's voice was strained and panicked. "Shaw is pulling the plug on both projects."

"What?"

Lord, how she disliked this man. She never should have let Edith go with him last night. She *certainly* shouldn't have let him back into the house after Edith fainted, and—most damaging of all—she shouldn't have let her mother spill forth what she had seen while Gavin stood listening, the veins in his little bird head pounding. Isabelle had thrown him out at midnight, with her mother passed out exhausted on the sofa. The last thing she told the lawyer as he left—and she was quite clear about this—was that he was to say *nothing* to *anyone* of what had happened to Edith at the digs.

"What were you *thinking?*" she demanded. "How much did you tell him?"

"He doesn't know a thing. He wouldn't even let me say what your mother saw. He just flat out shut me down."

"But why did you even *go* there?"

"He ordered me in. Called my house. He knew we were out there. I don't know how. I couldn't deny it, could I? He just knows things."

"Couldn't you make something up?"

"Frank Shaw isn't an easy man to lie to."

I could, Isabelle found herself thinking, somewhat to her surprise.

"He's going to shut down the projects." Gavin was practically sobbing now. "Put on the kibosh. No matter what's down there. We have to act fast if—"

"'We' nothing," Isabelle snapped. "You've done enough damage as it is."

"But what—?"

"I'll come up with something."

She hung up. Edith followed her into the kitchen. Isabelle put on the kettle. Clear thinking was in order. She wished Hal were in town, but he either was driving back from Oxnard (with news of his own, she hoped) or he was already here, getting ready for his game. She wouldn't trouble him before he played. He was pitching tonight against the Angels again, under the lights at Wrigley. She knew how much it meant to him. Afterwards they'd go someplace quiet to talk. They would take Edith along—maybe not what Hal was expecting, but this was an emergency. They needed a plan.

··

Vera called out from the kitchen:

"Would anyone like another slice of cake?"

"Come sit down with us, damn it," Charlie called out.

She came in with the coffee pot. Hal pulled in his legs to let her pass. Rose had done most of the talking for the last half hour. To him, to Charlie, and to Vera. To his family. That alone would have been enough to chew on for a few days, apart from anything she actually had to say. *Rose.* Jesus. She insisted on referring to Charlie as "Jackson," or "Mr. Pike," even after she'd explained why. It made Charlie laugh every time. She seemed to know an awful lot about him, and she had him slotted into a fantastic story that she told with the matter-of-factness anyone else might have used recounting a day at the county fair.

"We needed Mr. Pike all along," she told them. "But it took some time to find him. My father traveled from Mexico to Canada in search of him. He finally located him in Seattle. And brought him home."

Vera sat beaming in her usual corner of the sofa. Charlie put his cup down and folded his hands behind his head.

"Tell 'em why your dad was after me," he said, grinning.

Rose held up her hand, as if to say *I'm in charge here*. Which clearly she was.

"There were several reasons. One, of course, was to bring him in on this wonderful opportunity. And to reunite him with Mrs. Gates and his son ..." She nodded at Hal as though he was the barest of acquaintances. "But there was another reason as well. The boots. They are rather special to us. They figure in a story much older than we are."

"It's a hell of a tale, too," Charlie interrupted. "Seems there were two chiefs ... ."

Again, Rose held up her hand.

"My father was looking for the boots, and he was looking for Mr. Pike. As his quest continued they became one and the same. We are very happy with his success. To bring you all together here—that's a dream we've had for ages.

"The boots were stolen from us," she continued. "It may have been an innocent theft. Their keeper was—well, he had become careless with his things. Even those that had been entrusted to him as holy. There is a game they play in the mesa country, whiling away the heat of the day. A game of chance, somewhat like the dice games I have seen men play in the taverns."

"Craps?" said Charlie, leaning forward. "Them old Indians shoot craps?"

Rose shot him a look, and he shrugged and sat back.

"Your friend did not know what he took when he won the boots from my kinsman. We hold him blameless. Indeed, he has been of great use to us. But the important thing is this: the boots must be returned. They must go back where they came from. You and your father have been selected to return them. Together."

Charlie winked at Hal.

"Just like the old days. You and me."

Hal crossed his arms. Rose smiled at the gesture.

"Naturally you want to know more. The entire story would be long in the telling—longer than we have, I'm afraid. The bare bones are this: The legends speak of a star child who will deliver the boots back to their maker, deep below the mountains. The child must descend with his father. We've known that for many years. Only recently have we known who the child and father are.

"Make no mistake. There is treasure in this place. The very treasure you seek, we seek with you, though it means little to us as wealth. Our interest is in the golden tablets that are stored in the anterooms, on which is written the history of the first world. We want it with the same hunger that you want your riches. That is why we help you."

Bullshit, thought Hal. Even if he didn't know what the hell they might or not find down below, he was damned sure it had nothing to do with Charlie Gates or his boots. This was nothing but a scoop of malarkey ice cream on top of yet another slice of old Houdini pie. Apparently she had Charlie—"Mr. Pike"—believing it. His mother, too. (Hardly surprising.) Hal smelled a rat with a tail as long as Rose's hair.

She continued:

"If you had heard this story in Los Angeles you wouldn't have believed it. You certainly wouldn't have acted. You may not believe it regardless. But I think now that you will act."

"Damn right he'll act," Charlie blurted. "If we don't get us a pile of gold out from under that city, my name ain't Charlie Gates. Or Jackson Pike. Or whatever the hell it is." He guffawed and slapped his leg, then hiked up his pant leg to display the calf of one tooled boot. "I'll even swap these for it, if that's what it takes."

Rose wagged a finger at him.

"Careful, now. And remember your name isn't Charlie Gates—not where the City is concerned, that is. Not until we're done. Then you may call yourself anything you please."

Everyone except Hal laughed again. They were looking at him now. His arms still were crossed, and he had a look on his face that could have soured a bucket of cream.

"Why two holes?" he said.

Charlie leaned forward and rubbed his hands together.

"Let me tell him," he said. "This is the really good part."

Rose sat back and opened her hands in a gesture of giving him the floor. Charlie dug into a battered duffle next to his chair and pulled out a folded, tattered map. He smoothed it carefully on the floor in front of him.

"One way to get to the treasure," Charlie said, "would be to dig and blast down to the shallowest tunnels. That's what Warren figured to do. They're a hell of a long dig down, though—way deeper than he imagined. But there are other entrances a lot closer to the surface. You still gotta dig for 'em, but you can do it a lot quicker than the months it's taken Warren to get even as far as he is, which by the way ain't even close."

"We're almost two hundred feet," Hal said, though he hadn't intended to speak.

Charlie laughed.

"At the rate you're going you'd get to the first tunnel sometime, oh, the summer after the summer after next—and that's if nothing collapsed on you, and if you didn't hit any underground rivers, and if Shaw and his goons let you keep digging, and a bunch of other 'ifs' I bet Warren hasn't thought of. But you find one of these portals—that's what the Chief calls 'em—and you can walk right down into the old city like it's Union Station. There's a half-dozen on this map. The marks aren't exact, of course, but close enough to warrant a look. One of them is where the new dig is going in. We think we're goddamned close on that one."

"Then why in the world—" Hal was almost afraid to finish his question, for he suspected the answer. "Why did the old Indian let us dig as far as he did in the wrong place? What the hell were we doing?"

"Two holes, two answers," Charlie grinned. "First, it took time to pinpoint the right portal. A couple of 'em are under big buildings downtown. One is pretty much under the Public Library. Another one is beneath a swimming pool in Brentwood. Greenleaf wasn't sure he'd ever find a good one. So it made sense to get some work started as long as Warren had the City's attention. And second, well ..." he looked at Rose, who nodded. "Look at it this way. You needed to be, um, invested. If it had all been too easy it might not have kept your attention while the Chief went looking for me, and hell you'd be off playing baseball in St. Louis or some damned place by now. Like Rose says, he needs you. Us, that is."

"You mean we've been working our asses off on a two hundred foot hard rock decoy?" Hal felt his face turn red.

"It wasn't wasted time. We got the second permit, we got you here, we—"

"What about Warren? Does he know?" Hal interrupted

Charlie and Rose exchanged a look Hal could not decipher—conspiratorial, but something else too. Ashamed, he hoped.

"Warren's not what you'd call top dog on this thing," Charlie said. "He's been a big part, sure. He might even get a cut. But it ain't really about him."

Hal closed his eyes. It still was not clear what was expected of him. Rose spoke up as though she was reading his thoughts.

"We can drive back tonight. You have a car, so we'll all go together. There's a game tomorrow, and Warren won't expect you to work. After your game we'll start at the new place. We'll dig some shallow shafts—just until we hit rock, and then we'll know we aren't in the right spot for the portal and we'll move on. My father will be there. He'll let us know when we're close. You and Mr. Pike will descend together and we will join you, to see what we see. You'll leave the boots behind. After that, it's all up to you."

She got up and made for the door.

"I'll see you after dinner," she said.

She left. Hal was alone with his parents.

"Well, here we are together again," said Charlie. "It's about goddamned time."

CHAPTER TWENTY-ONE

THE GAME AT LARGE

T HOUGH this was just another charity exhibition game—this time raising a few greenbacks for the sorry farmers out in the Texas panhandle—it was going to be played for keeps. The Angels, first place in the PCL, were faltering. Halfway through the season the kranks were wagging their tongues about how the Blessed Boys were hearing footsteps. A loss to a barnstorming bunch like the Sheiks, Hal Gates or no Hal Gates, would wag the tongues even louder. The Angels were playing to win.

Hal was glad to be pitching. He needed to clear his mind. The goddamned strangest afternoon he'd ever spent got stranger still after Rose left yesterday, with Charlie breaking out a bottle of bourbon from a cupboard in the kitchen and regaling him and Vera with tales of his travels, acting like a man without a worry in the world. Vera was as normal as Hal could hope for, doting on Charlie like a fussy mama bird. At least Hal got filled in on some details about how Charlie had met Greenleaf, and what had brought him south—sheer persuasion, as far as he could tell, that and curiosity, and of course greed. He spoke little himself. He nursed a tumbler of bourbon, and tried to think outside the din of Charlie's incessant yammering.

Rose returned at seven o'clock for the drive back to the city. As Charlie was repacking his duffle and Hal was coming downstairs with his overnight grip, Vera rose from her place on the couch and announced that she would "just run upstairs for a minute to change," (as if she had run anywhere since before Hoover was president) and that if nobody minded, she would like to come along.

"I haven't been to the city since I was a girl," she said. "I used to love it so."

Hal nearly fell over. This was a development every bit as unbelievable as an army of gold-plated lizard-men cavorting in Plaza Park. Charlie clapped his hands and said hell yes. Rose seemed delighted. She even volunteered to help Vera pack, and followed her upstairs. Hal stood aside to let them pass. When Rose's shoulder brushed his chest he felt something like an electric shock, sharp and hot but not entirely unpleasant. He and Charlie packed the car. When he came back inside he saw Vera stuffing the crystal set into the top of her suitcase.

Now he was warming up with Payton in the visitors' bullpen at Wrigley. The crowded park was as gorgeous as before; a deepening sky above the towering light stands, a faint salty breeze. Hal supposed this was as close as he was likely to get to happiness anytime soon, and that he might as well enjoy it.

Isabelle was present, of course. And not just her. Christ, his father was there. Charlie Gates in the flesh. And *Vera* was there, for the love of God. Hal had half expected her to back out and stay put at the hotel he'd gotten for them up on Wilshire. But she'd insisted on seeing him play. Rose had come too. She'd announced on the way down that she was meeting not only Rex and Warren at the game, but that Greenleaf himself planned to attend.

The Angels' fans went nuts when their team was introduced, waving giant paper cut-out wings they'd gotten from hawkers outside the gates. It might have been a playoff game, the way they were acting. Hal was somewhat comforted by a not inconsiderable contingent of Sheiks' fans in the audience. They had no wings to wave, but many were sporting ridiculous cloth turbans, sold by the same vendor. The Angels had a brass band above their dugout. They played jazzy versions of gospel songs—"Rock of Ages," "Amazing Grace" and "How Great Thou Art, Jehovah," with a lead Negro trumpeter who hit his high notes with such piercing clarity that they seemed to be wafting down from the heavens. Not to be outdone, a group of Sheiks fans in the left field bleachers had located an East Indian player of some primitive, ear-splitting reed instrument that sounded like a rusty police siren. He played between the brass band's songs; brief, tuneless riffs in an eerie scale—the music of snake charmers, as near as Hal could figure it. As soon as the swami paused for breath the brass band would start up in answer, its snare drum popping like a rifle. It was a great night for a ballgame.

Behind home plate, ten to fifteen rows up, protected by a wire screen stretched between two light poles down the foul lines, the occupants of the V.I.P. box were glad-handing their way through the pregame festivities. Frank Shaw scanned the crowd around him, counting his supporters and detractors. It seemed to him that the former outnumbered the latter, which pleased him, but he was a canny enough politician not to take numbers for granted. He was wondering how best to spend whatever hand-clasping currency was available before the singing of the Anthem.

He'd already done his duty by the Police Chief, chatting him up in the limousine on the way over, agreeing without listening to everything he said about the rising crime rates, the new waves of Okies, the increasing gang warfare in Chinatown—all the usual police subjects. Shaw was confident by the time they arrived at Wrigley that he'd have the Department's continued allegiance, at least in the near term. Now he wanted to talk to somebody with a little more influence.

Three rows down he spotted Joe Vitorri, an alderman and owner of two of the city's biggest hotels. Joe also had more or less complete control, unofficially of course, over one of the gangs about which the Chief had been complaining. He was a good guy to have on your side. Shaw was getting ready to amble down and shake his hand when there was a commotion at the box entrance. A guard was clearing the way for a contingent of a dozen men, including several reporters with their bulky cameras held high over their heads, flashes popping. Two of the newcomers wore baseball uniforms. Word spread quickly that the teams' owners thought it would be a brilliant idea to bring the starting pitchers up to meet the dignitaries before the game—a great photo opportunity; publicity not only for both teams, but also for any politico who wanted to be photographed as a man of the people. Shaw liked the idea instantly. He would make sure that the shot they got of him was front-page quality. He pushed through the crowd to meet them. Joe Vittori could wait.

The *Times* did run his picture the next day, on the front page of the "C" section, but it wasn't the shot Shaw imagined. Some alert photographer had caught the moment when he was introduced to the Sheiks' star pitcher, Hal Gates. Shaw could be seen emerging on the right hand side of the photo, Hal on the left, a half-dozen men between them. The photographer had shot from a half squat, aiming up. In the photo Hal looked downright mythical, towering over the other men like a Great Dane in a litter of Dachshund pups. He was smiling, one massive hand extended, his hat cut off by the top frame. The photo did not flatter the mayor. It showed his eyes wide, his head thrown back, and his mouth in a little "o." Throughout all of Los Angeles men picked up the paper, flipped to the sports page, laughed aloud, nudged the closest fellow present and pronounced some variation of the city-wide consensus: "Looks like Shaw got goosed."

Shaw had no idea before the game that Hal Gates, terror of the bush leagues, was the self-same man-child who had stood in his office in March with that twitchy bald scientist. Gates hadn't done any real talking, Shaw remembered, but he did recall the one thing the kid had said when needled about their crazy plan to dig for lizard-gold: *It might be crazy to look, sir, but for sure it would be crazy not to.* That phrase popped unbidden to Shaw's mind as he recoiled from the surprise of seeing the near-familiar face below the baseball cap.

He couldn't tell if Gates recognized him or not—his face was oddly inexpressive, as if his mind was elsewhere. The other pitcher, the fellow from the Angels, was completely forgettable, although the Police Chief assured Shaw that he was a former big-leaguer. What Shaw remembered, and what echoed still in his mind the next morning when Dolores showed him the sports page, was that single comment:

For sure it would be crazy not to.

He heard it as they escorted the pitchers back to the field. He heard it as the brass band played the Star Spangled Banner. He heard it all through the game itself. *Crazy not to.* Despite the madness he'd witnessed it seemed just possible to him that it was, still, crazy not to. But if you wanted something done right, you did it yourself. He knew he'd done the right thing pulling their permits. But maybe it was a little soon to be filling in holes. Maybe it was worth a look-see.

He reminded himself that the giant supposedly was the holder of some sort of incriminating information about him. Shaw decided not to let that bother him. The man-child was busy now. Hell, he was a celebrity. Surely he would have better things to do than try to unlock skeletons he could hardly have been old enough to remember anyway. And if baldy or anybody else started making noises—well, thought Shaw, he was sitting next to the Police Chief, after all. Surely being mayor meant something when it came to self-protection.

The game began.

Lucky, bucking tradition, had Hal batting third. With a runner on base, especially against a fast-ball pitcher like Carter, he was the team's best chance for a run. From the start of the contest, however, the "runner on base" part clearly was going to be a challenge. Carter's stuff was as good as the Sheiks had seen. His fastball had a break so sharp you could hear it in the first row of the bleachers, a sound like a zipper, then the pop in the catcher's mitt, then a roar from the Angels' fans. Strike three was followed by one quick, lonesome wail from the trumpet, sounding for all the world like a baby's cry, at which the crowd laughed raucously. Hal watched the one and two batters go down. Nothing would feel better than to connect with one of those fastballs. He wanted Carter's best stuff, and he wanted to hit it hard.

He didn't even see the first pitch. He heard it hit the mitt behind him, the umpire's hoarse shout of "strike" and the answering howl of the kranks. He chuckled to himself: *This must be what it's like batting against me.* He stepped out of the box, took a vicious practice cut—more for show than anything—stepped back in and stared toward the mound. Carter stared back. Was there a slight curl to his lip as he went into his windup? Hal cocked his bat as the ball left Carter's hand, but held up on this swing as the pitch hit the dirt just in front of the plate and skipped to the right, out of the reach of the catcher. The ump dug into his pouch for a fresh ball. Hal ground his right foot into the dirt behind him and turned to face the pitcher again.

Another wind up, another throw. Hal uncorked a power swing, feeling the bat slice the air with a vicious whistle, doing his best to keep it on a level plane with the white sphere speeding toward him. There was a loud "click," he felt a sharp sting in the fatty part of his left hand, and out of the corner of his eye he saw the ball spiral up and to his right. It was foul, deep into the third tier of seats behind the plate; a long, looping arc of futility. Hal heard a few throaty hollers from the dugout.

"You're on it!"

"Straighten it out!"

"Next one!"

He resumed his stance. This time there was no doubting the curl in Carter's lip. *Nice swing,* it said. *Now hit this.*

Then something weird happened.

The next pitch came in slow motion. Not like a change-up. It was a fastball—Hal could see its rotation, end over end, moving so slowly that he could spot the individual stitches as it spun. It was as if the ball was being carried, instead of flying, toward the plate. Such a pitch, could anyone actually throw and control it, ought to be murder to hit; indeed it would break a hitter's back as he geared up for normal bat speed and then had to adjust to a ball so slow. But Hal knew as soon as he cocked his wrists behind his head that he was still in synch—that his swing, for no reason he could understand or control, was in fact going to be timed—was going to time *itself*—with the pitch. As his started his cut he realized that *everything* was moving in pace with the delivery—Carter's follow-through, the first baseman dropping into his fielding crouch, even the banners waving out in right field—everything moved s-l-o-o-o-w-l-y as he brought his wrists around and witnessed, for the first and only time in his life, exactly what it looked like when the sweet spot of a bat punished a fastball in flight—the explosion of fine white dust, the compression of the ball, the jump of leather off wood, the stitch rotation violently reversed, the bat coming around as the ball sets off on its new, surprise trajectory, in this case in a graceful, soaring, picture-perfect arc against the dark sky and into the third deck of the right-field grandstand. Then, as if at the flip of a switch, he heard the roar of the crowd and the wild cries of his teammates, and felt the bat fly out of his hands as he started toward first base. All was normal again.

A crowd of Sheiks spilled out of the dugout to greet him as he crossed the plate—hardly normal behavior for a first inning homer. As his grinning teammates half shoved, half dragged him back to the bench, Hal saw Lucky standing, hands on hips, a quizzical expression on his face as though he alone understood that what he'd just witnessed was more complicated than a well-timed swing. He nudged Hal in the shoulder as he passed.

"Nice piece of hitting, kid," he said.

Hal bit back the response on his lips: *Thanks. But it wasn't me.*

The Sheiks took the field with a 1-0 lead. Hal walked to the mound with slow deliberation. He didn't have any idea what had just occurred. He breathed deeply as the first batter stepped in, hoping that his mind would shut down and his body take over, relying on instinct to do his job. Hal took the sign from Payton: fastball, no surprise. He got set, went into his windup, and threw. Nothing weird happened. The pitch, a shade more outside than he'd intended it, still caught the edge of the plate, the ump signaled "Strike!" with a hoarse shout, and the Sheiks fans went wild. Hal caught the toss back, took another deep breath and leaned in for a new sign. Business as usual.

Or maybe not. Not that anything like his home run happened again—not for a while, anyway—but the game that unfolded was hardly run-of-the-mill. Hal retired the side in ten pitches. As he returned to the dugout he noted that the crowd was oddly silent, as if they sensed that this would be a contest to which they ought to pay close attention. As if they were settling in for the show of their lives.

One, two, three. One, two, three. So it went until the fifth, when Carter intentionally walked Hal, then struck out Barnes swinging—or flailing, more accurately—at shoulder-high heat he never saw. Both the crowd and the dugouts sat in silent awe at the pitching performances they were witnessing. In the sixth inning Hal's teammates moved away from him on the bench, heeding the age-old baseball superstition of not talking to a pitcher about a possible no-hitter in progress. And it wasn't just a no-hitter Hal was flirting with. He had a perfect game going—not a single base runner through eighteen hitters, then twenty-one, then twenty-four.

Any real fans will pull for the pitcher in the final innings of a possible no-no, even if it's their own team being victimized. There comes a point when the game at hand starts to take a backseat to the Game at Large. The kranks were juiced. They expressed their enthusiasm by becoming completely silent. No shouting, no running children, no brass band. Even the vendors shut up. The Angels' crowd had the solace of knowing that, should Hal pull off a perfect game, their pitcher had performed masterfully as well. No ball besides Hal's homer had gotten out of the infield.

In the top of the ninth the Sheiks' first baseman caused a little stir by fouling six balls off on a 3-2 count before grounding out on a change-up low and away. The next batter, Payton, struck out looking. The Angels would have but three more chances at the one-run lead. All the Sheiks had to do was hold on.

Hal wasn't bothering with signs anymore. He was throwing his fastball to batter after batter, mowing them down with pure velocity. The first two went down swinging and then came Jigger Statz, walking in slowly from the on-deck circle with the game on the line.

Payton called time and trotted out to the mound, his first such visit all game. He put his glove in front of his face to muffle his voice.

"We got him on a slider last time," he said. "Set it up with something outside."

"To hell with that," said Hal. "I'm throwing heat."

"Hey, this is Statz," Payton answered.

"I don't care if he's Babe Ruth," Hal answered, aware that he sounded like a whining schoolboy.

"Look," said Payton. "You've almost got—" Hal glared at him. The catcher trotted back to his spot behind the box.

"Play ball!" the ump called.

Statz looked at Hal. Hal looked back. Both men were smiling. Statz dug in with his back foot. Hal threw as hard as he could; thigh high, middle of the dish. He figured Statz would be taking on the first pitch, as was his reputation, and he wanted to establish who was boss.

Statz wasn't taking. He swung late but hard. The ball made an ugly sound coming off the bat—ugly to a pitcher one out from a perfect game, lovely to the man holding the bat. A crisp, solid rope down the right field line. No chance for Harris, even if he hadn't been playing way too close to center, to get to it on the fly.

A hit. A single. A base runner. A ruined perfect game.

But it was none of those things.

Statz ran like a man thinking double. For about forty feet. Then he crumpled to the dirt as though he'd hit a wall.

There was an explosive gasp from the crowd. Harris played the angle perfectly, fielding the ball cleanly off his shoe tops on its second bounce. Statz got halfway to his feet, took two steps forward and fell again, hard, as if the wall had scooted back a few feet just to taunt him. Another gasp from the crowd, this one laced with yells and curses. Hal stepped down off the mound in the direction of the first base line. He almost wanted to help, to take Statz by the arm and hustle him to the bag before Harris made his throw. It was hard to see a good ballplayer humiliated this way. But it was too late. Harris crow-hopped twice and fired a bullet to Harkness at first, who had one foot firmly on the base. Statz made his last effort and fell again as the first-base ump made the "out" sign. The crowd erupted: a storm of shouts, screams and protests, all directed at Hal. As if he'd done anything worse than serve up a fat one.

"Bum!"

"He shot him!"

"Monster!"

"Cheat!"

For the second time that summer Hal stood suffering the hysteric abuse of an angry Wrigley crowd. When he'd beaned Isabelle's date he at least had understood the outburst. This time he wanted to proclaim his innocence and defend his honor.

He quickly scanned the rows above the home team dugout. He spotted Isabelle right away, next to her mother. She had her hands clasped in front of her, as though she'd been in the midst of a clap but was frozen in motion. She saw him looking. To his relief she smiled.

Then he looked down three rows. There they were, the whole motley crew: Charlie and Vera, Rose and Rex, Warren and Greenleaf.

Charlie was half-turned, saying something to Warren, which surprised Hal a bit as their old friendship had been rather strained of late. Vera had her head down, searching for something in her purse. Rex was gazing at something off to his right. Chief Greenleaf was halfway down the aisle, headed who knew where. The only person looking back was Rose.

She winked at him.

CHAPTER TWENTY-TWO

A MAN WHO KNOWS WHAT'S WHAT

H AL was in no mood for noodles, and he didn't want tea. If he had to have noodles and tea he sure as hell didn't want them in the company of his girlfriend's mother. He wasn't getting anything he wanted lately though, even when he sort of was—as in, how many guys pitch a perfect game and wish they hadn't?

Isabelle had picked the restaurant. She gave the cabbie good directions, all on back streets, to Chinatown. Hal had his uniform in his leather bag. He wore a plain white shirt and dark pants but he knew it was naïve to think he could wander the city incognito. There just weren't many men his size around, and there were twenty-thousand people on the streets who thought they'd just seen him work some kind of voodoo on the most popular ballplayer in Southern California. Isabelle didn't want to go to Pico Rivera in case some strange chance brought Reggie home, and there was no safe place in Hal's boarding house to talk. So noodles and tea it was. And Edith.

Hal had asked the elderly waiter if he had any beer, and the old granddad nodded cheerfully and assured him yes, yes, beery beery, very good, then disappeared into the kitchen, from which he hadn't yet returned. Isabelle had talked since the moment they sat down. There was little chance anyone would eavesdrop on, or understand, their conversation here. Hal gathered that things had gotten even more impossible. The mayor wanted to shut them down. Hal couldn't say he blamed him. It was actually refreshing to see somebody thinking straight about all this nonsense. Shaw didn't have to contend with loony mothers or greedy fathers or mystical boots or a dark-eyed woman who could turn a ball game any direction she wanted without getting out of her seat.

Hal hadn't said his piece yet; hadn't explained what had happened in Oxnard, and how his own role in all this apparently had shifted; the star child and all that. Of course he didn't believe it, but it seemed that there was little he could do but go along with the program. Greenleaf and Rose had more tricks up their sleeves. Hal had just seen evidence of that. There'd been no talk so far of what had happened on the field. Maybe Isabelle thought it was just a lucky break. She hadn't even congratulated him on the win. She was all tunnels and visions and what happens now. She'd caught the bug for sure.

"We need to move soon," she said. "We may have only a few days. Or nights."

"To do what?" said Hal. "Hard-rock mining isn't something you take on with a couple of buddies by flashlight. We've been digging for months."

"I know," said Isabelle earnestly, and a bit impatiently. "But haven't you heard what I'm saying? There may be another way. My mother—"

"Had a glimpse of something. No disrespect intended, Mrs. Robinson, but that doesn't mean it's going to be easy to find."

Edith merely blinked.

"What do you mean?" said Isabelle. "What happened up north, anyway? Did you see your father?"

Finally she's asking, Hal thought. He took a deep breath.

"I saw all kinds of things in Oxnard," he said. And he told them. Isabelle's mouth fell open, almost comically.

"Why didn't you tell us this before?" she said. "This changes everything."

"I was going to tell you as soon as you paused for breath," Hal said. "I don't know who is going to do what. I don't think we have much to say about it, frankly."

"What do you mean? If we're the only ones with all the pieces, we ought to be able to make the best move."

"We might have information," he answered. "But they've got something we haven't got."

"What?" said Isabelle. "Aren't we all in same boat?"

Hal laughed. There was no race on anymore. There was Greenleaf and Rose calling the shots, and a bunch of puppets dancing on their strings. Hell, he was the biggest puppet of them all.

"Didn't you see what happened out there tonight?" he said, as gently as he could. "That was their way of telling us that they're in control. I didn't pitch that game. I didn't get that hit. I was just doing what they wanted. You saw Staz."

"He fell. Twisted his ankle or something. Accidents happen."

"That was no accident. I saw the way she looked at me."

"Rose?" said Isabelle.

"Of course."

"I just noticed you weren't saying her name," Isabelle answered.

Hal shook his head. It was hardly time for jealousy.

"They want us to go into the tunnels," he said slowly. "They'll find a way. No matter what Shaw wants."

"That's it?!" Isabelle blurted. "'They'll find a way?' Like you have nothing to say about it? All those hours in that horrible hole, all those years taking care of your mother, and now you're going to do whatever they want you to do? What about me? What about the treasure? Did you even get them to agree on your cut? You're the biggest man in Los Angeles. Doesn't it ever occur to you to take control?"

Her face was red, her hands flat on the table as though she might shove it across the room. Edith put a hand on Isabelle's shoulder and said her first words of the evening.

"Now, dear. No need to get upset."

Isabelle jumped to her feet, splashing the noodle bowls onto the table.

"If you're not man enough to look out for yourself, let alone me, maybe somebody out there is. Let's go, mother. Dinner is on the big fellow."

Edith gave Hal a look of helpless apology as she followed Isabelle out the door. The other customers—two middle-aged Chinese couples—watched Hal with obvious amusement. The staff spilled out of the kitchen to see what the fuss was about. Hal felt his face grow warm. He looked at the mess on the table. Noodles and tea. Jesus Christ.

He tossed a few bills onto a dry spot on the tablecloth. As he made for the door the old waiter returned, grinning, holding a tray on which was balanced the largest bottle Hal had ever seen—easily two quarts, sweating ice-cold condensation, with red Chinese writing and the single word "BEER" on a yellow label. The waiter set it on the table.

"Beery beery," he beamed.

Hal sat back down. He drank the bottle in three long gulps. Then he went home.

..

Timothy Gavin was not going down without a fight. No siree Bob. He was nobody's stooge and nobody's fool. It was a dog-eat-dog world the best of times; these days it was dog eat rat or pigeon or whatever dog could chase down and get its jaws around. He intended to be the one doing the chasing. And the chewing. By God he did.

He ordered another gin.

"Son of a bidge," he said for the fiftieth time that night. "If's down there, I godda fine it." The dark-haired bartender polished a shot glass from the drying rack.

"Well, my friend, whatever it is, and wherever 'down there' is, you ain't getting any closer sitting your ass on a bar stool. Why don't we make that your last one? You drink any more you're going to float away."

Gavin regarded him dully. What the hell did this guy know? There he stood, rubbing his damned glass, unaware that riches unimaginable lay below his big lead feet. Maybe he was right about the drink, though. His wife would be waiting up.

"Son of a bidge," he said again. "Is down there. Godda digs all y'godda do".

The bartender poured a glass of water and set in front of him.

"Bottoms up," he said. "You'll thank me in morning."

Gavin burped.

"Godda digs, all."

The bartender nodded, as if thinking this over carefully.

"You got a shovel?"

Gavin laughed.

"Need a damn big shovel," he said. "Ain't no lit' hole."

"They got shovels the size of buildings," said the bartender. "You ever been to a quarry? Man, they got some shovels at those quarries."

"No … quarries," Gavin said slowly. The bartender's image blurred, doubled and tripled before his eyes, then collapsed into a more or less constant form. Handsome kid. White apron. Black hair. Awfully young. Smart, though. A man who knows what's what. He reached for the water glass and tipped it back into his open mouth. What the hell? Worst gin he'd ever tasted. Maybe it was time to quit. He set the glass on the bar and cocked one eyebrow at the young man.

"Get you a big ass shovel," the kid said with a little laugh. "Dig you a big ass hole."

Gavin started to laugh along, then hiccupped again. He slid off his stool.

"Son of a bidge," he said.

The next day at lunch time he found himself standing in the offices of Tony Belucci and Sons Machinery, looking as decent and official as his hangover allowed. The bartender's wisdom had come to him over his morning coffee, which he had made and burned himself, his wife having left to spend a few days at her sister's house in Costa Mesa. As far as Gavin could recall he'd told her everything, thinking that a full confession might make her sympathetic to his trials and tribulations. It hadn't.

The Belucci offices were in a warehouse near the docks, a bustling, workaday part of town that Gavin didn't know well. He'd imagined the waterfront as a gritty, rat-infested, rough-and-tumble place where a swell like himself would be conspicuously out of place. So he was surprised that the Belucci offices were as flashy and up-scale as anything downtown: thick Persian carpets, heavy mahogany, leaded glass, Tiffany lamps, and a receptionist in a lime green silk dress who smiled so sweetly at Gavin that he almost forgot his hangover. Not to mention his fear. For he was doing something very illegal, not to mention dangerous: he was misrepresenting himself as a city official, on assignment from the mayor himself. He had requisition forms with him in triplicate, awarding a no-bid emergency contract to Belucci and Sons Machinery. They were to begin work as soon as practicable on a series of excavations in the Fort Moore Hill neighborhood. Today if possible. Gavin had prepared the forms himself, on his own typewriter, just an hour before. He'd signed them too, with Frank Shaw's name. He'd broken enough laws to land him in jail for a very long time.

Tony Belucci was short, fat, ugly and rich, even in times like these. His office was like the waiting room only nicer, with real art on the walls and a wet bar behind his desk. He poured Gavin a whiskey, which made the lawyer nearly vomit until he'd swallowed half of it, at which point he began to feel just fine. Belucci glanced at the ersatz forms and papers, and shoved them aside.

"So what the fuck is really going on?" he said.

"Excuse me?"

"I had me a little girl in this office not twenty minutes before you got here trying to sweet-talk my dumb-assed son into taking a rig up there after lunch. And now you come in here wanting the same damned thing. So what the hell?"

"You had you a which?"

"Hang on." Belucci pressed a button on his phone. "Get in here," he said.

Within seconds the office door swung open and there stood a younger version of Belucci; a little thinner, with a crooked nose that was purple on one side.

"My son Ralph," Belucci growled. He turned to his son. "Who was that little piece in here just now?"

"Just … just an old friend, sir. Her mother is a teacher at a school on Second Street. They have some water coming into their basement, and she can't get anybody to do anything about it. She wants me to take a shovel up there and look to see if there might be a burst pipe or something. She's, um, somebody I used to know."

"I bet," Belucci grunted. "At least you inherited my taste in dames."

He looked from his son to the lawyer and back.

"There's something going on here. This have anything to do with all that talk of buried gold and shit?"

Gavin was aware that his mouth was flapping like a screen door in a breeze.

"Hell, I read the papers," Belucci said. "Biggest bunch of bullshit I ever heard. Sounds like somebody's dippin' into the peyote. But what the fuck do I know?"

Neither Gavin nor his son replied.

"Tell you what," Belucci said. "I'm going to say go for it. Ralph, take a couple of rigs up there, and a crew of whoever is still sober enough to work on a Friday night. Take some lights. Dig your hearts out. Hell, we'll get paid. Even when those papers turn out to be as phony as I know they are, I'll get my money from the City. They know better than to cross me. And of course we all might get rich as Croesus. It's a red-letter day either way. Have the rigs back here on Monday morning. Now scram."

Six hours later Gavin found himself on Second Street with Isabelle and Edith Robinson. The Belucci crew had brought a diesel generator and klieg lights on tall stands, which Gavin had them set up in a circle around the area between the road and the school. He was ready to dig up the entire property looking for this door. They'd dig all night if they had to, and get some guys on the day shift as well. Once Shaw found out the jig would be up. He prayed that the Robinson lady would come through for him.

Isabelle held her mother's hand and glanced at her watch a lot, every once in a while peering down Second in both directions. Gavin started to ask who she was expecting, but he was interrupted by Ralph and one of the backhoe drivers.

"We're all set up," the kid said. "You point, we'll dig."

Gavin gave Edith a look. She smiled ruefully and shook her head.

"Start near the fence," said Gavin. Just a couple of big ol' trenches."

The backhoe driver looked at him sideways.

"What are we looking for, if you don't mind my asking?"

Gavin tried to sound official.

"Subsurface anomalies," he said, making up the term on the spot and feeling rather proud of it. "I'll be inspecting each excavation."

The drivers climbed into their rigs and started them up, filling the air with the roar and stink of engines. Gavin hoped the neighborhood wouldn't get too curious. As the first backhoe swung into position its blade lifted up high and slashed down into the scrubby grass, gouging out a section the size of a small steamer trunk. Gavin walked toward the activity, motioning Isabelle and Edith to follow him. His mind was a tumble of fear, excitement and dread. He was defying Frank Shaw. He was digging for gold.

..

Hal went to work the morning after the Angels' game. The day was hot and bright. The crew was on site, standing in a little circle, kicking at the dust, muttering in Spanish. The gate to the pit was closed. Warren emerged from the trailer he used as an office. He was carrying the X-ray machine in its canvas bag. He looked surprised to see Hal at first, but recovered quickly and nodded to him brusquely.

"Big day ahead," Warren said, approaching the group. "I won't be here—you're in charge as usual, Hal."

"Where are you going?"

"Chief Greenleaf needs my assistance."

"Where?" he asked, though he was pretty sure he knew.

Warren gestured with a tilt of his head that they should continue the conversation out of earshot of the crew. Hal followed him a few steps toward the road. They stood close together, their heads nearly touching.

"This other group," Warren whispered, "the one we talked about—the Chief seems to believe that they are onto something. He wants me to use the machine over there. Apparently he believes there may be another way into the tunnels."

So he knew a little, but not everything.

"What should I do here?"

Warren looked toward the crew.

"Dig," he said. "For now I intend to stay the course."

Hal nodded, biting his tongue. Dig. How could he dig?

"The crew is antsy," Warren said. "Watch them carefully."

He shouldered his machine and hurried away. In the little frame house across the street the curtains in the window fell closed.

Hal turned back to the crew. How could he tell them to spend the day drilling set holes and shoveling rock for nothing? They might not be happy about two months of wasted work even if they'd gotten their paychecks on time. They might have the guts that he seemed lack, to walk off the job and never look back. Better to keep them "invested" as Charlie would say, until the situation changed. Hal drew himself tall and gave them a workmanlike nod.

"Let's get to it," he said.

And once again they took their turns down in the shaft.

The rock was the hardest they'd encountered in two hundred feet. On Hal's first ascent he was trembling and soaked with sweat. He poured a cup of water over his head. As he wiped his eyes dry with the tail of his shirt he saw two cars approach slowly from the east. They were Bentley limousines; sleek, black and sinister, like something from a gangster movie. He was surprised when the passenger door of the lead car opened and there emerged Mayor Frank Shaw, coatless, wearing a white shirt, tie, and brown leather suspenders. His face was blotched and sweaty, but he was smiling.

"Ah," he said, approaching the fence. A half-dozen men, similarly attired, spilled out of the waiting cars. "If it isn't Cy Young the gold digger."

Hal unlocked the gate. Shaw walked in as casually as if he was strolling into his own office. He extended his hand and Hal shook it.

"Hell of a performance out there yesterday, son," said Shaw.

Hal said nothing. Shaw continued.

"So what the hell is a big baseball star like you doing working your butt off with a bunch of spics?" Shaw jerked his head in the direction of the Mexicans, every one of whom, Hal figured, was a better man than Shaw ever could hope to be.

"Guy's gotta eat," he replied, not meeting the older man's gaze.

Shaw's men roamed freely around the site, looking into the blacksmith tent, picking rocks off the rubble pile, examining the tools lined up against the trailer wall. Warren would have chased them off the property in a heartbeat. Hal remembered what Isabelle said about him not "taking control." He *was* in charge here, after all.

"Mr. Shaw," he began, "I think you'd better—"

"Your boss around?" Shaw asked.

"I—well, no. He's not."

"You're the honcho here?" Shaw asked.

"I am."

"Is the gadget available?"

Hal was thankful that Warren had taken the X-ray. Even he had never been permitted to touch it. What would these goons have done to it?

"He has it with him."

Shaw nodded, his thick lips pursed in disappointment.

With the mayor insisting that they "go ahead and act like we're not even here," Hal mustered the crew into their usual routine; lowering and raising the hoist, fussing with the generator, refitting the drill bits, taking their turns in the order of descent. Shaw and his men wandered the premises, looking, touching, and getting in the way. One fellow even tried the door handle of the trailer.

"Hey!" Hal shouted. "That's private!"

The guy backed off with a shrug. Shaw laughed.

"No secrets here son," he said. "We're all in this together."

Hal bit his tongue and went back to work. It was his turn again in the Hole. When the men lowered him down it was like being dropped into a hot oven. There were almost enough set-holes sunk into the rock at the bottom to allow for a blast; a few more and they could place the charges. Hal worked as quickly as he could by the light of his head lamp, wrestling the heavy drill and its impossible length of hose, squinting through the sweat that burned his eyes, his head aching from the screeching din that the drill made in the cramped shaft. When he was satisfied that the holes were sufficient to set the caps he gave three tugs on the safety rope and prepared for the ascent.

Hal rose to the top. Garcia, the hardest-working of the crew, stood by with blasting caps and explosives. He wore a sleepy expression, as though he already knew that the game had moved elsewhere, and this next explosion was all for show.

Hal freed himself from the harness.

"Blow it," he said. "And then that's it for the day."

Shaw stood nearby, mopping his florid face with a blue cotton kerchief.

"Not losing faith, are we?"

Hal didn't answer.

When it came time for the blast he herded the visitors away from the shaft, insisting that they stand outside the fence on the sidewalk while Garcia set off the charge. The last thing Hal needed was for some projectile to take out a bureaucratic eye, or even smudge one of those clean white shirts.

Garcia leaned into the plunger. There came the muffled growl of a subterranean explosion, giving rise to an instant bloom of fine dust, rising into the air as high as a tall palm tree. And then something new: Even as the black dust hung suspended in the breezeless air, it was followed by a geyser of dirty gray water that rose straight out of the shaft and higher even than the dirt had flown. Had there been any wind someone would have gotten a soaking, but as it was the stream, like the blast from a giant hydrant, fell almost straight back down. It lasted a full minute and subsided all at once, as though someone had turned a spigot. It took another minute for anyone to work up the nerve to approach the pit.

Hal grabbed a pickaxe, for no reason he could think of, and made his way to the shaft. It was now a well. The water level was clearly visible, no more than ten feet below the ground. Two hundred feet. Jesus. He took off his cap and scratched his head.

"Be damned," Shaw grunted behind him. "Look's like that's that."

CHAPTER TWENTY-THREE

A SELECT FEW

VERA had never stayed at a hotel before. According to Charlie, the Biltmore was a first-rate one. Ages ago, when Hal and Sarah were very small, they had dreamed about some distant day when they would be "flush," and able to travel to places foreign and exotic; stay in hotels and drink champagne and forget all there was to forget about Oxnard. She'd never actually traveled farther than San Francisco, and that was only once. So this was nice. She missed Hal, but she understood that he was busy after his big night. And he had a girlfriend now. A pretty one, too. She was proud of him.

Everyone seemed to be enjoying themselves. Of course they talked a lot about the Plan. It had been ages since Warren had talked to her about it, but she still believed in its magic. The group acted as though its success was now inevitable. Charlie and the old Indian man were especially animated. They pounded down whiskies in the downstairs lounge while the Indian proclaimed "our destiny at last," and Charlie nearly choked with laughter. Warren, who was putting them down as rapidly as Vera had ever seen him, had his own refrain, all about *vindication* and *scofflaws*. Rex couldn't stop talking about what he would buy—cars, a boat, a house in the Hollywood Hills. The Indian woman was mostly silent. Charlie shook his head from time to time, hiccuped a lot, and once, with a wink at Vera, muttered "Houdini pie, I swear," grinning as he held up his glass for a refill. The bartender kicked them out at 2 a.m.

A little after noon the next morning, they all—except Warren—loaded into Rex's car and drove to Second Street. To Vera's delight no one challenged her when she piled into the back seat next to Charlie. It seemed she was part of the gang now. Warren was waiting for them when they arrived, fiddling with his X-ray machine. He and the Chief huddled over it for a while, the Indian talking rapidly as Warren jiggled its knobs, peered into its eyepiece and made adjustments. Rose meandered in slow circles around them. Rex napped in the back seat. Charlie walked around the field with Vera close behind, pausing a few times at Warren's car and straining up on his tiptoes to see the machine. Greenleaf waved him away impatiently.

"Let the man concentrate," he growled.

The afternoon shadows were growing when the old Indian finally stood and summoned everyone.

"Our progress is slow," he announced. "It is telling us too many things."

Warren stared at the gadget as though it, not the Indian, had spoken.

"There is interference from something," he said. "Indications are strong, but—well, shifting. Nothing precise enough to go on. Not now at any rate."

"Tonight," said Rose. "All the signs point to tonight. This is the place. We don't need your contraption. We need darkness and moonlight and the star child. With these things we will find the entrance. Tonight."

"But ..."

"When the moon appears over the tree line. Bring your toy if you wish. Just make sure, Mr. Pike, that you and the boy are here."

There was no conversation in the car on the way back to the Biltmore. Warren wore a stricken look of frustration and embarrassment. Vera felt sorry for him. He had explained to her many times how difficult the X-ray machine was—delicate, fickle, and mercurial. 'Like reading a woman,' he had joked, back when they used to joke together. At the hotel the men headed to the bar. Vera was tired. Having spent most of the past fifteen years sitting on a davenport, she found the activity level of the past twenty-four hours exhausting. She lay down and slept fitfully for a while, and was just awake and washing her face in the marble bathroom sink when she heard a knock on the door.

It was Rose. She had changed into a pleated skirt and a crisp white blouse. Her hair was rolled in a bun at her neck. She had a box of chocolates she'd bought in the hotel gift shop, and she handed it to Vera as she came into the room as though invited. Vera stepped back blinking. This girl was not as young as she seemed. Not a girl at all, actually. Which made sense after all, being Greenleaf's daughter. Why, thought Vera, the old Chief must be—how old? Seventy-five? Eighty? So then Rose would be ... It hardly seemed possible. But at any rate, here she was.

"Charlie isn't here," Vera said. "Or rather, Mr. Pike. He's down at the bar. With the other men. Killing time, I guess. The way they do."

She laughed, a little nervously, and was relieved to see that Rose smiled too.

"It's not Mr. Pike I came to see," she answered.

She smiled again—a nice smile, Vera thought, but unsettling somehow. Warm and mocking both, as though she saw right through you but liked you anyway.

"It's us women," Rose continued, "who have to stick together."

"Oh. My. Well. Yes."

Vera felt herself blush. It wasn't often anymore that anyone said "us" and meant her, too. Even coming from this unusual woman it was a flattering inclusion.

Rose sat down and patted the bed beside her.

"Any luck yet with your crystal set?" she said.

Vera blinked as she sat. Rose had seen the radio at the house, had asked about it and seemed drawn to it, though there had been no opportunity to explore it at the time.

"Things have been busy," she answered with a little shrug. "To tell you the truth, I've never had much success with it. Charlie thinks I'm crazy to use it. He always has."

"Men don't have the best heads for these things," said Rose. "They only believe what they can see."

"Except for your father, of course," said Vera. "He's not like that."

"He's not much like other men in many ways," Rose agreed. She crossed her legs under her and settled against the pillows stacked along the headboard. "But even he has lost patience over the years."

"How many years?" Vera ventured.

Rose smiled.

"Longer than you'd think. Now what about that radio? You brought it along, didn't you?"

Vera knelt and pulled her suitcase out from under the bed. The radio was wrapped in the kimono Warren gave her so long ago. She handed it over and stepped back, folding her hands in front of her.

"Sit down," Rose said. "You're as nervous as a kitten."

Vera sat in the straight-backed chair by the desk. Rose turned her attention to the set. She seemed to be quite familiar with how to work it. She said nothing about its outlandish appearance—the old slipper, the bits and pieces of Sarah's life, faded and fragile now. She had the earmuffs on and was sliding the tuner slowly along the copper coil. Vera remembered how Charlie used to tease her when she was first experimenting with the set. She must have looked something like this, she thought—not as pretty, perhaps—but the same look of focus, even obsession. And all for nothing.

Rose held out a hand, her head still bent in concentration.

"Come," she said softly.

Vera leaned forward. Rose pulled off the earmuffs and repeated her command.

"Come. Listen."

Vera walked the few steps to the bed as though approaching the edge of a cliff. She reached out her hand. Rose pulled her down to the bed and slipped the moth-eaten earmuffs over her head.

Nothing. Not even the usual hiss and static. But the "nothing" was itself a thing; a kind of hollowness. A profound, engulfing emptiness; the very sound of silence itself. Though Rose still held her hand, and she could feel the bed beneath her, Vera had a sense of falling. She felt dizzy. She worried that she might faint.

Then she heard singing.

A girl's voice, so distant and faint that Vera thought it might be simply a ringing in her ears. She looked quickly at Rose, then closed her eyes. The singing was louder. She could identify no words, nor even a melody, but clearly it was song not speech; lilting, melodic, repetitive and familiar. Sarah. She'd have been able to pick the girl's voice out of a screaming crowd. Here in the eerie vacuum of the radio silence she knew without hesitation that what she heard was her daughter.

She felt Rose's hand gently pull away, and realized with a start how hard she had been gripping it. The singing was louder still. It was a child's play piece, more a chant than a song. She had not thought of it in years:

One two, buckle my shoe …

Then it drifted away again as though the singer—as though Sarah—was running in and out of a room, or swinging on a long rope swing, yes that was it, coming nearer, then flying away, then nearer again, chanting all the while. Vera mouthed the words to herself. It was Sarah, on the other side. Vera hoped that the girl would speak next, maybe even acknowledge her in some way. She took a deep breath, concentrated as hard as she could, and waited.

The room door rattled, followed by three dull thuds.

"Damn it woman, what are you doing in there? Oh hell, I got a key someplace ..."

There was a jangle of metal and the sound of the lock. It was Charlie, beaming, a little unsure on his feet, raring to go. He took a step back when he saw Rose.

"What the hell?" he said, then turned to his wife. "You ready?"

Vera stared at him. From the headset came a jumble of noise—static, squeals, an announcer's voice, a snatch of a dance tune. She pulled the muffs from her head, hurled them at Charlie and collapsed on the bed in tears.

..

On the return trip to Second Street Rex drove separately, with Charlie. Vera had stopped crying. Rose tried to talk to her about what had happened in the room. "These things aren't in my control," she murmured, stroking Vera's hair. Vera hardly heard her. She was so mad she could spit. She had heard Sarah's voice. She had almost spoken to her. And then Charlie had ruined everything. Damn him. Damn it all.

No one knew where Hal was. Rose asked on their way out to the cars, but the only one to have heard from him since the game was Warren, who shrugged and said he was probably with that girl of his. Charlie remembered that they had been ordered, essentially, to be there together. The star child and all that. But nothing could happen until they had found a passage underground, and he wasn't holding his breath. Let the kid go have some fun.

Things at the new dig had changed dramatically since the afternoon. Warren saw the site first, turning the corner off of Spring.

"What in the name ... ?" he began, slowing the car to a crawl. They had left the site abandoned. Now it was anything but. Though there was still light in the sky, the whole area from the street to the school was awash in the white glare of floodlights. A half-dozen cars were parked along the road, along with two flatbed trailer rigs. People were milling about. Most alarmingly, two full-sized earthmovers were at work, clanking and snuffling, churning up the earth in gargantuan handfuls and disgorging it in piles everywhere, leaving open pits like graves.

"Shaw," Warren snorted. "Damn him."

The Chief, still leaning forward, shook his head.

"Not Shaw," he said. "Strangers. What are they doing here?"

"That shouldn't be too hard to guess," said Rose. "They want to be rich."

She opened the door while the car was still slowing down. Behind them Rex also came to a stop. Within a moment they stood huddled by the parked cars while the workers slowly turned their attention to the newcomers. The earthmovers stopped growling. Only the hum of the klieg lights broke the silence.

"Be damned," muttered Charlie.

He was grinning, which Vera found infuriating. What could possibly be funny?

"Whoever's beating us to the punch has got a couple of women," he said. "And if my eyes don't deceive me, one of 'em is Hal's sweet young thing herself. Spot that figure a mile away. Hell yes, he's his Daddy's boy."

"But what do they know about this place?" said Rex. He seemed more angry than bewildered, as though he was watching the interlopers load bags of gold into their cars already. "Why wouldn't they be on Hill Street? At the dig?"

Greenleaf took a few long strides toward the lights. No one else moved. He turned back to glare at them, but they saw his gaze settle instead on something behind them. They all looked back, and saw the unmistakable silhouette of Hal, walking up Second Street, the last rays of the setting sun behind him.

"Evening," he said. "Looks like I found everybody at once."

Vera broke from the group and hurried down the road to meet him. She took both of her son's hands and smiled radiantly, her anger with her husband briefly forgotten. It took Charlie only a few seconds to ruin the mood.

"Look what the cat dragged in," he said.

"I wouldn't miss a party like this," Hal said.

He looked down the road toward the school. He'd seen right away that the "competition" included Isabelle. As they all moved down the road together, he began recognizing others—Edith, then a man he supposed was Gavin. There were a number of men in work clothes, including a fellow whose face was discolored by an ugly bruise. He took in the equipment, and the piles of dirt alongside the trenches, and it seemed to him that his life at last had reached some peak, or depth, of lunacy.

The two groups met within the circle of light from the lamps. They faced each other awkwardly. Isabelle kept her eyes averted. Rose stared openly at Edith. Greenleaf glared. Gavin was uncomfortable, nodding nervously at Warren and Hal, clearing his throat as though preparing to speak, though he did not. Rex looked as though the obvious next step was to start punching someone. Warren craned his neck, trying to see what the workers had accomplished. Hal focused on Isabelle. Charlie looked from one face to the next with a big, tipsy grin. Ralph Belucci, with his purple nose, stepped forward officiously, but when he saw Hal he backed off, and stood now halfway between the crew and Isabelle, fidgeting from one foot to another.

Greenleaf broke the silence.

"This is a sacred place," he said. "Who has cause to be here?"

He turned his black eyes from one to another, beginning with the workers. One by one they bowed their heads and shuffled their feet, unable or unwilling to answer. Ralph scratched his head and said nothing. The Chief turned to Isabelle. Despite her lowered eyes she seemed to feel Greenleaf's gaze, and blushed deeply. When he looked at Gavin, the lawyer's throat clearing became a full-fledged coughing fit and he staggered away, doubled over, pounding his chest. Only Edith seemed unmoved.

Greenleaf turned then to his own crew, and his gaze was no less stern. Rex could not bear it, and turned away muttering. Warren opened his mouth as if to answer, then closed it slowly, his shoulders sagging as his chin dropped to his chest.

When it came Charlie's turn he laughed.

"Hey, you invited me, remember?"

The old man grunted, and a smile tugged the corner of his mouth. Hal watched the drama from a short distance, holding his mother's hand. He too returned the Indian's stare, and smiled in a way not unlike his father.

"Here we are," he said, "just like you told us to be."

"Yes," Vera said. "What now?"

A fat, white moth flitted lazily into the air between Greenleaf and Warren, and then darted up toward the overhead lights. Greenleaf watched it a moment, then crossed his arms and spoke in a loud, impersonal drone.

"You have come here to steal the ancient gold of my people. Your greed does not interest me. We have come to give back to the old ones, not to take from them. But only a few may enter the old places. My daughter, myself. Only us, and this man and his son, who have been chosen. The rest of you go. Return tomorrow to seek your gold."

Hal smiled. Nice try, he thought: the old guy thinks he can spook everyone away with a little mumbo-jumbo, take care of business with no prying eyes about. Whatever "business" was. So far all they had here was a bunch of holes in the ground. Nobody was entering anything yet.

Ralph stopped his squirming and marched forward, wagging his finger in Greenleaf's direction.

"You wait a doggone minute," he said, in a voice like a mouse in a trap.

Rose turned to face him.

"Wait for what?" she said.

Her voice was hard, her eyes fierce. Ralph backed away, turning his head aside.

"Nothing, I guess," he muttered.

"Go on, then."

First the workmen and Ralph left, making their way to a few of the cars parked down the street. Then, with a sigh like a punctured zeppelin, Gavin shoved his hands in his jacket pockets and started for his car, pausing to motion that Edith and Isabelle should follow. Only now did Isabelle look at Hal—a beseeching look, it seemed to him. Gavin reached for her sleeve. She pulled away.

"She may stay," Rose said, pointing.

Isabelle pulled away from Gavin's grasp. She took a few steps toward Warren's group. Hal could tell that she was trying not to shout for joy.

"No," said Rose, holding out a hand, palm forward. "The other one."

Now it was Isabelle who stopped short.

"My mother?" she said.

Edith blinked.

"Me?"

"You have seen," Rose said.

Edith blinked faster.

"I … well, I'm … I'm not sure … what I've seen. Something no one else seems to see, at any rate. If that's what you mean."

Greenleaf gave his daughter a doubtful frown.

"She may stay," Rose repeated.

Edith looked baffled but pleased.

"I would prefer that my daughter stay as well. I rather depend on her."

Greenleaf rolled his eyes. He pointed to Hal.

"This woman is yours?"

Hal blushed. What sort of question was that? And how should he answer? He opened his mouth and closed again. Isabelle glared at him.

"Um, yes," he said. "She is."

"Yes," Isabelle echoed. "I am."

"Then it's your decision," said Greenleaf. "But be quick."

"She stays," Hal said. Gavin left alone.

"Very well," said Greenleaf when the lawyer had gone. He turned to Rex.

"You may go."

Rex drew himself up to his full height and scowled.

"Now just a damned minute," he said. "If that's his girl, then this one here is mine, after all, and …"

"Go," Greenleaf interrupted.

Rex turned to Rose.

"Tell him," he said, a whining note creeping into his voice.

"Go," said Rose.

"I …"

"Now."

Rex left, but not before staring menacingly at each of them in turn. His gaze lingered longest on Warren, who seemed to shrink beneath it.

"You and your stupid machine," Rex snarled. "See where it got us."

He stomped off to his car. That left Vera and Warren. Greenleaf looked at them in turn. Vera took a step backward, as though she meant to follow Rex on foot down Second Street. But she still held Hal's hands, and he did not release her.

"She stays," Rose said. "She has heard. That is sufficient."

Charlie snorted.

"Oh for the love of ..." he began. A quick look from Rose cut him off.

Warren leaned on his bundled-up X-ray machine, feet spread, in an obvious display of stubbornness.

"This was all my idea," he said.

"It was hardly your idea," said Greenleaf. "You have merely played your part."

Hal remembered the conversation in Oxnard. Was it possible that Warren had been coerced into the Plan simply to keep him, Hal, available? The notion was preposterous. So, it seemed, was the idea that his uncle would now be dismissed at the critical moment—even one of failure, or at least disappointment. As demanding, condescending and infuriating as the man had been, it would not be right to proceed without him.

"He stays," Hal said, his voice shaking a little. Greenleaf and Rose both looked sharply at him, as though he had departed from a script. Rose seemed amused.

"Didn't you hear my father? Only the chosen."

"Well then I'm choosing him," Hal said. He pointed to the X-ray machine in its sack. "He's seen things no one else has."

"That's for sure," Charlie chuckled.

"Enough," barked the Chief. "We're wasting time. No more talk. Very well. We are who we are. Now it is time."

With that he turned on his heel and walked toward the earth piles in the school yard. Rose followed, beckoning the rest, who fell into a ragged line—Edith and Isabelle, Warren, Charlie and finally Hal and his mother.

"Where are we going?" Vera whispered to Hal.

"No idea," he said. "None at all."

CHAPTER TWENTY-FOUR

EVEN CONSIDERING

G REENLEAF bypassed the first of the trenches, leading the group be- tween them. Hal peered into a couple as they filed by—nothing but yellow-brown dirt, mottled with gravel and rocks. Greenleaf beckoned Rose to his side, then Edith, too. The three clustered with their heads together, Edith glancing back over her shoulder at Isabelle. Greenleaf had pulled a paper from his pocket—the map, Hal assumed—and was studying it with a wrinkled frown. The deliberation took some time. Hal looked around.

Beyond the pool of light the darkness was impenetrable. Above Hal, thousands of tiny insects swarmed in the glow from the lamps. Every few seconds one would veer too close to a bulb and disappear with a *ssss*. Vera released his hands and inched her way toward the trio. Hal took a step in Isabelle's direction, just as his mother suddenly lifted her hand, one bony finger extended, and pierced the silence with a single word.

"There," she said.

Greenleaf's head snapped up. Rose spun around.

"There," Vera said again. Her pointing finger shook like a dowser's rod. All eyes followed it toward the shed at the corner of the field, be- hind the baseball backstop, well beyond the circle of light. The building was a mere shack, no bigger than an automobile garage, with no win- dows; just a tar paper roof and double doors secured by an oversized padlock that looked more suited to a battleship than a school.

Greenleaf looked at his map, then at the building, then at Vera, his eyebrows raised. Rose put her hand on his arm and whispered some- thing in his ear. He shrugged and nodded. She turned to the rest, who had all gathered now.

"Gentlemen?"

She held out her hands.

"Here goes nothin'," said Charlie.

Greenleaf walked with Charlie, and Rose with Hal, toward the shed. As pathetic as the building was its lock was formidable. Perhaps a hacksaw could cut its hasp, but as far as Hal knew no one had brought tools along. He wondered what the old chief had in mind. He didn't have to wonder long. The old man grabbed the lock, examined it front and rear, then took a single long stride backward and delivered a kick to the door that would have toppled a draft horse. The lock sprang open and fell into the dirt. The double doors rattled from the impact. Charlie clapped his hands.

"Goddamn! I've rode mules couldn't kick so good."

Rose fumbled with the latch. The door swung open with a rusty groan. Greenleaf produced an electric lamp from somewhere on his person and switched it on, aiming it inside the shack. Everyone stepped forward, craning their necks to see past him into the building. Hal sensed Isabelle off his right shoulder. He reached a hand back and felt her squeeze it once.

It was simply a storage shed. Greenleaf's light flitted like a sparrow, illuminating a bit of this and that: shelves along the back holding cans of paint, a few twisted sections of pipe, a stack of steel buckets, parts of a disassembled engine. Tools leaned along one wall: shovels, rakes, a post-hole digger. A roll of wire fence and a coil of chain lay atop a filthy green rug. Hanks of rope and wire hung from the cross-rafters.

Rose had a flashlight too, pulled from the pocket of her dress, and she flicked it on; another dancing light. Greenleaf peered into corners and looked overhead. The group inched forward. Now Warren had a light out too, and was moving it more deliberately from one object to the next, then across the dirty floor, back and forth. Something small scurried across the floor and disappeared under the rug. Hal ducked to avoid the dangling objects and the spider webs that looped among them.

"Well," Greenleaf said.

"Perhaps not *in* the building." Warren announced. "Perhaps *near* the building."

One by one they backed out into the field, the flashlight beams dancing on the bases of the walls and the surrounding grass and dirt. It was clear that no one had any idea where to look or what to do. Hal certainly had not expected to see the like of Rose and Greenleaf taking direction, or even clues, from his mother. But now they all seemed to be wandering about without purpose. It seemed a fitting way to end the evening. He hoped that they would simply go home, and leave the place to Gavin in the morning.

"Oh, for cryin' out loud. Am I the only person with eyes in his head?"

It was Charlie, drawing their attention back to the shed. He had his hands on his hips, his hat set back on his head and a smirk on his face.

"Didn't nobody here never hide anything?"

Charlie went in the door and moved to the opposite side of the rolled fence, which he kicked out of way. He gestured for Hal to join him, then picked up the coil of rusty chain and tossed it aside. He and Hal stood across from each other, the matted green rug between them. Charlie bent and grabbed one edge.

"Come on now. On three."

Hal knelt and picked up the opposite corner. It was gritty and foul in his fingers. Their lights were focused on it like stage lights.

"One … two … three … up!"

The rug folded as they lifted and tossed it aside. When the dust began to settle they saw that there was a door in the floor. It was about the size of a kitchen table-top, and appeared to be made of steel or iron, smooth and gray; a single trap door with one thick iron ring the size of a serving platter at its edge. It was oddly shaped, elliptical rather than round, with a single, massive hinge, crudely fashioned, on one side. Charlie laughed, his arms crossed on his chest.

"Any half-assed bootlegger could have told you to move the damned rug. Boy, I'm ashamed of you. Didn't you learn anything from your old man?"

The shack was suddenly crowded again. Everyone stood in a circle around the door. Greenleaf knelt and placed a hand on its smooth surface. Rose looked at Hal.

"Open it," she said.

Open it? Just like that? Hal squinted at the handle. The door must weigh a ton—there was no telling how thick it was, but the heft of its hinge suggested that it was as substantial as it seemed.

"Give him room," said Rose. Hal looked up at the rafters—perhaps they could support some kind of winch, if something could be rigged … . But that would take gear and time, neither of which they had. The others shuffled out of the shed. Only Rose and Greenleaf stayed behind, in the doorway, their lights on the door, their faces in shadow. Charlie winked as he passed and nudged Hal in the shoulder.

"Don't go anywhere without me," he said.

Hal took a deep breath of dusty air, blew it out and took another. He squatted, flexed his knees, and exhaled again. Then with one more deep breath he grabbed the ring in both hands and pulled as hard as he could.

The door opened so easily he nearly flew out of the shed. He caught his balance as he shoved it away from him. It slammed against the shelves, sending their contents clattering to the floor. Hal staggered backward, catching himself with outstretched arms against the wall. The beams from three flashlights played slowly over the yawning hole.

At first there was nothing to see. There was a lot to smell, however, as a powerful odor of decay wafted up from the blackness. It stung Hal's eyes and clouded his vision. He brought his hand to his face and turned away, struggling not to be sick. There was coughing from the others, and gagging, and Charlie's voice saying "Shit almighty!" Slowly Hal got a hold of himself, the bile rising in his throat, his eyes half-closed. He inched forward and peered more closely.

A dozen stone steps led to a small landing, then more steps descended into blackness farther down. On the landing there lay a pile of rags, poorly concealing a heap of human bones. Along the sides of the pit, on the stairs, on the landing itself and on crude wooden shelves as far down as the flashlights could illuminate, were bottles of booze. Hundreds of them. Whiskeys, gins and vodkas, all with familiar labels, all full. The torch beams played over them as they winked and sparkled. The lights refocused on the bones. The skeleton seemed intact, its grinning skull staring straight up with vacant eyes. Next to the skull was a crushed, tattered, desiccated object the approximate shape of an old-style top hat. At the skeleton's other end lay two objects that were slightly easier to recognize as boots, with wooden soles. On top of the rags lay an empty bottle.

The lights probed the blackness below. They returned to linger on the bones and the crumpled rags, then on the steps, then the shelves and the labels. They swept, converged, danced, bounced and flickered, then came to rest finally on the skull. It was Charlie who broke the silence. His voice was subdued.

"I'll be damned. It's old Abe."

"My God," said Warren.

"It can't be," said Vera.

"Who is Abe?" said Edith.

Hal had last seen his father's friend the day that Charlie himself disappeared. Vera always claimed no knowledge of his whereabouts. Warren said he'd not heard from Abe in twenty years. Yet this indeed was him. His signature hat and boots, however tattered and torn, could not belong to anyone else. What he was doing buried under a tool shed in Los Angeles was just one more question to which Hal had no confidence he would ever know the answer.

Charlie took off his hat and scratched his head.

"He's an old friend."

"Why is he here? Do you know this place?" said Greenleaf.

Charlie shrugged.

"Hell, I haven't seen Abe in ages. Figured he was dead. Guess I was right."

"But this place ..." Rose began. Charlie interrupted

"Hell, I don't know what it is. Looks like quite a stash he's got. I remember his ma taught school down here someplace—ran away from his dad when we were just kids. Maybe he looked her up. Damn fine front for a little business operation, I must say. Old rascal."

Vera and Warren moved to the edge of the hole. Isabelle took several steps back, outside the shack altogether. Hal wanted to comfort her, but he couldn't tear himself away.

Rose started down the steps. Vera gave a little cry of surprise, and Hal found himself making an involuntary motion to stop her, then pulled back. There was nothing obviously dangerous about the hole. It was dark and it smelled bad, but clearly it was a place where people had been—someone had dug it, and built the stairs, and the shelves, and stocked them. But with the crumpled clothes and bones on the landing, the place seemed more like a grave than a storeroom, and Rose's descent was unsettling. She stopped on the landing where she bent and examined the remains. Then she stood and looked back up at the group. Greenleaf's flashlight illuminated her face.

"Someone shot him," she said. "His breastbone is shattered."

She turned away, probing the lower darkness with her flashlight.

"The steps continue. They are steep."

"How far?" asked Greenleaf.

"Farther than the light," Rose said, peering ahead. She picked the empty bottle off of Abe's remains and hurled it unceremoniously into the blackness. Hal tensed and strained to hear it shatter on the stairs below. But there was no sound.

"Christ," Charlie muttered.

Greenleaf took a tentative step. He was excited, making little clicking noises in his throat and passing his flashlight back and forth from one hand to the other.

"Can you see anything?" He called to Rose.

"Only stairs," she answered.

Charlie's lips were clamped in a tight, thin line. Clearly he didn't like the idea of going down those stairs. Neither did Hal. But he was awfully curious about what lay beyond the bottles. Greenleaf was descending now, tentatively, letting his lamp play alternately on the steps and the bottles. He walked down a few more stairs to Rose's side, and together they began to descend. Within a few seconds there was nothing left to see but the weakening glow of their lamps, and no sound but the soft echoes of their shuffling feet. Then Rose's voice: soft, firm, and distant.

"Come."

Hal looked at Charlie, who was chuckling now, a little nervously it seemed.

"Hell, it's only a hole in the ground. Ain't this what we was after? Whatever's down there I guess we gotta go see it. But ..." He paused, reached down and pulled off first one boot, then the other. " ... I don't plan to have these on my feet in case anybody—or anything—really wants them. So let's go." He started down the stairs.

Hal felt Isabelle's hand on his shoulder. He removed it gently and looked back. Edith was pulling her daughter away.

"He's got to," she said.

Charlie was on the landing now, the boots tucked under his arm, lifting the rumpled rags with one bare foot.

"Poor bastard," he said softly. Then he nodded at Hal.

"Let's go," he repeated.

Hal squared his shoulders. Warren offered his flashlight.

"Take this. Pay attention to everything."

Hal walked down the steps and stood with his father next to the bones. There were even more bottles than it looked like from above. A spectacular stash, worth a fortune even now that it was legal. He kicked gently at the battered top hat. A small shadow scurried out from under it and disappeared. Along with Charlie he moved slowly to the edge of the landing and took the first step down—it was taller than those above, more roughly hewn from the stone. They took another step, then a third. It felt as if they'd fallen ten feet so quickly did the landing recede behind them. Hal turned to have a last look at the others. He could just see the tops of their heads, peering over the edge, watching the descent. He had an urge to wave goodbye.

Just as he felt Charlie tugging at his sleeve, the space above them came suddenly alive with light and noise—shouts, footsteps, bright lamps and the sound of scuffling. Without pausing to think Hal grabbed his father by the elbow and pulled him up the stairs they'd descended, back to the landing. Brilliant search beams blinded him. He heard Isabelle scream and the sound of his mother shouting *No*. He stepped over Abe's body, his father stumbling at his heels.

When he reached the lip of the hole he stopped abruptly. The area inside the shed door was now almost as bright as daylight. Edith, Isabelle, Vera, and Warren stood against one wall, their hands atop their heads. In the doorway stood the unmistakable silhouette of Frank Shaw. His hands were on his hips. Next to him stood an unfamiliar man in a police uniform. They were both laughing.

"Lizard gold my ass," Shaw said between hoots. "Looks like we have nabbed us a couple of old-time bootleggers."

"That we have," said the cop. His big torch beam played on Abe's bones and boots. "At least. Maybe murderers too. Looks like all kinds of mischief afoot here."

"Well, hell," said Charlie.

He took the boots from under his arm and tossed them behind him. They made one sound as they hit the top step. Then nothing.

"What's that you threw?" said the cop. "Come on up out of there, now."

Seconds later Hal and Charlie were back at ground level, outside the shack in the muggy night air, surrounded by lights, a dozen plain-clothes policemen and the rest of their group, clustered in a knot against the wire fence. Shaw had his arms crossed officiously. One of the cops held a revolver, causally pointed in Charlie's direction. Another was eyeing each of them up and down in turn and scribbling in a notebook he'd pulled from his pocket.

"That everybody?" he asked, snapping the notebook shut.

"We ..." Hal began. Shaw was watching him, one eyebrow cocked. Charlie cleared his throat.

"What we were doing, you see ..."

"Save it," said Shaw. "I'm not sure I want to hear what you were doing. Not yet anyways." Shaw hunched his big round shoulders and went back inside the shed. He reached for the massive steel door. As easily as Hal had pulled it open he yanked it upright and let it drop back into place with a deafening clang. Then he dusted his hands together and came back out into the night. As he passed Hal and Charlie, Shaw paused. He looked at the older man as though Charlie was a puddle of something he didn't want to step in. Then he turned to Hal, squinting and cocking his head to one side. He took a step back and looked from one to the other. Shaw shrugged and let out a long, theatrical sigh.

"I guess the apple don't fall very far from the tree," he said. "Though who would have thought it would go rotten so fast?"

"You ..." Charlie said. Hal shot him a sideways look, shaking his head quickly. Shaw laughed.

"That's right boy," he said. "You keep the old man in line. Before he says something he regrets." He nodded to the cop.

"They're all yours now," he said. "I got work to do."

EPILOGUE

W HO got them off, Hal never knew. Gavin? It seemed unlikely, but what did seem likely any more? For whatever reason, after a perfunctory couple of hours at downtown headquarters the whole crowd was released. They even found cars waiting for them on the street, with tight-lipped drivers to ferry them to their various homes and hotels. Hal waited almost a week before he ventured back to the schoolyard. He and Isabelle went on a Saturday. The shed was gone. In its place a group of workers were pouring a concrete slab the size of a dance-hall floor. The contractor in charge was Ralph Belucci himself. When Hal and Isabelle appeared he made himself scarce. A talkative laborer explained that they were working on an expansion of the school building. Over the next few months that was exactly what happened—a brand new gymnasium, built squarely over the location of the trapdoor. It was Shaw's first project as mayor, for which he received all manner of public acclaim. (He was impeached a few years later and hounded out of office for graft and corruption. Hal never heard what happened to him.)

The original dig also was closed. The wooden fence was torn down, the shacks and tents and overburden pile disappeared, and the shaft entrance was sealed, again with a concrete slab. A one-paragraph story appeared in the *Times* explaining that the exploratory mine on Fort Moore Hill had been closed due to underground flooding, and that no further excavations would be permitted. Eventually the site became an automobile garage. The frame house across the street burned one night in the autumn, leaving only a pile of black ashes.

Hal was approached in mid-September by the Angels with the offer of a contract for the following year, which he accepted to the dismay of Lucky and the Sheiks, though they said they understood. At an off-season practice two weeks after he signed he took a foul ball in the side of the head while sitting in the dugout. The force of the impact knocked him unconscious. When he awoke in the hospital an hour later he found that his left eye would no longer focus in concert with his right. His baseball days were over.

Isabelle marveled at how calmly he took the news. They planned their wedding for the next summer. Hal got a job with his father again, running a laundry business for hospital linens—a most unlikely line of work, Hal would have thought, but again it was Shaw of all people who provided Charlie with the connections. Hal worked as a driver, then a dispatcher, when the business grew enough to need more than one truck. Charlie oversaw the operation from an old warehouse on Figueroa Street. Vera kept the books. They sold the house in Oxnard. Vera put the crystal set away in the attic of their new place and never spoke of it.

Edith reestablished her old business. Her experience with the Plan had transformed her, much to Isabelle's dismay, into a caricature of her former professional self. She now saw herself as a legitimate psychic, and wandered the house in her robe and turban, a look of furious concentration on her face; as though she was searching too hard for something she'd had once but couldn't locate again. As for Gavin himself, his wife never returned from Costa Mesa. He maintained a small, shoddy law practice exactly suited to his skills, and stayed away from City Hall.

Isabelle found Rex in his room a few days after the incident at the shed. He was packing a bag. Though he remained outwardly as surly as ever, his bile seemed more reflexive than heart-felt, and when he said goodbye—destination unknown—he actually kissed her cheek and wished her luck. Isabelle received a card some weeks later from Texas, where he was over-wintering with a traveling circus. She never heard from him again.

Warren disappeared. After they were all released from the station, he took a taxi alone to his boarding house. Hal and Isabelle went to see him a few days later. His room was vacant. The elderly Irish landlady said that he'd paid his rent current and left no forwarding address. The more questions Hal and Isabelle asked, the more suspicious she became, closing the door a few inches at a time until at last only her nose poked out.

"You're not mixed up that business with the lizards?" she asked.

"He *told* you about that?" Isabelle sputtered.

"Sure I couldn't shut him up," said the woman. "The man made no sense."

And she closed the door in their faces.

As for the gold, and the place they'd found Abe, Hal's many questions remained unanswered, as Shaw quite literally had slammed the door on any possible revelations about what in the world they'd all gotten mixed up with. He never learned where Greenleaf and Rose went;

nor, for that matter, where they had come from. Charlie told him not to worry.

"I doubt the two of them ever got into anything that they couldn't get out of."

"Then you think they survived?"

It was December 1934. Charlie and Hal were sitting in a bar a couple of blocks from the laundry, ostensibly celebrating the purchase of a new truck, but it was a rare conversation that Hal didn't try to turn back to the Plan. Charlie said it was a waste of time to dwell on it—"like going over and over a poker hand you didn't win." But he was a bit more talkative today—perhaps on account of the good Scotch he'd ordered for the occasion.

"What I don't think," he said, swirling the golden liquid in his glass, "is that the old fox would have gone down those steps if he didn't know where he was headed."

"So what do you think is down there?"

"A damned nice pair of boots."

"No treasure?"

"No treasure for me is all I know."

"Lizard men?"

Charlie snorted.

"Houdini pie."

They drank in silence a while. But Hal couldn't let it rest.

"I do wish," he said, "that we hadn't just off and left poor Abe like that. He deserved a Christian burial at least."

Charlie drained his glass.

"Hell, what does he care? I should do as well when my time comes. But you know, it was nice to see him again after all these years. Even considering."

"Maybe whatever's down there is what killed him," Hal offered.

"Nah, I don't think so. Plenty of folks had reasons otherwise."

It was hard to believe that the adventure was over. Surely someone would be unable to resist the lure of what might be down there. Stories like the Lizard gold didn't go away for good. It would come round again like the comet Hal was named for. Someday, somebody would have another try.

Charlie sat seriously, his brow furrowed.

"I do miss them boots, though. Despite all the trouble they caused me."

Hal laughed. His father was an irascible old reprobate, but he certainly wasn't dull. He wondered how long this laundry business would pan out. A guy like Charlie wasn't going to stay happy washing sheets for long. There'd be more trouble down the road. But for now, things were good. What more could he ask?

He tapped the table to get his father's attention and pointed to his empty glass, one eyebrow raised in question.

"You bet your ass," Charlie said. "I'll buy."

Well, thought Hal, the world is certainly full of mysteries. He held a finger up for the bartender, who hurried right over.

..

About the Author

Paul Michel is an award-winning short writer. *Houdini Pie* is his first novel to be published. He lives, writes and performs in Seattle. You can read more about him at www.paulmichel.com.

AUTHOR'S NOTE

While *Houdini Pie* fundamentally is a fictional invention, its inspiration is rooted in historical fact. While doing internet investigation for an entirely unrelated story in 2002, I came across an excerpt from a 1996 *Los Angeles Times* article about the city's Brentwood District, home today of celebrities and super models. The piece related a bare outline of events that took place there in the early 1930's featuring one G. Warren Shufelt and his "subterranean sonar" hunt for the buried gold of a 4000 year old tribe of Lizard People. There was mention of help he received from a Hopi Indian Chief named Greenleaf, and the visions of a local psychic named Edith Robinson. I did more research and found that the written record, apart from a few period articles in the *Times,* had little more to offer. There is no mention of a sidekick for Mr. Shufelt, but I felt that he ought to have one, and Halley Gates took shape as I immersed myself in the news and culture of Southern California in the Great Depression. Frank Shaw was a real person and mayor, driven out of office during his second term due to allegations of corruption. Many of the baseball players in the novel are based on actual stars of the Pacific Coast League. Everyone else is a figment of my imagination.

I am grateful to the staffs of the Los Angeles and Oxnard Public Libraries for their help with my research. The books and articles that inform the histories of bootlegging, mining practices, professional baseball and everyday life portrayed in the novel are too numerous to enumerate. I am indebted to Celeste Bennett, Adam Finley and Larry Cyr for their good work on both the inside and the outside of the book. I owe thanks as well to my family—my wife Ann and my sons Colin and Pete—for their faith and patience, and to supportive friends and colleagues too many to mention without fear of forgetting someone.

DESIGN NOTES

This book was typeset using fonts used in the era in which the story is set. Title fonts are in Kabel and text fonts are in Cooper Light, developed by Frank Cooper (a student of Goudy) in the 1920s and popular throughout the 1930s and '40s.